The Wondrous Life of a Long-Ago Man

Val Edward Simone

A Morningside Publishing Book
Payson, Arizona

The Wondrous Life of a Long-Ago Man

A Morningside Publishing, LLC Book

Text and Illustration Copyright © 2011 by Val Edward Simone.
All Rights Reserved.

Printed in the United States of America

First Edition

Library of Congress Control Number: 2011904428

ISBN 978-1-936210-11-4

Cover illustration and design: Val Edward Simone

For more books please visit:
www.morningsidepublishing.com

Dedication:
To all you other yearning souls like
me who wish to travel further
than life will ever allow.
~Val

With Special Thanks To:
Forever My Greatest Supporters
My mother and father

Musical Inspiration
Kevin Kern
Secret Garden
Edward Shearmur
Yanni

Editor
Rita Samols

Advance Readers
Rick Cavaliere
Stephan Pavlik
Michelle Walbert

Chapter 1

Welcome to my wondrous life!

I am Thomas Bartholomew Cantfield, presently thirty years of age and holding dearly in my mind a magnificent story bursting with intrigue, adventure, excitement, and brutal honesty.

Today, dear reader, I set my hand, by way of quill and ink, to these parchment pages to tell you an astonishing tale.

Before today, I could have written volumes and imparted unto you great and informative narratives regarding my unusual birth and unique upbringing in the great city of New York. Or I could have begun this record with the exciting account of how I came to be on that forsaken ship torn asunder by a mighty tempest.

I might have given you a detailed description of the wonderful men I met while on board that fated ship, during my travels through those dreadfully frightening and unpredictable waters of the fabled South Seas.

I considered beginning my tale in the midst of the great gale itself, or by well expounding on the glorious deeds of the good and brave Captain Elias Watson, who offered himself as a sacrifice by courageously taking the precious time to lash me to the top of a large broken table with nary a thought for his own safety. I could have told how he pushed my fingers into holes in its top to assist with my grip, and placed a large skin of sweet water around my neck just before the ship broke up and sank out of sight. How he stood bravely on the prow of his ruined ship as it slipped quietly into the watery bowels of evil itself, accompanied by the mournful wails of lost and dying men screaming their lungs to utter depletion before forever sliding under the waves as Satan himself howled in scornful delight. That cur, that beast, so lacking any mercy whatsoever in his heartless chest, that unconscionable fiend who tossed me here so unceremoniously so very long ago.

That damnable hurricane!

Yet still, I could have begun my saga at many other points in my life, but each of those accounts would be but a pale shadow of the story I shall tell you now. No, today truly begins an amazing tale, about my extraordinary life.

I washed ashore on the island precisely on my thirtieth birthday, March 30, 1830, that infamous date now being fully thirty and seven days past.

Remaining joyful and thankful, I celebrate my continued survival every day, for each new day brings with it new challenges and opportunities for triumph.

The true inauguration of this astounding anecdote, however, began when I abruptly awoke upon the shore of this island, still lashed to the tabletop, alone, with the new day's sun in a cloudless sky bringing great heat upon my face and the endless waves washing over it and cooling it, again and again.

By all accounts, I should have perished with the rest of that valiant crew into that cold, black sea, but there was I, lying safely on dry land, alive and apparently none the worse for wear, the white, sandy shoreline of this amazing island stretching away from me in both directions toward ends too distant for me to see.

From its initial appearance, I deemed it to be a large island, and it gave me pause to rejoice in the moment, for if it was indeed a large island, I reasoned, then it was almost certain to be inhabited, especially in the general vicinity of these South Seas in which I knew our ship to be located.

When last I had inquired as to our whereabouts, Captain Watson had informed me that we were about twenty-eight or twenty-nine hours out from the safe harbor of Papeete, Otaheite, and only thirteen hours from the mild lagoon of Bora Bora, sailing in a southeasterly direction. Four hours later, the fateful storm struck us without clemency. We had watched its approach with trepidation, but by virtue of its speedy advance, we could not outrun the monster.

I had previously sailed through these same waters only one year before, though upon favorable seas and in a westerly direction. At the time, it was told to me that many of the islands in this region were inhabited, though some of them reportedly by soulless man-eaters — cannibals.

While lying upon the shore, I had felt a sudden chill flash through my body, but not from the air surrounding me, for as I have stated, the sun was bright and warm. Nay, the chill I felt was caused by the invented eyes of an unseen ravenous man-eater glaring at me from somewhere in the inland bushes, well hidden and regarding me as his next belly-stuffing meal.

If such a creature had haunted the near bushes, it would have been impossible for me to repel his attack, for I had no weapon with which to defend myself. He was either, and with not a doubt, a skilled hunter or a fearful warrior. In any regard, he was sure to be an expert with both spear and knife. Without my blunderbuss or sword, I would certainly be no match for the savage's killing skills.

I trembled with fear when I heard the rustling of leaves coming from the bushes well ahead of my current position on the shoreline. My eyes desperately searched the undergrowth for any clear sign of the source of the sound.

I waited nervously for an expected assault, but after several minutes all yet remained still and quiet. I calmed my fears by insisting that no one was lurking in those bushes and it must have been only the wind, although I felt no breeze upon my face.

After several more peaceful moments, the only sound being from the waves gently lapping onto the sandy beach, I concluded my anxious expectation by deciding that the noise I had heard earlier was perhaps playing only in my frightened and confused mind.

Seconds later, however, another rustle of leaves and branches again captured my full attention and brought me abruptly to a state of highest alert. Having removed my lashing, I now stood up and planned to meet my attacker with a square and full-front facing of courage and defiance. If I were to be attacked by the man-eater, I would make the battle one to remember, for I intended to take his wicked life from him if I were at all able to do so. At the same time, however, I considered this point also: if this wretched creature feasted upon my flesh this evening despite my most ardent efforts to prevent it, I intended to put him well to the task of earning his meal.

In my youth, I was never considered a lad of violent tendencies or intents, yet I was neither of a cowardly nature. I was known for choosing to resist an altercation whenever the opportunity presented itself to me. Yet also was I known never to back away from a fight when such was forced upon me. As was I known always to go to the aid of an innocent when an unseemly brute sought to take unfair advantage of a weaker individual.

In all things, over the years prior to my inelegant arrival here on the island, I stood tall when I needed to, but I strenuously labored to avoid conflict whenever possible, first with a gentle, understanding mind and then with soothing and kindly words.

In this case, however, faced with the possibility that I might soon be confronted with a man-eating savage, I harbored no naïve belief in my ability to successfully assuage the beast.

I looked about me and noticed a loosened plank on the table. I yanked at it mightily and it quickly gave way. I now stood with at least something I might use to momentarily shield me from a tossed spear. I then took up a sturdy stance and awaited the inevitable assault, which, to my great joy, never came.

I must confess my foolishness to you for such a response to an unidentified sound, for only seconds after my taking up such a defensive posture did a large bird burst forth from the brush into the bright blue sky and wing happily upon its way, far from the fool below observing it in perspiring relief.

In my defense, however, I submit to you this question upon which to ponder: in the moment of uncertainty, having heard tales of the man-eaters throughout the region, might you also have taken such a posture when confronted by such a sound? Still, even after the passage of so much time, I find myself on occasion giggling as at a buffoon when recalling the event.

Concluding a search of the immediate area, I soon suspected that I was alone, for I found not a single sign of the island being inhabited, at least at the moment, by anyone other than myself and a steady flock of edible fowl.

In the days shortly following my untimely arrival, and prior to chronicling my exploits here onto this page, I made a complete tour of the island that was to become my home, at least for a while, and found that I was, indeed, utterly alone.

The island was of an oval configuration, with the longer ends being laid out in an east-west direction. I had washed ashore on the southern shoreline. In terms of distance, I cannot with any accuracy say just how large the island was. What I can say is that walking from one end of the island to the other, on an east-to-west line through the center, required about two hours. I estimated my average pace to be approximately three miles per hour. That calculated to make the island between five and six miles from one end to the other. From north to south, using the same method, I calculated that distance to be approximately three to four miles. Further, during the exploration, I established an inventory of what the island possessed necessary for my survival.

Said inventory of the island's resources included a single spring of sweet water positioned almost dead center of the island and very near a large outcrop of basalt rock at the base of the island's extinct volcano, which rose upward at least five hundred feet and covered most of the eastern end of the island, creating a gently sloping and sandy shoreline.

The westerly end, being substantially flatter, was much easier to traverse and provided good soil for a small orchard of trees laden with ripe papaya, mango, coconut, and breadfruit, the center of the orchard being only 250 or 300 yards from the spring.

The island's fowl were quite passive and easy to trap, and they made splendidly hearty meals. I also found wood aplenty for maintaining a vigorous fire whenever I wished.

Also in those early days I found, washing up onto the beach and continuing for several days thereafter, many useful artifacts from the doomed ship. The most helpful items were found in chests belonging to some of the crew and included several knives, hatchets, sharpening stones, assorted thicknesses of twine, and the like.

Even vast yards of torn canvas sails washed ashore. Coupled with poles of wood, they made a wonderful and sturdy tent snugged away in the basalt outcropping, to keep me from both the heat of the sun and the pounding of rainfall, which was plentiful and often, but not overly so.

It was what happened ten days after my arrival, however, which has since proven to be most thrilling and fortuitous, although I did not regard it to be so at first, for on that day I found, washed up on shore and partially buried in the sand, a sealed chest.

Excitedly, I dragged it to my new home, taking several hours to do so because of the weight of it. But such weight was welcomed, for it told me the chest must contain wonderful and useful things that I might use to elevate my status from merely a shipwrecked survivor to a man of means—the prideful owner of an island estate, surrounded by things of comfort.

The lock, which was securely affixed to the hinge, proved to be most resistant to my attempts to open it. Additionally, the chest was waterproofed with paraffin sealing wax, further hindering my opening it. In fact, it took a full half hour and a hatchet to finally bash it open. But when I did open it, my otherwise hopeful and smiling countenance must have surely dropped into a sorrowful pout and filled immediately to capacity with dismay, for the chest contained only hundreds of pieces of new parchment, several ink wells filled with rich black ink, and a single quill pen.

Quite obviously, sealed as it was, it had been intended that the contents of the chest survive the moist air of the ocean voyage, unharmed and in such a state as to permit someone, possessing a mighty will, no doubt, to write a document of great length and presumed importance.

I set the chest aside during my initial disappointment, for in coping with the snares of the island, I saw no advantage to me in having parchment, ink, and quill.

After three weeks or so, however, it dawned on me that perhaps discovering the chest was of good fortune after all. Having such instruments would allow me to record my exploits on this island for posterity. Also, they would certainly be of great value should I wish, at some future time, once my rescue was successfully achieved, to publish the account of my thrilling experiences while marooned here.

As a burgeoning youth, during my time in school but outside my normal studies of accounting and finance, I had the good fortune to read Daniel Defoe's exciting account of Robinson Crusoe's life as a castaway, as well as the published accounts of well-known survivors of actual shipwrecks such as Alexander Selkirk and Henry Pitman.

Since my arrival, and based largely upon the remembrance of those now hallowed pages, I had fabricated many important items which I have since used every day, they being a bowl for eating, a cup for drinking, and gourds with which to keep handy several pints of fresh water, to mention only a few.

Having the means, then, and possessed of the will, I resolved myself toward emulating those exciting dissertations, although not to the same level, of course, as I was aware of the fact that I lacked the skills equal to the great authors who not only owned them in abundance but also used them matter-of-factly every day with wonderful precision and grace. No, I set myself to the simpler task of merely recording only the most notable events and important thoughts concerning my efforts to survive my time here.

Therefore, be troubled not, dear reader, for I shall make no attempt to deceive you into thinking that I am as gifted a writer as the great Daniel Defoe—a man truly gifted with the command of language and the knowledge of how best to present his gems that were his words and phrases. Soon after beginning my own modest journalistic efforts, I came to a fuller appreciation of Mr. Defoe's immense talent for storytelling even up to his unflattering end, cowering away as he did, hiding from his creditors and eventually dying in squalor.

I, on the other hand, wished only to record my adventures here in the audacious hope of one day being allowed to pass them on to another person who might find them of some mild interest, or to those who fancy such tales of intrigue and struggle, although at that time there was little intrigue, and even less struggle.

Chapter 2

Contrary to the style devised and presented in the tale of Robinson Crusoe, that of a daily journal, I had already determined not to endeavor toward such an end. Instead, I chose to keep a less detailed chronicle. Further, and in deference to Mister Crusoe, one point should be duly noted. During his time on his island, Mr. Crusoe experienced a wide range of exciting and challenging events, which necessarily supported that particular style of record keeping.

On this island, such excitement was not a daily event. Were it so, I fear I would not have had adequate time to chronicle them so profusely, consistently, and in such fine detail anyway.

Shortly after my discovery of pen, ink, and parchment, and if I had been born with the mind of an imaginative storyteller rather than a brain better suited to the ordinary and pragmatic details of accounting, I would have invented and set down wild and fanciful stories to delight you and to better occupy my time, which I seem at present to have plenty of, not having a burdensome need for anything in order to survive.

The trees freely gave me the fruit of their branches when I needed to eat. The nearby spring always patiently waited to quench my thirst when I wished to do so. And I had more wood than I could have burned in two lifetimes to keep a roaring fire ablaze when I so desired. The flints I had discovered in one of the chests that came ashore made my efforts to set the wood ablaze no task at all.

I did not have the necessary material for making a proper fishing net, but neither had fishing been difficult. I had much twine and hooks aplenty, found in one of the other chests. And there was an ample number of large insects roaming around which I used as bait on the hooks for fish most eager to impale themselves upon when they were provided the opportunity to do so.

One thing upon which I worked diligently to improve was the manner in which I harvested the fowl, for on more than a few occasions it had taken me well over two hours just to snare one. If you then factor in the time it takes to properly dress and cook them, one could easily see how most of my afternoon was consumed by that single chore alone. It thus proved to be an ineffective method for preparing my meals.

After a time, it became my considered opinion that the birds had become very suspicious of my snares and seemed more and more resistant to my attempts. They seemed almost clever as to my ways of entrapment, and within a short while it became a test of wills. I believed them to be actually taunting me to invent new ways to trap them. After that, the taunting rose to the level of a concentrated battle of wills, and it was a battle that I did not intend to lose.

There was one particular breed I had found to

be especially tasteful. I knew not what it might be called by scientists and hunters, but it was a large bird with gray-and-white-speckled feathers above and a white underbelly, and I had estimated its average wingspan to be approximately twenty inches, although I had seen a few larger and many more smaller than that. After suitably dressed for the fire spit, they averaged about two pounds and provided a filling meal.

In any event, they presented me a substantial challenge to capture. I concluded that they were much smarter than the other edible birds I had captured thus far, and neither as gullible nor trusting. I had found, however, that they were much more susceptible to capture very early in the morning and very much worth the effort.

And so by the end of the third week, I had already given much consideration to building a large pen in which I could stock the birds for easier capture. I thought long and hard on the design for several days prior to undertaking the chore, hoping to avoid the folly of beginning a fool's errand and building it improperly, for as I have already stated, I was an accountant, not a carpenter.

It took two full weeks to perfect my design, but upon its completion, that being on the thirty-fifth day since my arrival, I set about capturing as many of the birds as I could using several snares at once. Within four days more, I had captured twenty-two fat fowl and now held them securely within the pen, its dimensions being approximately four feet wide by eight feet long by four feet high.

Thus was the battle of wills brought to a swift and final conclusion, with me standing as victor and one them naked and hanging over a daily flame. Within a brief time, I hoped to domesticate them and husband several new flocks, enjoying a new food: fresh boiled eggs.

In short, by the end of the first month and a half, my life ceased being any struggle at all. In fact, except for the great loneliness I felt upon several occasions, there was not much that I could justifiably complain about.

Soon thereafter, as I thought hard upon the matter, it seemed to me that Robinson Crusoe must have been a very demanding fellow to draw such controversy into his life as he so often had.

I began to think him a foolish man, but such thoughts ended with me seeming to be the pot calling the kettle black, since I also was a castaway and destined to a similar fate, albeit I had a much easier time of it than he.

On the day of these thoughts, I noted that I had been marooned on the island fifty and seven days. On this, I was forced to admit another point. My time here had not been all that unpleasant, but I still felt pressed to improve my lot somehow.

I had, by this time, fully undertaken to scribbling into my journal, writing during the daylight hours, sitting in the sand with my back pressed against a large log. One day I noticed that the broken table upon which I had floated ashore on was leaning up against my tent. I decided that I needed a sturdier and flatter writing surface upon which to record my journal, and thus the next morning, my sixty-eighth day on the island, I set out to replace the piece I had yanked out on my first day, in fearful preparation for the nonexistent cannibal, and sculpt legs for the table. At the same time, I was forced to give serious thought to devising an appropriate method of attachment. I remind you again that I was not a carpenter; thus such an undertaking proved to be a delicate task, for which I was ill-trained, and I became quite frustrated in my attempts to properly attach the first leg to the table.

It was during the sculpting of the first leg, however, that I realized I had forgotten an essential chore, one which might have led to an adverse effect on my expected rescue if left unattended much longer, and one which I should have thought of doing immediately upon my arrival, but had failed to do so.

In response to such an important need, I set aside further sculpting efforts and set for myself on the morrow, instead, the strenuous task of moving a significant portion of wood to the southern shoreline in order to build a large signal fire, which I estimated should be twenty feet high when completed.

My reasoning for building the signal fire on the southern shore was simple: that was where I had landed. On this basis, I presumed that our course was south of the island prior to the storm. I considered that to be the normal course for ships in that region, but I must admit that in the fury of the storm I had lost all sense of direction and knew not our exact position relative to the island at the time of the sinking. Still, and regardless of the direction, it was my most fervent hope that the tall column of smoke and fire would not only alert the crew of a passing ship to my distress but also guide them to my exact location, thus bringing about my glorious rescue.

I quickly found, much to my dismay, that I was neither suitably formed nor well enough conditioned for such strenuous physical labor. The nearest stand of trees to where I had intended to build my stack near the southern shoreline was, again by my crude method of measurement, only about a quarter mile inland. However, I discovered the hauling of logs that distance to be particularly brutal for a man so ill equipped as I. Yet eventually I was successful in building a large spire of wood for the signal fire. It took an immense effort to drag to the shoreline the larger logs necessary to build a fitting foundation, but the structure was completed and made ready for its assignment.

As one fascinated with numbers, I recorded precisely eighty round-trips to complete my task. With it being approximately one quarter mile from wood source to fire stack, I calculated that I walked around forty miles over the twelve days that it took to build the spire.

After tugging on heavy logs for half of those

round-trips under the hot sun and under the other arduous conditions such as elevation changes, rocky outcrop formations, and the ever presence of scrub brush in the path, I barely made it to my bed on the night of the twelfth day.

In the last few moments of that day I was struck by an observation. Had I been a man of substantially more years, or of diminished health, or perhaps lacking the necessary willpower, it most likely would have taken me much longer to accomplish my task, or, and I think it more likely so, the signal fire stack would have been much smaller. In either case, I do not think that the effort would have been as successful in the end.

And here is the truly frightening point of such an observation. I wondered what my life would be like in several more years should I not be rescued before then, when, by that time, I no longer would be possessed of my youthful strength and vigor. This troubled me greatly. It was then that I knew that I very much needed to get off the island as soon as I was able to do so. It was the last thought I had before collapsing into near unconsciousness.

Suffice it to say that I awoke very late on the thirteenth morning following the start of my signal fire chore, eighty-two days since my arrival on the island, still very much exhausted. I had grossly miscalculated just how fatiguing it would be to move that much wood that far away. The resistance contributed by the sand was considerably more than I had expected. But with the task completed, I felt I had made a substantial effort toward my security and survival.

I daresay that through all of the effort, I came to believe myself a more recent incarnation of Robinson Crusoe. At least, I began to have a new appreciation for his travails and accomplishments.

That afternoon I made a meal of fresh ripened mango and breadfruit. Together, they tasted delightfully sweet and by then mango most surely had become my favorite fruit. And the breadfruit, with its doughy center scooped out and the rest used as a holder for the ripe mango, made the meal seem almost a cobbler. Interesting fruit, this breadfruit, for it seems to be neither bread nor fruit. It proved very easy to prepare and to eat, and I must say that after a few times preparing it, I found it most enjoyable, and it was then that I understood why the British Admiralty had commissioned Lieutenant Bligh to bring the breadfruit plants back to England.

I bathed in the spring the following morning, my glorious 83rd day here in this paradise, and though bathing in the spring was not extraordinary in any way, afterward I felt especially invigorated.

That sensation was short-lived, however, because in building the bird pen, I had unknowingly surmounted my last real test. The removal of my final challenge would later prove to be a fact more damaging than I could ever prepare for, but that is a story for another time.

In the matter of the fowl, the time necessary to both dress them for cooking and to cook them forced me to make my midday meal my most important and basic meal, eating fish or fowl along with fruit. My morning and evening meals converted to eating fruit and coconut within a breadfruit bowl.

If the truth be told, I found that I slept much better and awakened more refreshed in the morning with less food in my belly from the night before. I had been accustomed in the past to eating my nightly meal at eight o'clock, as that was the more gentlemanly time to dine back in New York City. However, there on that peaceful island, a heavy nightly meal seemed most inappropriate and much less healthy.

I decided that I would maintain this schedule, for health and energy reasons, once I was rescued and returned to civilization.

On the 130th day after landing on this tropical delight, I reflected upon the time I had spent here and concluded that it had been so far quite an adventure. I believed that upon returning to New York and recounting my island life at the society banquets sure to be held in my honor, my exploits would excite those of the upper crust such that I should be, no doubt, the talk of the town for a long while thereafter. I expected to be the envy of every other young man in the city. I further expected to have the ear of many of society's most sought-after women, and much more than just their ears, I believed. For the shameful desire of it, I expected to taste many pink lips upon my return.

Speak it not, kind reader, for I know that I am a cad of sorts. This, I fear, tends to occur within a man's heart and mind when he is alone for too long, of an idle mind, and without a woman's touch, which I fear has been weighing more heavily on my unchallenged brain of late.

By the time I recorded my 180th day trapped on this confounded island, it seemed to me that the life of a castaway was not nearly as exciting as I had once thought it to be. In fact, I found island life to be quite boorish and tedious.

I had given myself over to additional consideration of that charlatan Daniel Defoe and his alleged adventures of Robinson Crusoe. I concluded that his account of the life and times of Crusoe were nothing more than a cruel and bitter hoax inflicted upon the reader by that madman. For Defoe to suggest that being a castaway was an exciting adventure proved that he thought his readers a gullible lot.

And if I am to be considered an honest fellow, then I must admit it necessary to count myself among the naïve many, for he had me well fooled also.

On the morning of my 185th day of imprisonment, I awoke with yet another conclusion swimming about in my head regarding my admiration for Defoe, or, dare I say, my lack of same.

I concluded that he was a vulgar man whose disrepute now seemed well founded and deserved. I came also to the close of such thoughts finding his drivel of a story to be an offensive and pitiful attempt to deceive the reader into believing that the life of a castaway is somehow heroic or noble.

This thinking led me then to my considered opinion that his shameful tale represented only a rude, crude, and vile exposition absent any care or consciousness for his readers. I judged it to be the complete and total embellishment of what life itself is truly like, and I found it to be almost immoral and sorely in need of avenging consequences. But alas, the scoundrel already had rotted in his grave. Good riddance to you, sir, I say. May the worms pick your bones clean and may you find no peace anywhere in the next world, if there be such a world fit for a despicable character such as you.

In yet further consideration, I also imagined that the accounts of both other true castaways, Selkirk and Pitman, were also similarly embellished in some sick and unseemly manner.

As I pondered the matter, I drew to the further conclusion that Defoe was nothing more than a fraud, and that his horrid depiction of life on a deserted island was a bold-faced lie—an unadulterated exaggeration even unto criminal proportions.

I, for one, was glad he was dead.

Thus, having awakened to continue the 186th day of my undeserved sentence, I then judged my imprisonment in solitary confinement, such as it was, to be wholly unjustified. I certainly did not recall ever having done anything to deserve such a punishment.

In that moment, if I could have struck out at the one who had sent me here, I would have done so gladly, with a willing heart and soul, and filled with the full intent to destroy his life as he had destroyed mine.

On the 249th day, that day being 63 full days since I had last taken up the pen and recorded anything in my journal, I awoke to a new temperament.

During that time, I discovered that I had several

personal issues of a deeply troubling nature which I must needs overcome. On that morning, I took some time to review what I had written heretofore. I completed my read feeling deep shame and embarrassment for some of what I had written, nay, for most of what I had written. For those ill-chosen sentiments expressed herein, I judged myself harshly. I intended to rip up the last few pages I had written in my journal, but upon reconsideration came to the conclusion that these bitter thoughts and actions were a necessary part of what has come to define me. To have hidden them from you would have been heinously disingenuous of me.

Therefore, in all humility, I had to admit that those sentiments were an accurate depiction of what I had truly felt at that time. Upon a deeper study of why I would have written such acerbic opinions, I reasoned that those thoughts come to one who is instantly and abruptly removed from normal society and left to the ills of a lonely heart and a fearful mind—the telling screams of insecurity and despair, the mournful regrets of a once joyous life now seemingly lost forever.

I went through a period of several weeks, during which time I became confused, frightened, and terribly vexed. Yet, upon honest self-reflection, I realized that while all of these emotions were real and may have been necessary for the moment, I could not allow them, nor should they ever be allowed, to control my life thereafter.

Thus I acknowledge that I was for a time in a dark and desperate place. I also admit that, at first, I had viewed my marooning as an exciting adventure to be embraced and enjoyed, but it was only because I expected to be rescued quickly. Having cleared the web of self-deceit from my brain with the sharp stick of reality, I then saw my dilemma clearly and for what it truly was: a frantic battle for survival, emotionally, spiritually, mentally, and, possibly, even physically.

Please understand this, dear reader: it was only when I realized that my rescue would not materialize as expected that I felt my mind and spirit revolt in disappointment and cower away in the fear that I quite probably would die on this island, all alone, forsaken, and utterly forgotten by all who had ever known me.

I felt then a surge of appreciation fill my heart, coupled with gratitude that I was alive and not presently in the form of the alternative state. Despite my horrible and regretful acts and, as well, my undisciplined scribbling, I realized that there must have been some greater purpose to it all, although at that moment, I must confess, I could find no lofty purpose to any of it.

During such a dispirited time, however, I discovered that loneliness is not of a cavalier nature, but, being both a conniving and unpredictable villain, should command great respect.

I was a man used to being around many people. In my former life, I had never known loneliness on the scale experienced on the island. I think it was the abruptness of such a change that my brain and senses had difficulty confronting, and thus, rejecting reality, became ill and confused.

It is a frightening thing, you know, to suddenly realize that being marooned on a deserted island is not the same as a simple weekend's adventure in the forest—a short vacation to be enjoyed until you are once again home and performing your normal activities.

It is also most unnerving to realize that all of your friends back home are continuing on with their lives as normal, the parties planned, orchestrated, and executed in your absence with nary a thought for you.

In all honesty, I cannot say that the last statement was true, but I suspect it was. I sorely missed the camaraderie which friends share without thinking about it. My mind struggled with the thought that all of this and much more was going on back home without anyone wondering where I might be or in what state of mind and spirit I existed. And all the while, I sat on this desolate island, wondering if I was destined to spend the rest of my precious life struggling against my demons, both inwardly and outwardly, simply for the right to exist, afflicted with the knowledge that I might have to do so in complete and utter isolation.

The original voyage, the device used by some nefariously devious and malevolent creative force to place me here in this situation, was originally intended to be a thrilling two-year journey, a magnificent respite from the otherwise mundane life of an ordinary and low-level company accountant.

The other, more senior accountants were married, some even with children. They were not at liberty to make such a voyage, which demanded the full two-year commitment necessary to complete the journey.

The shipping company, wishing an audit of all its dealers and suppliers, including a highly sophisticated and onerous assessment of the productivity of establishing such expensive and distant routes, was, for a humble accountant such as I, a once-in-a-lifetime treat and a career-advancing opportunity the likes of which do not come often enough to men of simple means, the brood which I was kindred with.

The itinerary was to include visitations to company offices situated along both coasts of South America, then westward to company offices throughout the lesser South Seas nations, and finally to the larger Western Pacific cities of commerce and business and back home again. It was to be a simple expedition absent any danger, except what the weather might unleash. At the time of our departure, we did not consider the weather to be a threat.

We were so wrong.

Upon the completion of my duties and my return home, heavily dependent, of course, on the quality of my audit and assessment, I expected to be elevated to a position that, without this assignment, would have been well out of my reach for at least several more years. So it was by either greed or Providence that I willingly set out on the voyage, and therefore in doing so, it fell to me to absorb the responsibility for any end, be it for well or for ill.

I had struggled exceedingly for several weeks with the genuine possibility now confronting me that I might have to spend the rest of my life here.

Finally, I came to accept such a fated possibility, and I regretfully admit that I tried twice to take my own life when I was writhing in deepest despair during that disconsolate period.

Both times I fashioned twine into a hangman's noose. However, in miscalculating, on both occasions, the tensile strength necessary to support my weight, I soon found my face pushed deeply into the sand.

I often found myself, over the next several months, giggling about those two events. I further submit to you that it would have been quite a comedy for any audience witnessing the look of utter surprise upon my face after I plummeted off my bench, heard the snap of the twine, and pulled my contorted face, now suitably caked with dried sand, up off the ground.

Oh, the folly of a true fool.

I shall not be offended if you should find yourself also giggling at the foolishness of it all. But I tell you this: until these incidents, I had no idea that I was possessed of such showmanship demonstrating a propensity toward comedic ends, a true harlequin. I snicker even now, as I write these very words.

I think it important to note that I forgave myself for attempting such nonsense, and soon thereafter I was right in my head once again, or so I hoped.

I should tell you also that the second time I attempted my own destruction brought me comfortably to a new place within, for I recognized that it may have been my destiny to exist on this island a while longer, and after the failure of the previous attempt to end my sorry life, I seemed to have lost both the courage and the will to make a third attempt. And so, on the 200th day of my incarceration I found a new reason to continue on in spite of the full ills of my desperation and lost in the terrible throes of my loneliness.

I fashioned a companion out of crushed twigs, leaves, and grass, all bound together with what twine I had left. And while it was true that she was only a grass woman, and stood quite still and silent, having a wooden pole shoved up her backside for support, I found she gave me a small measure of comfort. At the time, it seemed enough to keep some semblance of sanity flowing through my diminished brain.

Or so I had thought.

By late afternoon of the 210th day, I became aware

that I sat near my cooking fire unexplainably steeped in comedic form, light of heart, a wily twist upon my lips and my head crammed with some silly-conceived truth as yet hidden from me.

I then slowly recalled the events of the previous ten days.

The morning of my 201st day, stepping out from my tent, I bid my grass companion a good morning. The world around me was oddly silent and yet all seemed normal for the most part. The trees continued freely giving fruit enough to eat each and every day. The spring continued spilling forth sweet, refreshing, thirst-quenching, clear water. The foolish fish continued believing that the delicious morsel drifting in front of them was provided without consequence. The wood remained plentifully piled and awaiting to be burned whenever I wished to enjoy a fire.

Nothing, seemingly, was out of order.

This silence was not unusual in and of itself, for often enough much time passed on the island when all was still. This particular stillness, however, was unlike any I had known before on the island. As I recall it now, the silence contained an almost ominous tone within it.

During that day and the days that followed, no deep and abiding truths were revealed to me. I received no special dispensation from the universe for thought or deed, as both were of a bland nature and absent of either fair or foul intent. I had no otherworldly visions. Neither were there any great insights given unto to me concerning the hidden workings of the universe. One day simply melded into the next almost without notice.

All in all, I was seemingly just a delighted soul, and I attributed much of my lighter disposition to my grass lady, with whom I had chosen to spend a good deal of time, engaged in riveting conversation or dancing together to wonderfully soothing music from an unseen but definitely heard orchestra.

And although pressed to discover the orchestra's hidden location at first, I finally came to accept the musicians and their gift of music for what it was without knowing where they dwelled—a simple gift to be enjoyed.

Thus, we danced for hours on end and in this bliss we continued on for several more days. I was happy, contented with my new friend and all that she had to say. Her soft words of encouragement filled my heart with hope. By the 209th day, I had found that both my spirit and my mind were in a new place.

By late afternoon on my 210th day, however, I realized both the folly and the truth of it all. I also discovered the real reason for my uplifted spirit: I had gone utterly mad from the ills of a great fever. Not a fever of the body, but of the heart, mind, and soul.

On the 211th day, my fever fully broken and gone, I awoke clearer headed and was able to look back over the preceding ten days with eyes now wide open and a soul now purged. The extent of mental clarity, however, was a question yet to be accurately discerned.

Looking back upon the episode now, as these

words form upon this page through the efforts of both quill and ink and my will to record, and having given the matter extended thought, I realize that the full effects of my isolation had set in hard upon me. And I see clearly also that the joy I believed I felt was nothing more than the bliss of a mind descended into lunacy.

Mind you, I did understand during those preceding days just how fragile my mind truly was, although I did not understand how such an awareness could be possible given the state of that mind—the ravaged result, no doubt, of my deteriorated mental condition. Still, I must have existed in some steady state of mind to continue recording events as I did.

To this day I do not know how I regained my sanity, but I remember giving thanks to whoever rescued my mind from the brink of such darkened oblivion, delivering me graciously once again into illuminated reality. Whether it was through grace or good fortune, I can never be certain, but one thing was clear enough to me. Had I remained in the depths of insanity for any length of time thereafter, I can only guess where I would have ended up, or in what further adverse condition I would have emerged from my time in that state of being. Most likely, however, I would have died a mindless wretch, completely unaware of the truth.

But then I wondered, had I remained in that state of mental decay, would I have ever known that I was insane, or for that matter, being then lost in some forever fragile fantasy, would I have been at all aware of my own existence in the real world, or might I have indeed gone on to eternity lost within that daydream?

Nothing, anymore, seemed certain, except that I was still marooned.

Sad is an empty heart. Tragic is an empty mind. Lost is an empty soul.

Chapter 3

During the time of my emotional infirmity, when I was consumed by that delusional state, my journal contained the bizarre thoughts of a man deeply ill. Yet even in my sickened condition, the nature of the accountant obviously felt it important to record such thoughts, and it is only because of the notes made by me while in that circumstance that I have any memory at all of the events that occurred over those sixty-three days.

How odd the human mind and its need to remember.

My writing during this period lacked style and eloquence, though the message was transmitted clearly enough. This lack of articulacy was due largely, no doubt, to the despair felt by a man too confused of mind and too desperate of spirit to chronicle his condition with any sense of fluency or propriety. By this account, I saw that I had clearly been a deeply troubled soul during this agonizing period.

Although I clearly recall my joy at having a mate to speak to, most of my recollection was surely in my head. And while I noted that nothing of any real importance occurred during that period of my insanity, upon further consideration I now contend that the joy I felt, in and of itself and despite my mental struggles, seems justification enough. I was happy during that period, and sometimes, when there is no other reason for it, being happy suffices. For the glory of it, then, at least I had not tried to end my life.

I had recorded my banal conversations with my grass woman. Such notes brought to mind how I had sat for hours on end in front of my new friend discussing deep and meaningful beliefs and points of view, engaged in wonderful discourses on the very nature of man and his proper place within this strange and crazy world.

Of course, in time I came to realize that my lady was built of grass and twigs and could no more speak than dance, the wooden pole shoved up her backside remaining sturdy, plumb, and holding her fast.

Upon further reflection, having nothing else more important to occupy my mind, I discovered that during my time infirmed, and in addition to the great despair I felt, I lived in the depths of anger and frustration. Anger, because of my obvious predicament. Frustration, because I did not know who I should blame for my being put ashore on this miserably silent atoll, forsaken and all alone. Was it the captain's fault? Should he have been better aware of the worsening skies—the telling signs of an approaching storm? Was it my employer? Could he have better arranged this voyage to avoid this area of ocean during the months when hurricanes are known to be more frequent? And if not the captain or my employer, then whom could I blame for this plight and my misery? I pondered on this matter often, even unto roaring with great rage and anguish at whomever was to blame, sending my echoing cries of agony and torment throughout the hillsides and scattering terrified fowl in every direction.

Then a chilling thought struck me. Was I, alone, responsible for being here? Had I overlooked what is truly good in this world and fallen victim to an underlying greedy and ambitious nature that had remained hidden from me before? In my quest to attain a greater position in the company, had I lost all perspective and disregarded the tragic consequences of such an inherently dangerous voyage? Dear God, I thought, am I indeed responsible for my fool's journey and thus for my own uncelebrated end therefore?

Then again, perhaps God was to blame. Or perhaps culpability lay in the act of some other hostile deity. The more I questioned, the more confused I became.

To be more succinct and avoid dragging you further through every varying thought I had regarding my need to place blame, I tell you now that after much soul searching, considered thought, and honest evaluation, I came to the unhappy conclusion that I could find no singular source upon which to lay the mantle of blame, except, perhaps, the Principle of Chance itself.

Hundreds of people perish on the ocean every year. Some of them are spirits of good and decent intent, others are cruel and spiteful beings. Neither form, it would seem, is a necessary prerequisite for such a fate.

Further reflection suggests that from time to time these things are bound to happen, given the very hazardous and unpredictable nature of ocean travel, and all who venture out onto the open seas know this without question.

I reasoned, therefore, that the Principle of Chance was strongly in evidence regarding my own misfortune. Out of the thousands and thousands of travelers setting out upon the ocean on any given day, it is the simple application of the Principle of Chance that determines which arrive safely at their destination and which do not. Chance also determines which of those who do not arrive die or become castaway on an island such as this one.

In time, and in an attempt to reconcile the reason for my state of existence, I found this conclusion: I had done nothing to deserve such a fate, yet neither had I done anything of an exemplary note that would warrant any special consideration in avoiding it. Sometimes, simply put, bad things happen to good people, or to bad people, or to people who just happen to be in the right place and the wrong time, or the wrong place and the wrong time.

In any event, call it Chance or call it Fate, here I was. It took time, but I finally accepted my fate willingly and decided that I should go forth into each new day, first with gratitude for having been placed on an island requiring very little effort or struggle to survive, and then with the hope that my internment here would last only a short while longer. I committed myself each new day toward the conscious effort to be happy and grateful regardless of what issues or challenges might confront me.

If you look about yourself, kind reader, and I suspect it need not be far, you will spot someone who is living more desperately than you are.

In conclusion, and in an effort to put an end to such a morbid perspective, let me leave you with this thought: such a choice is for you also, a simple choice that you can make each and every day for yourself and to the benefit of all those around you. In whatever life you find yourself living, be it rich or poor, be it hard or easy, be it wild or tame, your only true duty is to yourself, to simply arise each morning and choose to be joyful and grateful, and in so doing, radiate the gentle light of such truth, through grace, upon all others.

That mess was now behind me, and I had decided that I must make the best of my time while here. Certainly complaining about my predicament would not change it. Thus, on the 213th day, I arose early, suddenly refreshed from a wonderful night's sleep and in full ownership of a fresh new passion to begin a life as a writer. Not merely as a *recorder* of events, but as a *creator* of them. I wanted to write as an author would write.

During my time away mentally, I had seen and done some wonderfully strange things. In the heat of the moment I did not—nay, *could* not—begin to understand what ills my heart, mind, and soul had had to endure. Now, having fully recovered, I found that recording such events wrapped in the finely woven detail of an exciting narrative might, one day, prove to be most propitious toward my complete recovery after I was finally rescued. And seeing that I had both the means and the will, I then decided that I would write a book.

No, I had not been suddenly blessed with any more skill than I had possessed the day before, or the day before that, or the day before that. I had, however, received blessings of both inspiration and curiosity, both of which I had determined should be no longer wasted. I believed that they, being new blessings and therefore full of vim and vigor, would be sufficient to allow me to begin writing in earnest. I also believed those blessings would extend enough to allow me the dignity and opportunity to maintain my sanity, now that it was once again in my possession, and help me to pass my time more productively.

Therefore, on my 214th day as a prisoner on

this island, I began again to sculpt legs for my table and to make a better stool as well, reasoning that if I was to be a writer of tales, then I should have the proper tools.

Possessed, then, of a good spirit and the noble will to succeed, I managed, in only three weeks to build both my table and a bench, as it ended up being, instead of a simple stool.

On the 235th day, that day being the day I completed my carpentry work, comfortably seated on my bench and my arms now supported by a stout table, I began to write my book.

A portion of it was already written, of course: the chronicle of my fortunate, albeit unceremonious, arrival and the events following. From that beginning I embarked upon an adventurous journey into the hidden and untested mind of a new author—me.

Over the next few weeks, I started writing sometimes at night, for the ideas burst forth uncontrollably at times and would not allow me the peace given by sound sleep. Being forcefully awakened by arousing visions, I was forced to leave my bed and write down the scenes in my head before returning to my slumber.

As I had found several large candles in some of the chests in those early days, I now decided that they should be put to good use lighting my passages on those special nights when inspiration struck.

Of course, the candles were finite in number, and I had to weigh their use carefully to make them last as long as I was able, for I lacked the necessary materials to make more. Thus, most of my writing was accomplished during the daylight hours, when the sun was high and bright.

I had cut the candles into smaller portions so that I could better control their use, fearing that I might fall asleep and allow a much larger candle to burn down, wasting it.

I then took the opportunity offered while fishing to think about the plot structure of my new book and the characters that should play important roles resolving the challenges faced by my favorite protagonist, once again, me.

I began to understand what allured the great authors to take up the pen, the need they had to create, the passion that burned within them to set their imaginations free, to let those fanciful thoughts flow into ink and then down through the quill to land upon paper, the willpower and the discipline that drove them toward their own writing desks.

As a side note, I also found the task very therapeutic and calming.

To begin my book, I went back to page one of this journal seeking to give an appropriate title to my work. I searched my mind for such a title and came up with the following offerings. "The Tragic Account of Thomas Bartholomew Cantfield: a man once long-ago marooned" had a certain flair, but it was such a laborious title and reflected neither the true nature nor the disposition of my actual life here. After a time, I then came up with "The Marooning of Thomas Bartholomew Cantfield." That title was less laborious to both the mouth and to the mind, but it failed, once again, to properly invoke a true vision as to my adventures on the island. After much deliberation, and discarding other titles even less appropriate to the cause and therefore not worth mentioning here, I came to what I believe is a suitable and appropriate title: "The Wondrous Life of a Long-Ago Man."

How did such a title come to my mind? you might have already asked yourself. Well, to be honest, in a moment of calm, it simply sprang into my head. You can surmise why it is called "The Wondrous Life," for I stated clearly at the very start of this chronicle that it is intended to impart to you my wondrous life. As for the "Long-Ago Man," well, in truth, as I committed those words to parchment, I had then no sufficient reason for doing so. I was confident, however, that in time such reasoning would become clear to me.

The 240th day of my captivity began similarly to every other day since I had begun writing seriously. I spoke a cheerful good morning to my lovely grass woman, whom I had finally named Gretchen, having recalled a beautiful, flaxen-haired young woman whom I had noticed time and again ambling about the campus of the accounting college. In that other long-ago life, she had paid no attention to me, for she was from the upper crust of society. She was a comely beauty, as I recall, thin but possessing a fine and shapely figure.

Being the headmaster's daughter, she was often seen wandering around the school unescorted. She was not a student of accounting, of course, those endeavors rightly so being in the domain of men, but because she was the headmaster's daughter, Gretchen was as smart as they come. Compared to her, as I later discovered, I was but a dolt.

She chose Richard McGilliam as her beau, which was not at all surprising and a most natural choice, for Richard was the kind of man all the available women of the town, which hosted the College of Financial Preparation, a professional school specializing in the acquisition of accounting skills, would fancy. His smile was white, broad, and very friendly, and it alone attracted many a young maiden's attention. Richard was also very wealthy. His father, being a successful giant in the merchant trade, sent him to the school to learn the ways of high finance as part of his grooming to take over the family empire. Richard was a kindly sort, and I never had any adverse issue with him, but being myself from a much lower level of society, we did not, of course, consort together.

On this island, however, Gretchen was *my* grass woman, who had eyes only for me, and she told me so each and every morning as I greeted her.

Fear and courage, I have heard, are brothers who have coexisted long before time even began. I do not recall where I heard such words, but I do recall them being spoken or read to me.

I have also heard that fear is a relative experience, gripping some much harder than others. I will tell you this: I thought that I had known fear in my life, such as during the storm which sent me to the island in the first place, but I had never experienced the paralyzing effects of true fear before this day.

Later that same morning, my 240th day, along the path of my normal daily walk about the island, I spied what I thought to be the masts of a tall ship peeking above the distant horizon. Being on the opposite side of the island, the north side, and far from my signal fire, and feeling an immediate sense of panic setting in upon me, I began waving my arms and shouting as loudly as I could in a lunatic attempt to attract their attention. Of course, being so far away, they had no chance at all to see me. It was, simply put, the poor attempt of a desperate oaf, but one which proved to be fortunate in the end.

Being high above the shoreline, on an upper trail, I strained my eyes to see what kind of ship it was, and during this time I saw also the hint of a second ship on the horizon. From what I could tell, one appeared to be leading the other, and they were very close together. Excitement swelled my chest at the thought of finally being rescued by one of those beautiful, heavily sheeted ships.

I could only watch them approach, but with delight I saw that they appeared to be on a course directly toward the island. My delight, however, was woefully short lived, for the ship following, having soon come alongside the lead ship, suddenly belched smoke and fire. It was several seconds before I heard the boom of the cannons vibrate the air surrounding me.

"Oh, my," I uttered aloud, for 'twas surely a battle in the making, not a rescue.

From my vantage point high on the mountain, I watched as the horror of the grotesque fight played itself out before my saddened eyes. It was obvious to me that the following ship was of a specific evil intent. Whether they were pirates, I could not tell at that time, but the following ship was clearly a ship built for war, not for hauling cargo. I could plainly see the many cannon ports in her side, and there was an obvious disagreement being voiced at that moment and it shouted loudly enough.

The ships continued tracking southward toward the island, and within two hours, which time I calculated from the movement of the sun through the cloudless sky, they were just a short ways off the coast and battling hard. I could plainly hear the shots being fired from roaring blunderbusses and could clearly see that the following ship was giving much better than it was receiving.

Just then, ropes were slung outward from the following ship toward the leading ship. Within seconds, the lines now having been secured, brazen fellows from the trailing ship swung over onto the lead ship. Hand-to-hand battle then ensued. Steady pistol shots echoed out over the water and bounced off the mountains. I could see many men falling under the savage sword as well.

From my perspective, I could finally see that the trailing ship was indeed manned by pirates with deadly designs on the lead ship, which was now clearly a private merchant vessel under American registry, the Stars and Stripes flapping wildly about in the wind.

The battle did not last long once the pirates boarded the merchant vessel. I became very afraid, but at the same time I considered myself to be most fortunate, for had this battle taken place on the other side of the island, I would have already lit my signal fire, foolishly announcing my presence to that murderous breed which had just set upon those gentle men of the merchant vessel.

From the safety of my mountainside, I bore witness to the slaughter. One by one, the pirates murdered the helpless crew of the merchant vessel, tossing their bodies into a heap upon the deck of the ship.

To my wide-eyed amazement, a small launch emerged from the far side of the merchant vessel. I counted two men rowing for their very lives away from the carnage and toward my shore. I wanted to run down to the shore and lend assistance to them, but fear gripped me tightly, anchoring my feet to the path.

My temporary paralysis turned out to be another embrace of good fortune, for I saw some of the pirates firing at those men in the small launch. Then I saw one of the pirates, an officer, I presume, signal other men who quickly commenced a launch of their own. With several crewmen rowing as one, it did not take long for the pirates to gain closure on the small boat being propelled by only two men.

As the merchant launch struck the shore, the two men jumped from their boat and began running as the pirates fired several balls at the men in advance of their steps. I then heard shouting, but I could not make out the words. More shots were fired. The running men stopped suddenly and remained very still. The pirates, having landed now themselves, quickly approached the men and took them into custody, returning them to a man I presumed to be their officer.

I watched in horror as the pirates knocked the men to their bellies. I heard more shouting, and then one of the pirates pulled his pistol and pointed it at the men. The pirate officer then drew a cutlass and apparently ordered the men to rise to their knees, whereupon he immediately proceeded to behead them.

I trembled terribly, thinking that the pirates would wish to then remain on the island. If they did, it would be only a matter of time before they discovered me, and I had the terrible thought, *Is it to be my fate also to leave my head here on this sand, separated from my body?*

I tell you now that a horrible fear swept over me, and I am not ashamed to admit it. I watched as the pirates looked around. One of them, I was certain, even looked directly up at me. I froze, unable to stir my still paralyzed legs into movement. To my relief, however, he moved his head more left and then right. It became apparent that he had not seen my cowering form.

Within minutes, the pirates were in both launches and rowing back toward their ship. Then, for several hours more, I watched them remove virtually everything of any worth from the merchant vessel. I hoped against hope that they would leave the ship behind, but alas, that was not to be. As the pirate ship moved away, several of those detestable men tossed fiery torches onto the decks of the merchant vessel. Within moments, the entire ship was ablaze.

Almost immediately, the pirate ship weighed anchor and departed from the island heading due west. Left safely behind, I sat down to watch the cargo ship burn brightly late into the night, until all that remained of a once proud vessel were red-hot embers glowing on the waterline. Even that image did not last long, as she finally capsized and sank beneath the waves with an evil-sounding hiss, leaving me once again all alone and without hope of escaping the island.

That evening, sitting now calmly by my fire, I experienced a deep shame suddenly rushing over me. Why had I not been able to move during the attack on those good men? What had held my feet so still? What had caused me to stand by and do nothing to help those two distressed souls?

I began to think hard upon the matter. The simple answer was clear: surely it was fear that had fastened me to the ground, but *why*? Why had it held me so fast in its grip? What is the true nature of fear, I pondered, and how does one overcome it? What is it that makes one afraid? And conversely, what is it that makes one brave? How does one summon courage while paralyzed by fear? How do soldiers, in the midst of battle, find the daring to become heroes?

The more deeply I reflected on the nexus between fear and courage, the more questions filled my mind. What is most curious, however, is the fact that only questions came to me. I received no answers at all to my introspective inquiries. Simply put, then, without any answers to consider the matter on a deeper level, I could come only to the conclusion that I was a coward, and for a coward, it seems, there are no justifiable answers, just a pitiful and shameful existence.

What is shamefully true is that two men died because I could not summon the courage within to offer them any assistance. It matters not that I most probably would have failed to save them anyway. It matters to me only that I was unable to even try. I stood by as a frightened child and did nothing to intervene. Perhaps this is why I have been confined to this island. It seems that I am not fit to live among the good and the brave. It is fitting, then, that I should be marooned here, for being here requires no acts of heroism. It requires only that I cower away and do not protest.

I judged myself therefore a pathetic and loathsome creature, because there was no one else who could.

On the morrow, after a night of well-earned self-condemnation, I took myself to where the men lay and moved their bodies slightly inland, to the line of underbrush, where I then gave them a proper burial. It took me only a few minutes to dig the graves to a suitable depth with only my hands in the soft sand.

I then presented myself to them as what I was, a coward, a shameful and contrary excuse for anything useful in the world, a man, nay, not a man, but an unworthy waste of human flesh, completely undeserving of the honor to bury them.

Nevertheless, to them I said aloud: "Forgive me, you gentle men. Forgive me for being of a weak and cowardly nature. I have no excuse for my being so gutless and pitiful. I can only express my deep regret for not at least trying to offer assistance. I am fittingly here on this island, kind sirs, because the world has neither need nor want of a man born of a faint heart and a craven disposition. The world needs heroes, and I am not one to be counted among them. I further regret that you now share a part of this island with the likes of me. May you sleep well in your forever slumber."

I filled in the graves and walked back to my camp. That evening, I sat quietly by my fire and thought of nothing at all.

I am forced to confess to you this also. If being a coward was not enough, I might now appropriately be labeled a thief as well, for I liberated their outer garments so I might have something more to wear other than my torn trousers and a single tattered blouse. Even now, I wear one man's pair of shoes as I write this. I am at this moment, and once again, self-judged to be an immoral man and well deserving of my fate.

I feel it critical to my cause that you understand this: I had not intended to plunder the dead, but I was sorely in need of replacement clothing. To my good fortune, despite my despicable act, the men were approximately the same height as I, although both were much larger in girth it would seem due to the ill-fitting clothing. The cause, however, for this may yet be attributed to my restricted diet, for I remembered being a bit more portly than I am at present.

52

I am not, by any stretch of the imagination, a religious man, nor have I ever been known to possess any saintly qualities that I am aware of, and certainly, based upon my recent acts, you might agree with me, but on the evening of the battle I did take time to send a hearty thank-you out into the cool night air, to whomever or whatever had protected me from those inhuman beasts, if indeed I had been so protected.

On the morning of my 244th day on the wretched rock, I had, over the previous two-day period, contemplated something of a serious nature that I would now share with you presently.

Upon reading the stories of those other castaways, both real and fictitious, it had seemed strange to me how someone, finding himself in great need or very frightened, seemed always to find religion in some form or another.

I cannot say for certain that there is no God. Neither can I say for certain that there is a God. I can say only that in my years on this earth, I have not seen any clearly sufficient evidence to support either conclusion.

I suppose, then, it comes down to pure and simple faith, being the full of it, or the lack of it. It must be this simple, for in that I have no evidence either way, I am not at all certain of anything, whereas others become so certain of what they choose to believe that they search hardest for it and to no end, being in constant search of what they hold fast onto.

To those who find their faith in support of some

loving deity, I must congratulate them. It seems they are among the precious few who find some peace in their faith. I do not say this is a bad thing. However, to those who discover confirmation, in their own heart, that we are alone in this world without any One being above or around, watching out for us, then I say unto them they should seek to find some measure of peace to comfort themselves in their own way and by whatever means best suited to them.

For me, personally, I would rather choose to live in peace than to live in strife—if for no other reason than it requires less effort to live peacefully. For a coward such as I, this is preferable.

Seek not an answer from me as to what I believe, for I have no idea which camp is right and which is wrong. But if I be pressed to give an answer of sorts as to what I believe for me, my answer would be thus: if there is someone above who cares for me, then make yourself well known to me by sending a rescue ship. If so, then I shall give a good and faithful account of that being and try to live a more honorable life, singing its praises unto my end. If I do not see such a rescue ship, then I will conclude that I am nothing more than I am at present, just a timorous individual infesting this earth, deserving of nothing better, and in possessing no real value to this planet, nor to anyone else then, I shall quietly die when it comes my time to do so.

From what I have seen already in this world, I must conclude that we are born, we live, and we die, and given that I see nothing special about our species, the only consideration that remains, therefore, is in what manner shall we live and in what manner shall we die. In that, I fear, my lot has been already cast in stone.

Having deliberated on this matter a good while longer, I wondered what those men who died on the sandy shoreline believed. I wondered if they believed in a God who would protect them from those pirates, and if so, what then did they conclude just before the pirate's sword sliced through their necks?

I only pose questions. I offer neither solution nor criticism, for who could truly know what belief lived in their hearts in that final moment? I feel assured of only this: I was frightened to paralysis and am relieved that the pirates are gone.

In conclusion, I will add only this to what I already know for certain. The island is no longer a paradise, a place of light and harmony, of peace and joy, a place untouched by the ugliness that dwells in this world. It is no sanctuary for the afflicted of heart and soul. It is not a place of rest.

And if I ever dare think again that this island is anything other than a horrible prison, I have only to bring to remembrance the bodies of two dead men, my cowardly manner—and those damnable pirates.

Chapter 4

I did not sleep well the next evening, with the nightmarish visions of those sailors being slaughtered rudely assaulting me during the night along with the continued revisiting of my timid nature; I worried that those events might take some time to fade from memory. Therefore, on my 245th day of captivity, I visited their graves and offered kind words to them.

Fear not, for I offer you this assurance: I remained fully in control of my sanity, and I knew well enough that they were dead and buried and wholly incapable of any physical intercourse, but like my grassy Gretchen, it gave me some peace to sit by the graves and converse with those men, even though the conversation was devised and carried out in my brain alone.

During our conversation that day, those gentle beings forgave me my sins, and in subsequent conversations we became close companions, sharing stories of our lives and fates.

By the 250th day, I had been spending a great deal of time with my murdered friends.

One of them I named Matthew Bodine, for I knew not his given name nor his surname, of course.

Matthew was an older man, some ten years my senior, and well gifted of a very gentle persuasion. He was most kind in both thought and deed, and was usually first to offer words of comfort when I began feeling overwhelmed. He possessed little propensity for humor, however, and was given more over toward serious thoughts. He was married to a wonderful woman he called Tilly, for short, her full name being Matilda. They had married over ten years earlier and had a son, James, who had just turned eight years old the previous month, and a daughter, Chelsea, who would become six years of age the following month.

Matthew was on his way back home to Boston from an extended voyage to India, where he took some advantage of his stay and collected jewels, spices, and other exotic gifts for his wife and family. I found him to be certainly a generous and considerate man, albeit appearing to be stern and reserved.

On the ship, known as the AMERICAN DESTINY, he held the position of cargo master, the man charged with the placing of the cargo into the ship's hold so that the ship rides evenly upon the ocean. He was well respected by both the crew and officers equally. As I have said, he was a serious-minded individual and one not given to wild exaggeration. His wise and often pertinent counsel kept *me* well balanced also.

I was certain that during the passage of time, I would come to value his opinions more and more. His words usually included an accurate assessment of the underlying reasons for my moments of despair. His counsel, more often than not, eased my delivery to a good conclusion from any dilemma that challenged me. He possessed the unique ability to put my mind right again, over and over and with good speed. He pushed me to think.

My other friend was named Charles, or, as I was fond of calling him, Charlie. Charlie McShane. Charlie was a man without a mate, same as I, and very near my own age, although a bit younger. Like Matthew, he hailed from Boston, from a good solid family, albeit a family of common means, such as my own.

He was a much different sort from Matthew, for he was given widely to jest and merriment. Through this attribute, he had been largely responsible for, and my inspiration for, any comedic thoughts that entered my head. We had great fun together, Charlie and I.

His position on the ship was seaman, somewhat trained but lacking many skills that men with positions more senior possessed. He was new to his task, that fateful voyage being both his first and his last. Lacking certain skills, he was at that point in his career, at the time of his untimely death, little more than a landsman. He was a man with tendencies leaning more toward the mischievous at times, and substantially lacking in maturity. Yet, when I was trapped in my most serious and reflective frame of mind, it was Charlie who often crept up behind me and startled me with the most outrageous stunts of surprise. He was quite accomplished at renewing my spirit. He made me laugh.

All things considered, then, I was very blessed to have two such companions with which to share the island, one to give me good and sound advice when needed and one to make silly with when *that* was needed.

So, having released these new friends from the limitations of their graves, at least in my mind, we three companions traveled about the island, making new discoveries. Within hours after visiting their graves that first day, I had created their forms in the same fashion as Grassy Gretchen and even given each his own elevated position next to her so that they could converse with one another while I slept.

I was abruptly awakened the next morning, the 251st day, with a sudden splash of cold water. With a startle, I rose up from my bunk of leaves and wooden poles and noticed an empty bowl of water on the ground. I realized that my arm must have knocked it over onto me while in a fitful sleep, but then I heard that tiny familiar chortle behind me. I turned my head to see Charlie grinning at me, holding an empty gourd.

"Time to rise, Thomas!" he laughed, his silly tongue wagging from his mouth as if he were a madman. "And I've reclaimed my clothing, you mill thief." He giggled loudly and then darted from my tent.

"Splash *me* with cold water, will you?" I shouted in forged anger. I then stepped out from my tent to see Charlie scampering away, with already a substantial lead, down the path toward the fruit trees.

"Good morning, Gretchen," I said calmly to my grass woman.

I then spied Matthew sitting by the morning fire, redressed in *his* own clothing and calmly cooking eggs. "Good morning, Matthew."

"Good morning, lad. Charlie's at it again, I see."

"That he is," I replied just before breaking into a dash to chase after Charlie.

I pursued the jester past the trees and several yards further before catching up with him and tackling him to the ground. Then after wrestling each other, very much in jest, for several minutes, we finally parted, each lying on his back and panting like a dog, laughing uproariously.

After several more minutes, having stilled my laughter and rising up to rest on my elbows, I noticed Matthew, ever the serious one, approaching. He did not slow his pace, but continued walking past Charlie and me.

"Enough of that, gentlemen. Let us be going. There is much to do today."

"And what would that be, Matthew?" I shouted.

"I'm sure the sooner we begin searching for it, the sooner we will discover what it is. Up off the ground, you two. That is no place for gentlemen."

Having imparted those words to us, Matthew disappeared down the path and through the thicket. Charlie and I glanced at one another. Charlie chuckled.

"Gentlemen!" he said, snickering. "How dare he."

"How dare he indeed," I laughingly responded.

"Perhaps we should follow," he said.

"To what end?" I asked. "I know of no task that needs to be undertaken today."

"That's the fun of it, silly man. It's the discovery that's important, not the task."

With that, Charlie jumped to his feet and dashed after Matthew.

I, too, then stood up and dusted myself clean, uttering aloud, "It's going to be a good day, I think." I then gave chase.

I quickly caught up with my two friends, and together we walked and chatted about most everything we could think of. We discovered no task that needed undertaking, however, save a brisk and rejuvenating walk to the far westward end of the island and back again to the grove of fruit trees. For our afternoon meal, we settled for fresh mango and bits of coconut meat and coconut milk. It was delicious.

The sun was warm. The skies were clear. It was in fact, and as I had earlier declared, a very good day. I laid my head back against the mango tree and within minutes fell fast asleep.

I awakened abruptly to a loud snap, as if by a twig under a heavy foot. I sat up quickly and wondered whence the sound had come, for I had never before heard such a sound on the island. I clutched at my knife and then pulled it fully from its scabbard in preparation for an attack from the unseen assailant quickly approaching.

I shuddered when I realized that it must be the pirates, now returned to the island. I suspected that they had perhaps found my living quarters and had set out to locate the occupant. It is possible, I reasoned, that they simply followed the path leading here or are following the foot tracks in the sand. But by whatever means they had used to follow me, I was not eager to meet them.

I admit that my heart began beating so hard that I heard the pounding of it in my ears with grand lucidity. I slipped behind the mango tree and strained to hear the sound of the approaching entity, attempting to ascertain from what direction I could expect the attack.

I heard another snap directly forward of my position, and so I backed quietly away from the tree and then turned to begin my hasty retreat when I heard a soft female voice call out my name. I stopped dead in my steps in dumbfounded shock.

The voice called my name once again, this time drawing nearer. I returned to the tree and peeked around its trunk and nearly fainted with both relief and shock, for walking along the path through the thicket and into the clearing was Grassy Gretchen, in human form, alive and exactly as I recalled her image from school. Her long, flowing dress of dark blue silk buttoned up the front and had small white ruffles at the ends of the sleeves and around the neck. Sitting on her head was a hat made of matching material and adorned with peacock feathers swooping from its left side. She carried an open parasol over her head to protect her from the sun. She was, in fact, perfectly dressed for strolling around the college campus on a mid-June afternoon. She looked absolutely wonderful.

I staggered out from behind the tree and was instantly greeted by her warm and loving smile. I stared with what must have been an odd expression because she stopped in her tracks and twirled her parasol in front of her.

"And what have you been doing, my darling?" she asked.

I tried to speak. My mouth moved, I felt it move, but no sound issued from my lips.

"Have you nothing to say, Thomas? That look on your face tells me that you must have been making silly with Charlie again. Is that so?" She laughed as she trotted to me, hugged my neck, and kissed me on the mouth. She then wrapped her arms tightly around my body and stared up into my eyes. I swear to you now that I saw a sparkle, as clear and bright as the sun itself, in those eyes.

I tell you, truly, I still did not—nay, *could* not—find words to say, try as I might to search for them. In a short time after, I did find them, but they refused to come forth and make themselves heard.

I tell you this also, her lips tasted as sweet as ripe mango, and I was amazed at how soft they were. I tried once again to urge even a mumble from my throat, but there came no sound still. All I was able to do at that moment was stare back into her gloriously blue eyes, as if they were the spring pool that supplied me my sweet water.

"Are you not speaking today, Thomas? Or is it just for me that you hold your tongue?" she asked in a teasing tone.

Finally, I summoned my full concentration, but could force only a single syllable from my lips, in the form of "I." "I" is a word, and I know it such to be, and I spoke it clearly, truly I did. But even to my ear it was no more than a grunt. Nevertheless, it was all that I could bring to muster for all my effort.

Gretchen smiled broadly. "Did you say 'aye' as in 'Aye, aye, madam' or 'I' as in 'I am so glad that you are here, sweet Gretchen'? Her lips then parted to form around a white grin. She was teasing me without mercy. I knew it such, but I stood as the dumb lunkhead that I seemed always to be around her and could only stare at her for several more delicious moments.

Finally, with the shock of it all beginning to ebb ever so slightly, I formed my lips and forcibly pushed the air out of my lungs. "I am so glad that you are here, sweet Gretchen."

She smiled and began to respond, but before she could, I continued, "But how are you here? Have I now gone completely insane? How is this possible?"

"Are you in such a desperate need to know these things, my love," she gently inquired, "or are you able to simply accept the fact that I am here right now, with you? Is it not enough just to know that I am here and no longer made of grass and twigs?"

"It is, sweet woman, for the moment at least. It is enough to know that I am holding you and staring into your loving eyes. Yes. Unto heaven above I cry thus. Oh, sweet, sweet Gretchen, I sing *yes*, it is more than enough!"

"Then relax, dear Thomas, and kiss me yet again to give me assurance."

I instantly obeyed and kissed her for what seemed like several blissful hours, and then, hand in hand, we walked back toward my tent chatting as if we had known each other for years and had never parted.

"Please do not think badly of me, my love, but I feel you are attired for a place much beyond these meager surroundings. You must be very uncomfortable at present."

"Do not trouble yourself so, my darling. I am so dressed only for greeting you. I shall dispense with much of this later for the sake of comfort."

"Very wise. Very wise indeed, for this climate would weigh heavily upon you should you remain in like stead for my sake."

As we continued walking together, I felt that something was amiss.

"Is it me, my love, or does something feel absent?"

"All seems right, my dear. Why?"

"I don't know, but I'm certain that some important aspect is missing."

Then I realized what it was.

"Where are Charlie and Matthew?" I asked.

"They have returned to the tent, Thomas. All is well. Have no more thoughts as to what is missing, for all is as it should be for now."

With a full heart of joy and nothing more to give me pain or doubt, I walked with my Gretchen along the sandy path in the sole delight that she was with me, and knowing the confident truth of it: she would never leave.

Upon our return to the tent, I found Charlie and Matthew sitting around the fire, each with his own plucked fowl skewered on a stick and being cooked over glowing embers.

"We would have prepared a bird for you both, but we were unsure as to when you might return," said Matthew.

"No need of that, Matthew," I responded. "I am still full from our afternoon meal." I turned to Gretchen to ask if she felt hungry, but she anticipated my question and shook her head.

"Well enough, then," continued Matthew. "There seems to be a sufficient amount for us."

"I think Thomas lives on love now, Matthew," teased Charlie, wearing his usual mischievous grin.

"There may be some truth in that, Charlie," replied Matthew stoically. "There may be some truth in that."

I was struck shortly dumb once again when I looked over to the three now empty poles which once supported my grass friends.

"I tell you this, Thomas," said Charlie, noting my stare at the poles, "I was getting mighty tired of that pole up me backside."

Everyone laughed loudly. I laughed as I had not laughed since coming to the island. And after a bit, with tears of elation streaking down my face, I fell into a joyful silence, just gazing with delight and wonder at my new living friends. At that moment I felt all the horror of loneliness vanish from my mind.

Later that night, lying lazily around a zestful fire, with its orange glow reflecting off my new friends' faces, I glanced skyward only for a moment, but whispered my gratitude once more to whomever or whatever had graced me with these fine people.

Watching Charlie teasing the others with his usual mirth and hearing their laughter, I suddenly realized that I was as home here as if I had been back in New York, in the house of my parents.

With disbelieving eyes, I looked once again at

those empty poles, the fire's glow now dancing on their bare surfaces, and finally admitted to myself that I possessed no understanding whatsoever of how such a thing was possible, but I felt warmed and thrilled that it was so. I resisted the desire to raise the question, for I dared not risk finding that it was all just in my imagination after all.

I was here and holding Gretchen tightly to me. I felt her body move in rhythm with each breath she took. I smelled the aroma of her hair and skin. I felt the warmth of her body. I saw Matthew and Charlie clearly sitting across the fire pit from me. They were real. It was all real.

I sat in silence, but I was truly glad hearted. It was then that Matthew turned his head from the conversation of the others and stared at me. A slight smile formed on his lips, and then he bobbed his head at me as if to say, "Steady, my boy. All is well now." I returned his smile, and my heart swelled with happiness. He turned his attention back toward the others and began listening to them once again as I sat staring at him, knowing that my days of despair and loneliness were now and forever behind me.

On that night, finishing the 251st day of my fortuitous arrival, a new man was born. A man of promise. A man whose heart was now filled with perpetual hope, a man who would nevermore doubt the creative force behind fervent willpower, desperate desire, and skillfully employed intention.

Chapter 5

I opened my eyes in the warming light of the new day's sun, and once sleep had left them, I found myself outside and seated on the ground, my back against the log next to the fire pit, whose embers were now cold and dead. Gretchen was seated next to me leaning against my chest, my arms coiled around her, and Matthew and Charlie were curled up across the way, both sleeping soundly. I tell you now that it was a most glorious awakening for me.

I then glanced up at the empty poles where my grass friends had once hung together. Although I had seen those poles clearly absent any grassy forms the night before, I still could not believe my eyes and was forced to ponder once again what creative force could have given life to grass people. I recalled asking a similar question the previous night, to which I still had no answer; I knew only that I had never slept so soundly since my arrival on the island. I realize that I repeat myself, dear reader, but I think it worthy to restate here what a glorious evening the preceding night had been and what an incredible awakening that next tine morning.

I tried not to disturb Gretchen as she slept and so remained very still, but she stirred and soon opened her eyes. Instantly, another beautiful smile formed and her eyes sparkled once again.

"Good morning, my love," she whispered.

"Good morning, my love," I returned in kind.

"I don't want to move."

"Nor do I want you to. I am quite content to sit here like this forever."

She smiled warmly up at me. "And I would want to please you to do so, but my stomach cries out for ripe mango."

I chuckled. I heard the gurgling of her empty stomach calling out for satiation. "Then ripe mango you shall have, my dear."

We separated and I stood up, shaking the sand off my trousers, adding, "Rest yourself, my sweet woman. I shall return momentarily with your morning meal well in hand."

I stirred the dead fire and discovered still glowing embers under the ashes. I laid dried weeds over them, and within seconds a resurgent flame arose. I piled more wood onto the fire, smiled at my Gretchen, and then strode off down the path toward the grove of mango trees.

As I made my way along the path, I felt my spirit take wing and soar high above me. My whole being surged with reinvigoration, my heart filled with joy, my mind crystal clear, my spirit renewed. As I walked, I also experienced a new swagger, as it were, in my step. My attitude had changed during the night, I knew it had, but until that moment I had no idea of the extent of the transformation I had undergone. Something else had changed in me, something shrouded in mystery and not yet identifiable, but it felt good and right. A new thought boldly landed upon me.

"Is this what being in love is like?" I asked myself. Of course I had no answer, mind you, for I had never been in a loving relationship. You might think that odd, my being now thirty years of age, but I entreat you to understand that I had gone straight from my youth to school, and thence immediately to work. Since that time I had been concentrating on establishing myself in my trade, completely unaware of what effect the love of a good woman can have on a young man. I had felt infatuated with a woman before, certainly, but I now realized that my previous feelings were nothing compared to being in love, and knowing it.

Love is unique. Love is special. I had never, before my awakening, understood its power and its majesty. I was then, and I still am, a simple man, 'tis true, but love has a way of making a simple man feel as if he is something much grander. Love gives a man a confidence that he may have lacked otherwise. By some magic, it gives him reason to believe that all things are possible. Love can compel a man to think that he is stronger, wiser, and funnier than he actually may be.

How did I know these things? you might ask. I knew these things because that was the way Gretchen made me feel.

I picked several mangoes and tossed them into

a heap in the middle of my blouse, now spread upon the sand. Having filled the shirt to capacity, I then slung it over my shoulder and carried it back to camp, whistling a light tune, its name forgotten but the melody keenly remembered.

The morning air felt perfectly delicious against my bare skin, neither too hot nor too cold. I thought of what we might all do together that day. Perhaps we could walk to the eastern end of the island, and have our midday meal by the ocean. Perhaps I would do some fishing there, something I had never tried before. I intended to ask Gretchen if she would like to fish with me. The thought excited me, and so I almost danced back to camp.

As I approached the site, my heart sank. Gretchen and my two friends were not to be seen. I felt suddenly very ill. I called out loudly to each of them and received no response. I called to each again, more loudly this time, but only silence returned to my ear.

Had I imagined them? "Oh, dear me," I gasped.

I dropped my blouse to the ground, spilling the mangoes, and, instantly overcome with nausea, collapsed onto the log clutching my stomach. I fought the spasm of my belly trying to extricate its contents, but I was able to stave off such an event although the sensation remained for a while after. My head began to swoon. I no longer knew what to believe, and I wondered piteously, *Have I created them all in my head? Have I lost complete control of my senses?*

"*Why?*" I finally cried aloud.

I felt a sense of betrayal I had never felt before. If there was a God, He must surely be a very spiteful being to taunt me so, I reasoned. *Does He have no one else to plague? Must I always be the brunt of His cruelty?*

What was I to do, now that I was again alone?

No answers came to me. I was utterly lost once more, lost in a mire of complete confusion.

I heard the rustle of leaves on a nearby bush, and a second later my Gretchen walked out from them. She stopped when she saw me and smiled.

"You're really here!" I shouted in glee. Then Matthew and Charlie walked out into the open also. "You're all really here, aren't you?"

"Of course we are, darling," said Gretchen, her face now formed in a confused stare. "Where else would we be?"

I was so overcome with relief and joy that I could not hold back my tears. I wept into my hands like a baby, and I tell you, dear reader, I am not a man given to such outbursts of emotion. Not, at least, to this extent. I did not care, though; I had to relieve all the tension and stress that had overtaken my body and mind, and so I wept openly and unabashedly.

Within seconds, Gretchen was at my side, her arms wrapped lovingly about my head, soothingly stroking the back of my neck and giving me what comfort she could.

I cried for a long while, I can admit that to you

without fear of losing my masculinity, and when my tears had finally dried, I sat on the log and recovered in Gretchen's arms as would a child.

After a while, Charlie came crawling over on his hands and knees and put his face near mine. He stared at me for several seconds and then pulled a silly face. "Are you done with that now?"

I laughed and reached out my hand and caressed the top of his head. He made another odd face. "Now he pets me as a dog?"

I laughed harder. A few more tears of joy trickled from my eyes.

"Dear me, here we go again," Charlie teased.

"Leave the man be, Charlie," said Matthew. "Can't you see that he is still overcome? With what, I know not, but he remains in an emotional state."

"But it makes his face look funny. All contorted and out of sorts," kidded Charlie.

I laughed again.

"Are you going to stay sappy all day?" he asked.

"No, Charlie," I finally managed, with my own smile. "I just thought that I had lost all of you. I thought you were just figments of my own crazed imagination."

"Well, silly, as Gretchen said, where else would we be if not here with you? I think you've gone daft, old man." Charlie giggled and rolled onto his back, staring up into the sky. "I think Thomas has bats in his belfry, Matthew."

"I think *you* have bats aplenty in yours, dear boy," Matthew rejoined.

Charlie giggled.

"I didn't know where you all had gone," I began to explain. "When I returned and didn't see you, I called out to each of you but received no answer. I then thought that I had imagined you and that the spell had finally collapsed."

"It is difficult to hear you, lad, when we are so near the falls of the spring. It's quite loud there, you know."

"I understand, Matthew."

Gretchen stroked my face and held my head in both of her hands as she turned my face toward hers and spoke very softly. "I understand your fear, my love, but you had only to look to the empty poles and you would have known."

Those words she spoke were said with love and reassurance, but still I felt the fool. She was right: if I had only looked to the empty poles. It was the obvious thing to do, and yet I had not considered that simple act because of my deep anguish. She had a wonderfully calming effect on me.

"We went to the spring to wash up," said Gretchen in her most soothing tone. "That is all there is to it. I'm sorry you experienced such terror, my darling, but we three are here with you. All is well."

"Yes, it is," I uttered in glad relief. "All is well once again."

That afternoon, the four of us took a walk to the far easterly end of the island, as I had hoped. We spent the entire afternoon there, and Gretchen tried her hand at fishing. I was well pleased, for she caught several large fish and all of them quite on her own. I believe she enjoyed most of the experience very much, but she balked when it was time to affix the insects to the hook.

"Thomas," she yelled, time and time again. "I simply cannot do this. Please help me."

I laughed and, of course, baited her hook, but she managed to land, by herself, the fish she subsequently caught. She even had the nerve to 'shoos' me away when I tried to help her.

Of course Matthew, in his ordinarily calm state, lay back against a tree and just took it all in from afar, while Charlie, also his normal playful self, teased Gretchen with the dead fish until she chased him away.

I laughed very hard seeing Gretchen chasing Charlie up and down the shoreline for quite a while, the two tossing sand at one another and making fun of each other.

I had no idea that Charlie was as fast as he was, nor was I aware how tenacious Gretchen could be once provoked into action. It was all in good fun, of course.

We were all such very good friends.

I looked to the west and was witness to the glorious and fiery end to the sun's daily journey across the sky. Having made a great fire near the beach, we all sat in a circle, each sequestered in our own contemplative quiet, listening to the rhythmic songs of the ocean, the waves rolling in and splashing upon the shore.

I, myself, sat there scribbling my final thoughts of the day into the journal before the darkness came and stilled my hand, lost in wonder as to how many more miracles I was to receive. I had both my love and my good friends to keep me company. I had still winds and fair weather to comfort me. And, it even seemed to me, the island itself, although still very much an entrapment for us all, was continuing to bless us with sustained moments of enjoyment.

The darkness finally closed in such that I could no longer see the page well enough to write, and that being the end of my 252nd day on the island, I laid down my quill and took my rest, Gretchen's head upon my chest, still wondering what new adventures awaited us on the morrow.

The next morning, after the night on the beach, we packed up the things we had brought and returned to the camp without incident. As we reached the site, I spied a large albatross sitting by our dead campfire.

By the way it flapped about on the ground, it appeared to be injured and unable to fly.

"Oh, Thomas, the poor thing is injured. Catch it so we might heal it. Please, Thomas. Quickly," Gretchen pleaded.

"Yes, Thomas," added Charlie, "catch it. I've never eaten albatross before."

Gretchen scowled at Charlie, and as the saying goes, if looks could kill, Charlie would immediately have been transformed into a corpse, but he only smiled devilishly in response to Gretchen's agitated stare. "Joking, dear sister. Only joking."

I crouched low and walked toward the bird, but upon seeing me approach, it scampered off into the underbrush and toward an outcropping of basalt, its wings flapping wildly but unable to lift it off the ground.

I followed it into the brush, which was so thick that I had never before attempted to penetrate it. But seeing that there was now good reason to do so, I pushed my way through at least twenty feet of thicket, following the sound of the wounded bird, twisting this way and that to escape the branches trying to snag me, until I popped out into a very small clearing. I was shocked to see the bird hobbling toward what appeared to be a cave entrance.

My chase had apparently exhausted the bird, and it could resist no further. I approached it slowly and gently so as not to cause it any more stress than was necessary to capture it. As I neared, it quickly scratched at the sand and appeared to bury something, then moved away. It looked terribly frightened, but it could no longer move away from me. I reached out toward it very slowly and stroked its neck carefully and then picked it up in my arms. I studied the bird for several seconds and determined it was female. I could feel her little heart beating hard and fast from what I guessed was a combination of fear and exhaustion. I continued stroking her neck gently, and as I did so, I felt her heartbeat slow.

"Fear not, my little friend," I spoke softly, "for I harbor no ill will toward you nor do I intend to harm you. Take heart instead, beautiful one, for I shall mend your wound. I have a place to keep you safe until you heal, and then I shall see to it that you continue your travels, dear friend. So calm yourself. You are among gentle and caring beings."

After several minutes, the bird seemed calm enough that I was able to carry her to the mouth of the cave and peek inside. My eyes, not having yet adjusted to the diminished light, made out enough detail to give evidence of a naturally well-built structure. I decided that I would explore it more thoroughly later; attending to the bird's injury was a more urgent task requiring my attention.

I worked my way back through the underbrush, taking great care not to allow the branches to harm my new friend.

When I broke through the final section, Gretchen was there to greet me, tears streaking down her worried face.

"Gretchen, my love, dry those tears. Our new friend yet lives and is at this moment calm and safe."

A huge smile formed on her beautiful face, and her blue eyes sparkled with joy. She reached out and stroked the bird's neck as well. The bird must have recognized that she was in no danger, for she sat calmly in my arms, blinking her large, dark eyes and twisting her head all about, taking in the view of friendly hands reaching toward her.

I carried the bird into my tent, stopping first to pick up a handful of collected seeds that I normally feed to my captured menagerie. I held my opened hand up to her beak, and she promptly pecked away at the free food. I knew this to be strange, for it had been my experience that birds, once captured, did not immediately eat. But my new friend must have felt safe, for she pecked away until she had eaten every seed.

I set her gently down upon my new desk, expecting her to attempt to fly away the moment I released my grip upon her. She did not, however. Instead, she stood on my desk and patiently allowed me to thoroughly examine her wings. Of course, not being experienced in bird healing, I could not tell what was wrong with the bird. A gentle touch of its bony wing construction did not reveal any feeling that broken bones were the cause, but clearly something was amiss that prevented the bird from taking wing.

After my examination, I stood up, perplexed as

to the cause of her inability to fly.

"I have no idea what I'm doing, my love," I said to Gretchen.

"Can it fly?"

"I know not, but for tonight, I shall put her in the pen with the other birds and give her time to rest."

"Her?" Gretchen asked.

"I believe so."

A perfect smile formed on Gretchen's lips. I believed that she felt some sense of instant sisterhood with the only other female on the island. I was never sure and did not ask. It was sufficient enough for me to see Gretchen's delightful smile.

"Tomorrow," I said, "I shall then set her free if she appears able to fly."

I stroked the bird's neck with the back of my hand. "Tonight, my little friend, I offer you the safety and hospitality of my menagerie. Hopefully, tomorrow you can continue your journey to wherever your destination lies. I just wish I had wings, for I would gladly join you."

I picked her up and put her inside the aviary. At first, the other birds seemed bothered by the huge bird's sudden presence, but after a short time they settled down and fell back into silence.

My new friend now suitably secured, I turned my attention back to the cave. I gathered up my hatchet and within the hour had cleared a path through the underbrush. My friends followed me through the brush and gathered in the clearing, each staring at the cave through mesmerized eyes.

"Did you know this was here, Thomas?" asked Matthew.

"No, I had no idea. I found it chasing the bird."

"I believe it would make a wonderful home," added Gretchen.

"So do I, dear," I responded while calculating how long and how much effort it would take to make it ready to become our new abode.

I stepped through the portal, let my eyes properly adjust to the diminished light, and immediately found myself within a large, rounded structure with a ceiling rising upward to almost fifteen feet in the center. The floor of the cave was soft sand that stretched out into a circle which I estimated to be at least twenty feet in diameter.

"This will make a splendid dwelling," I remarked. "The air is cool, and the entrance can be hidden in case the pirates make an unscheduled return."

"I agree, Thomas," said Matthew. "We should undertake the task to move as quickly as possible. No telling when those animals will return, but they *will* return, of that I am certain."

"Tomorrow, then, Matthew. Tomorrow morning we move."

That evening I sat in silence pondering what memory Matthew and Charlie had of the pirates and of their subsequent murder. I was hesitant to bring up the matter, fearing that any mention of it might bring unwanted emotions to them. One day I would inquire, but not this day.

For some reason, still unclear to me after all this time, I arose before sunrise and gingerly stepped outside my tent into the cool morning air. I placed more wood onto the fire and blew into the embers until the heat resurrected the flames. I fashioned a torch and lit it, then went to my menagerie to check up on my new feathered friend.

She was awake as well and staring back at me.

"Are you able to fly now, little one?" I whispered.

As if she understood me, she flapped her giant wings until she lifted off the ground, but being in a small pen, she did not rise high. It was enough, though, for me to see that her ability had returned to her.

"Ahh," I said in response, "you can once again take wing, I see."

I opened the pen just enough for her to get out, and out she came—on foot, however. I secured the latch once again and stood back, giving her the freedom to take off, yet she remained firmly on the ground.

"You are free, little one. Off you go, then."

The strangest thing then occurred. The albatross waddled past me and over next to the fire. She tucked her legs under her body and squatted down as if she wished to warm herself by the flames.

I stood in wide-eyed amazement as she then turned her head to me as if inviting me to join her. I walked slowly to the fire and sat on the ground next to her, my back, as usual, against the log.

"So you wish to stay and keep me company this morning, eh? Well, madam, I could not be more pleased."

The bird next stood and walked over to me and squatted again, right next to my leg. She then laid her head directly upon my thigh as if it were a pillow to her. I reached out and began stroking her neck and body. And there we sat together, man and fowl, at peace with one another.

"What should I call you?" I asked. "Do you have a name?"

She, of course, did not reply.

"If you do not already have a name, may I give you one?"

She picked up her head and looked at me. I took that as a sign that she wished for a name.

"Very good. Then a name you shall have." I thought about it for a moment or two. "How about Alma? Do you like that name?" She remained quite still. I took that as a no and thought some more. "How about Beatrice?" The bird remained silent and still. I thought once again. "How does Abigail sound to you, my little friend?" She raised her head and looked at me. "Abigail, then. Is that the name you wish?

Abigail?" She seemed to nod, but perhaps it was a normal gesture for a bird. In any event, I took it as confirmation. "Then Abigail it is. Abigail Albatross. That is how I shall introduce you from now on."

She again laid her head upon my leg. Thus did Abigail and I sit by the fire and converse for the rest of the hour, watching the sun peek its head over the eastern horizon. The conversation was one-sided, of course, but Abigail was an excellent listener. It was a good thing, for I was in a chatty mood.

As the early morning sunlight streamed through the lightly spaced clouds, I decided to gather fruit for the others before they awoke.

"Abigail. I shall take a walk to the mango tree and pluck some of the fruit for breakfast. Would you care to join me?"

I swear to you that Abigail understood my words, for she immediately rose to her feet. I did also, and Abigail and I strolled very slowly along the path to the orchard and plucked a few ripened mangoes from the branches and walked back to the fire, steeped in deep conversation all the while. I remember considering it quite an important and illuminating conversation at the time, although I cannot recall a single word of it now.

Upon arriving back in camp, I immediately cut up a mango and offered Abigail the first succulent piece. She gobbled it up hungrily. "Ahh, so mango is also your favorite, I see. You should know this, then, Abigail: mango is a favorite of mine as well. Having so many wonderful things in common, I expect that we shall get along famously, wouldn't you agree?"

She looked at me once again. I learned then that that meant "yes." Thus, I learned to speak Albatross that morning, if such a language there be, or, better still perhaps, Abigail learned to speak English. I'm not sure which it was, but we communicated quite well nevertheless.

After several more minutes passed, Abigail then stepped away from me and took to flight. I watched her fly into the rising sun and soon she was gone.

I tell you, great sadness swept over me, almost bringing me to tears. She was merely a bird, but I missed her as if she were a long-time friend. I reasoned that she had snuggled with me to thank me for helping her with whatever had ailed her the day before, and now it was time to go about her life. I silently bid her good-bye and wished her well, but I was feeling a bit selfish at that moment as well. I wanted her back.

What was it about Abigail that had touched me so? She was a bird and I was a human; there should be no emotional attachment, but there had been a specially shared moment that I would not forget.

I laid my head back against the log as the morning light warmed my face. I closed my eyes and gave a silent 'thank you' to whatever force was watching over me. My time on the island was unique. I had friends to comfort me, and I had come to know a bird as a friend. Was it that the island held some magical power quite unlike any other place I had ever been? Were such occurrences the norm for the island? I couldn't answer those questions, of course, but if not magic, then how else could it be explained that grass people could come to life and a man could communicate with a bird?

Some time went by, and then another island miracle happened. Abigail returned with a fish in her beak. She landed and waddled up to me and laid the fish upon my lap. I was stunned.

"For me, Abigail?"

The look.

"So, you are retuning the gesture and bringing me a fish for breakfast? Do I understand correctly?"

Again, the look.

"Why, thank you, Abigail. What a lovely gesture, little one. I accept your gift with gratitude and humility."

I cleaned the fish, giving the innards to her. She ate them eagerly. I then hung the fish over the flames until the meat was ready to eat. I felt it necessary to share with her, but she refused. Apparently Abigail did not eat cooked fish, or perhaps it was my fish alone to eat. Either way, I ate the fish and was grateful. Abigail then pecked at a mango.

"I see. You would like more mango." I pulled out my knife and sliced the mango for her. She loved it.

So there, seated together on the sand next to the

fire, in the early morning of the 254th day, Abigail Albatross and I, Thomas Bartholomew Cantfield, became family.

Chapter 6

Gretchen emerged first from the tent. She stretched and then snapped to alert, seeing Abigail seated next to me with her head again resting upon my thigh.

"What is this, Thomas? Have you found comfort with another woman?" She then smiled warmly, as she always did, and sat down next to us.

"Good morning, my love. I think I should introduce you. Gretchen, I would like you to meet Abigail Albatross. Abigail, please say hello to Gretchen."

Abigail looked up at me and then stood and walked directly into Gretchen's lap and squatted back down.

Gretchen's face beamed with joy. "Hello, sweet Abigail. It is so wonderful to make your acquaintance." Gretchen then stroked Abigail's back and neck and looked with elation into my eyes. It was as a child opening a present on Christmas morning.

"Abigail has chosen to join our family, my dear," I said.

"Well, she is most welcome. I'm sure that she will make a wonderful addition, too."

I split a mango and handed it to Gretchen. "She is much like me, my love. She fancies mango as much as I do."

I handed Gretchen my knife, and she cut slices

and shared them with Abigail. Abigail, of course, could not refuse.

"Good morning, lad," came Matthew's voice as he exited the tent, stretching as well. "Good morning, my dear."

We both greeted Matthew. Within seconds, Charlie emerged.

"And what have we here? Breakfast already in hand?" teased Charlie.

Gretchen cut Charlie a wicked look. Charlie struck a comedic pose, raising his hands in mock surrender. "It was a joke, Gretchen. As before, it was only a joke."

Within a short time, introductions completed, we sat sharing breakfast and light conversation. Abigail, of course, willingly gobbled every piece of mango handed to her. I believe it was her way of bonding with each of us, and also to fill her greedy little belly—but I jest here.

Although she showed a strong partiality toward me, she demonstrated nearly an equally powerful affection for each of us. Even Charlie, in his own teasing manner, showed his true affection toward Abigail. He would tease her about her becoming lunch, whereupon Abigail would kick sand at him. We all laughed, except for the ever-stoic Matthew, but I saw the sparkle in his eyes. He was delighted.

The morning congregation completed, it was time to move the camp into the cave.

While Matthew and I moved my belongings, Charlie and Gretchen fed the birds in the pen.

It was decided that the pen, being full of squawking birds, was too difficult to move. We did not want to risk accidentally destroying the structure and setting loose our supply of fowl, so we agreed that the tent and pen would remain where they were. Charlie and Matthew would continue on in the tent together, while Gretchen and I would live in the cave. And Abigail, too, of course.

Therefore, with less to rearrange, and none of us possessing any belongings in great number to begin with, the move took only minutes to complete, and very soon we returned to the easy life of enjoying our family time.

It was not long before I saw Charlie and Abigail again teasing one another. Abigail flew around Charlie as he tried to catch her. I laughed so hard that tears filled my eyes. I even saw a smile crack Matthew's face eventually. Finally, worn out from the mock chase, Charlie collapsed onto his back and lay panting. Abigail then landed on the sand and crawled over and laid her head on Charlie's heaving chest, and they rested.

Looking out over it all, I suddenly felt warmly blessed. I realized that although I still saw the island as a prison, I also saw it as an opportunity unlike any other. Nowhere else could I imagine such a scene.

Grass people coming to life and an albatross adopting us as her family were completely beyond what I believed to ever be possible.

Perhaps I had judged the island incorrectly, I reasoned. The storm which brought me here was not the island's fault. But after I washed ashore, a desperate and lonely man, the island had immediately provided everything necessary for my survival. And in abundance, I should add.

The murders were not the fault of the island either. That responsibility lay with horrible men and their terrible manners. In fact, despite those evil cads' despicable acts, it was the island that had brought Matthew and Charlie back to life and then gave being to a woman made of grass and twigs. And when needed again to save a life, the island had provided a resting stop for an ailing albatross.

The more I considered it all, the more I came to regret my words spoken against the island. It seemed that I was wrong. The island was not holding me here; rather, it was trying to make my life as pleasant as it was able to do so.

I thus began to see the island very differently, and then it struck me hard: the island was in desperate need of someone to care for. She must have wished for a family of her own, and by whatever force responds to these desires, we were brought to her shoreline in fulfillment of her yearning, in great need of her to care for us. And care for us she did.

I laid my hand against the sand and bowed my

head.

"Thank you, island. Thank you for all your blessings and good care. I apologize to you, madam. I was cruel and thoughtless before when I accused you of being my prison. I was wrong. You, dear island, are my salvation. I will honor you thus, from here on out. Until the day I am rescued and even after, until the end of my days, I shall call you sister."

I cannot explain what happened next, except only to say that I believe the island acknowledged my apology. It shook as if an earthquake had struck, but there was no violent jolt or damaging upheaval. Instead, it was more of a gentle rocking. It was as if the island shuddered with joy and gratitude of its own. The ground rolled a bit and then all was still again.

"Yes," I said, "I love you also, sister."

My struggle against the island was over.

I would never speak ill of her again. From that day forward, whenever I received a blessing from the island, I would pause, kneel, and lay my hand flat against the ground and say a private 'thank you' to my benevolent and caring sister. She received each thanks with both grace and humility, but never again did she shudder.

A week passed, and we all shared wonderful days together. Wherever we walked, Abigail would either waddle along behind us or take to the air and land next to us when we stopped and rested. Sometimes Abigail flew away for several hours at a time, but before nightfall each day she would return to her special spot within the cave.

Early in the morning on the 261st day, I witnessed a scene so alarming that recalling it now still sends sharp chills up my spine.

As I exited my cave, with Abigail next to me, I looked immediately eastward toward the rising sun, expecting to see the birth of a beautiful yellow orb and clear skies.

I swallowed hard.

On that morning, it seemed that the fires of Hell itself were fully ablaze in the sky. I immediately knew what that meant. A rainstorm was soon to come, and given the constant need for fresh water, it was not an unwelcomed sight. But the sky was much redder than I had ever seen it, the reason for my immediate apprehensive reaction.

This would *not* be an ordinary rainstorm.

As if my previous experience with fear and deficiency of courage was not enough, the following several days were apparently the opportunity presented to me by some evil deity to revisit more terror.

When I was tested by that first storm which

landed me here, I did not think I could have imagined a worse fear, but then I had faced the challenge of confronting murderous pirates.

I did not pass either test well.

Over the coming days, I came to a new level of understanding fear and its effects on an already fragile mind.

One very important element in that understanding was that fear appears to be guided by backward thinking. It seems to be always founded on what could go wildly *amiss* and never on what could go absolutely right. Fear, I have since concluded, is absent any measure of optimism whatsoever. It is a primal reaction to an unexpected terrible event or to an event not well prepared for. I found it a most curious emotion when studied objectively, although, until recently, I had little opportunity to be objective. Additionally, there seems to be little logic involved in fear, being more motivated by the instinct of survival and irrational thought.

I noted along the way this observation also: just when you think a situation cannot become any worse, you often discover the real truth—it can.

As I began before, I continue now and say that that morning was a surprise to me, but I had no idea at that moment what Hell, once again, was about to unleash upon us.

What began as mere precaution on my part would soon and forever change the way I thought of fear and courage.

Upon seeing the rich redness of the morning sky, I immediately awakened everyone and urged them to begin securing the camp. We gathered up everything that was not lashed down, and even tightened the lashing on what already was lashed down, making the bindings extra tight.

All that day, we watched the clouds building higher and higher into the sky. By the afternoon, I realized that what was coming toward us was an enormous storm. I had no idea how large it would be, but it seemed larger than any other I had ever endured in my life—including the monster that had sunk my ship.

Mind you, it was a common event for it to rain for a day or two, and often enough it would come in torrents, at least for a while, but then it would pass harmlessly onward and we would return to our normal activities. I felt deep within my soul, however, that this approaching storm would be much different, and so, as the lone survivor of one great storm already, I took the precautions necessary as I thought best to protect those under my care. I was, after all, the first inhabitant of the island. This made me responsible, at least in my mind, for the lives of all the others. At that time, though, as concerned as I was, I had no concept of what was to come.

Being a cautious fellow by nature, I decided that we should pick enough fruit, coconut, and breadfruit to get us through several days. Considering the size of the forthcoming tempest, I anticipated that it might be difficult to get to the trees to pick them while in the throes of the storm. We all worked together in bringing in as much fruit as we deemed necessary for our needs and then brought extra rations for good measure just in case. Charlie, of course, contributed the least amount of manual labor during our preparations, but his mirthful spirit and jolly words kept our spirits high. That was all we needed from him in completing our tasks.

Not possessing an abundance of extra clothing to share, we tried to preserve as many dry pieces of clothing as necessary in order to maintain our comfort. It is an awful feeling to be soaked to the skin and not have a change of clothing. So whenever the rains came, we all preferred to remain in the cave until the storm passed.

As we gathered extra water from the spring in gourds, I thought it a bit ironic and humorous. In a short while we would have an abundance of water, but I wanted clean extra rations in the cave in any event. To my mind, it was better to have supplies well in hand than to seek for them later.

After gathering the supplies needed, we managed to bring a large store of dry wood into the cave so as to keep it arid and available when the storm had finally passed. A previous storm a short time before, although much less severe and of no particular note, had taught me about storing dry wood. It was a lesson well learned.

I looked eastward, and the frightening red of

the skies I noted in the morning had now softened to a bright pink, but glancing westward often during the day I could see the angry-looking rain clouds fast approaching. It would be nice to see the soaking and cleansing rains again, for it had been nearly a month since the island had last received the benefits of any measurable rainfall, but a damaging deluge would not be welcomed at all.

Over the previous few months, I had come to enjoy the time just after a good rain. Things smelled different—cleaner. The air was fresher, and the plants seemed to react quickly to the rain by producing fruit soon afterward. It was the sense of renewal after a small storm that appealed most to me.

Later in the afternoon, as I made my final trip to the cave with a shirtload of papaya and mango, I glanced up at the sky again and noticed it worsening very quickly. Also, no longer were the clouds a simple dark gray, filled with needed moisture. They were taking on a much more threatening appearance. The large, puffy clouds now reached higher into the sky than ever before, and the lower clouds grew darker than I had ever seen them, almost black.

I realized the approaching storm was going to be even larger than I had first estimated. My earlier precaution was now turning toward extreme alarm.

I called out to the others and expressed my deepest concerns. Matthew and Gretchen heeded my warnings and continued checking the camp for anything that could be dangerously tossed about in the expected coming winds. Charlie, however, sat still, his usual mirthful expression upon his face.

"Charlie," I shouted out, "take me seriously on this matter. This is going to be a very large storm. Help us secure the area, please. The storm will be fully upon us within hours."

"Unfurrow your brow," Charlie responded in his typical cavalier manner, "or your face will bind up into that frightful frown forever. It's wind. It's rain. Nothing to be overly alarmed about." He laughed loudly and then skipped around the camp shouting out with an obvious lack of concern, "Rain and wind, that is all it is, Thomas! Nothing more than a sound sprinkle and a zestful breeze, silly man. Let's go for a walk to the island's end and greet the storm's approach."

"Charlie," I cautioned, "this is no laughing matter. It will be a much larger storm than you expect. Please help us."

But Charlie was not the sort of person to take anything seriously. I suppose it was in his character to live a carefree life, but whenever I glanced westward and saw the growing storm, fast approaching, I wondered how anyone could feel so unconcerned about this potential catastrophe. Still, and paradoxically, his mirth calmed me. I was able to rationalize this coming event with more objectivity because of Charlie's childlike exuberance and his obliviousness to its destructive potential.

Most of you would probably call Charlie a

person of limited awareness and ability, but to me he was almost a rock of steadfast consciousness. He possessed an irrepressible expectation that nothing was completely bad or hopeless, that everything would always, somehow, end up for the best. Nothing ever seemed to alarm Charlie. No matter what harsh thing confronted him, he walked without fear or concern. I daresay that if he met a man intending to run him through with a sword, dear Charlie, with his infectious grin and laughter, would find a way to make the man a friend instead.

He took nothing life offered with any degree of seriousness: "He left the worrying and the fretting to us." "Worrying is not for me, silly man. It creates too many wrinkles," he would say. Somehow, Charlie always managed to find comedy in every threatening situation. In fact, I'm quite certain that if Charlie ever took the time to consider his own beheading, he would manage a way to find some humor in it. He was an amazing fellow, and I think that it is what I found to be most endearing about Charlie: his keen and uncompromising sense of humor.

I was not a fool, I knew the coming storm would be dangerous, but through Charlie's gay approach to life, I was able to hold onto hope when most would have buckled in fear and woe. In fact, because of Charlie, the only fear I felt at that moment was the fear that had it not been for Charlie's indomitable spirit of mirth and joy, I might have soon collapsed into a terrified and paralyzing state.

I cannot suitably enough express to you how much I valued my new friends.

Gretchen and Matthew, on the other hand, took my warnings seriously, but with an air of calm and dignity. They understood the somber nature of the impeding storm and helped me secure the camp. Together, we retightened the lashings holding the tent to the stakes. They helped me recount the necessary provisions of food and water to be certain that there would be enough to wait out the storm's passing.

I, alone, took great care with the manuscript, returning all writing utensils and parchment to the safety of the chest so as to preserve them should our surroundings become exceedingly wet.

Late in the afternoon, the winds picked up in intensity and speed. I could tell that we were in the preceding moments before a great storm, and these winds were only the portent of much greater winds to come very soon.

It was then that I fully realized this would not be just an unusually vigorous hurricane, like the one that sank my ship. This was going to be a monstrosity. A life-altering event if ever there was one.

Matthew, Gretchen, Abigail, and I gathered together in the relative safety of the cave. Without any door, however, we were surely going to feel the wind to some degree. Still, the cave was far more secure than anywhere else I knew on the island. Charlie, of course, refused to yield to any concern and would not come into the cave.

"Come on, old man. Enjoy the breeze," he shouted, just outside the cave entrance.

"Charlie, come hither, you fool! The storm is almost fully upon us."

Charlie would not capitulate to the common sense of it, though. Instead, he raised his arms as a bird would its wings, and reveled in the increasing intensity of the wind, that impish grin now fully extended across his face, heralding only more excitement to come, as far as he was concerned. He then began laughing and shouting in unrestrained glee.

I pleaded with Matthew to speak to Charlie with more reason than I could apparently muster, but Matthew just shook his head and refused.

"The boy has his mind made up, Thomas. Who am I to say that he is wrong? Perhaps he is the wise one and we are the fools."

"How can you say that, Matthew? Can you not see how the gale grows in intensity?"

"I see it, Thomas. So does Gretchen, and, I suspect, even Abigail knows what is about to descend upon us, but Charlie, Thomas, Charlie just sees another opportunity from which to take sport. Sound reasoning and Charlie are not compatible. You should already know this."

"No, Matthew, I see only that he lacks normal common sense in these matters."

I called out again to Charlie and urged him to come inside with us, but he only laughed all the harder and grinned even wider. I steadied myself and determined that the only way I would get him to safety was to rush out into the storm myself and forcefully pull him back into the cave with us.

I prepared myself. I stood and dug my right foot into the sand.

"What are you doing, Thomas?" asked Gretchen anxiously.

"I am going out to get Charlie before he gets injured."

Gretchen grabbed my arm. "No, Thomas! It is already too dangerous out there. You might be struck by flying debris. Stay here. Charlie is a fool, and he subjects himself to a fool's end."

"He is my friend, Gretchen. He is *our* friend. I cannot leave him out there, fool or not."

"I could not live without you, my darling. I cannot exist without you. Stay here with me. Protect *me*. I'm sorely in need of you right now."

I could see the worry in her expression. I sensed a mortal dread within her.

"If you try to save Charlie, then a fool you are also, Thomas," said Matthew. "And it will be a fool's journey toward the same end as Charlie. Leave him to his unwitting ways. The wind is too great now. You will put yourself into harm's way unnecessarily, my boy."

"No, Matthew. I will not leave him out there. I would do the same for you. Charlie is no less a friend. It is my job to protect him from himself."

At that moment, the wind's intensity grew fivefold. I heard the Devil howling once again, just as he had done on the night the great gale sank my ship and just before being tossed into the sea.

As the terror of that evil howl revisited me, so did I sense the return of paralyzing fear.

I was truly afraid, and yet I could not leave Charlie, now a sniggering imbecile, out in the storm, unprotected. I had to try and rescue him even if it meant my own life. A true friend does not abandon another just because he chooses to act imprudently.

A large gust struck the tent, causing it to flap about violently. From what I could see of it from the safety of my cave, I was surprised that it remained lashed to the stakes and did not blow away. And there was Charlie, leaning into the gust as if planted in the ground, giggling.

I continued to the entrance under the protests of both Gretchen and Matthew. I looked out at Charlie, still standing like a bird ready to take flight, his arms stretched out to his sides, his face turned up and directly into the wind, that crazy giggling now turned into full maniacal laughter, as if in a direct challenge to the gods to send their very worst to him.

"Charlie, please!" I screamed. "Please! Come inside, now!"

Charlie turned his head and grinned directly at me. "Not me, silly man. For on this evening I shall learn to fly." Another crazy round of laughter filled the air before being drowned out by the Devil's howl.

I prepared myself to dash from the cave, grab Charlie, and pull him back into safety when an even larger gust struck. It lifted Charlie off the ground as if he weighed nothing at all. Within a second, Charlie had disappeared from view, leaving only his demented screech of delight quickly melding into the storm's wail.

"No!" I screamed. "Charlie!"

It was too late, however. Charlie was gone.

Matthew grabbed me by the back of my britches and tugged me fully into the cave an instant before a large section of broken tree trunk smashed into the wall where I stood only a second before, shattering into small pieces.

Despite my near death, I continued screaming for Charlie. "No," I bellowed, "Charlie's gone!"

Gretchen cradled my head in her hands and tried to calm me with soothing words, but she could not assuage both the terror and rage that I felt bursting forth from me.

I felt that I had let Charlie down by not rushing out sooner to rescue him. I cried remorsefully and continued calling to him for a long time thereafter.

Matthew assumed his usual stoic pose and shook his head. "Charlie made his choice, Thomas. It is not your fault. Take no responsibility for his idiocy."

I heard his words, and somewhere inside both my head and my heart, I knew them to be sound advice, but they also did nothing to alleviate my feelings of guilt nor my sense of betrayal toward my jester friend.

At that moment, I felt myself fully enter the tragic domain of fear. Without my friend of mirth to guide me through the troubled moments with his gift of joy and hope, I lost all sense of balance and, once again, tumbled back into the darkness of my mind's troubled places.

I submit to you, dear reader, that the fear of losing one's mind can, at times, exceed that of physical fear. With a physical menace threatening you, you can perhaps reason your way through it. When you lose your mind, you lose all sense of reason and control. You then may find yourself in the unholy blackness of your self-invented terror, a prisoner of your own beliefs, where salvation may no longer be conceived of nor recognized if it should appear.

Some, I think, might find this state of lost senses more tolerable than others, for the question arises, does a madman even know that he is mad? And if he does not, then is the convention of rational thought regarding sanity, with its strict framework and limitations, also abandoned? And if rational thinking is thus abandoned, is it possible that he may live out his life in the fullness of insane bliss, even unto some gloriously imaginary end that a man of normal sanity may not have the possibility to envision at all?

For me, at that time, I believed the loss of control over my right to choose my own destiny represented a greater loss to me than some physical loss. An imbecile does not understand his fate, nor can he choose his own path, for his infirmity has chosen for him.

I wanted the ability to choose what is most and what is least for myself, but then would that not be the coherent thought of one who was not an imbecile? And there, in the mired depths of that paradox, lay my confusion, for it then seemed to me that it was only a person of sanity who toiled most with those thoughts of choice and destiny.

I remained lost in my grief throughout most of the night, but if memory serves at all, I do recall that as the winds roared in anger, the clouds unleashed a deluge of rain onto the island in such torrents that I thought all cover would wash away, leaving only bare rock.

I lay cuddled next to both my friends, clutching them as tightly as I could, fearing that the storm might take them also. Matthew, however, ever indomitable and calm, smiled at me through understanding eyes and said, "Fear not, lad. We shall remain with you. Take joy in that, for there is not much else to take joy in on this night."

Abigail was taking all of this in stride on the far side of the cave, squatting in the sand, quiet and uninvolved, very unusual for a bird in these conditions, but then Abigail was anything but a normal bird.

I could hear the tent flapping violently all night long, and had it not been made from the sturdy material of sails, it might have been torn apart and flung away.

For hours and hours the storm raged on. I could not see how we would survive the night in the midst of such a squall. By my estimation, this hurricane was many times larger than the one which had brought me here. Thus, I could find no reason to fight off the fear that had finally overtaken my senses, and so I lay trembling incoherently for most of the night, it seemed.

Very early the next morning, when it was still very dark and stormy, I finally recovered enough to peek out the entrance of the cave and, aided by the flash of lightning, I watched as trees were uprooted and tossed away as if they were twigs. I also noted that my bird pen was completely dismantled and my birds gone. I wondered how the tent could remain standing in such a fierce wind. I had no idea how it was possible, and yet there it continued to stand in spite of the terrible gusts.

Some might call it Providence, some might call it plain and simple good fortune. As I have stated before, not being a religious man, I surmised that it must be the way I had raised the tent in amongst the basalt rock formations at the base of the former volcano. Perhaps the height of the surrounding rock protected my tent from such tearing gusts. Whatever may be the truth, be it Providence, luck, or stout engineering, it proved to be most sufficient.

The hurricane continued near full strength well into the second day, that being now my 262nd day on the island. We had water and food enough to sustain us through it all, and as I now look back on it, I found that we were in no particular danger as long as we stayed where we were—deep within the cave.

Of course, during that time, I continued mourning the loss of my dear friend Charlie, but Gretchen and Matthew, being the rocks of reason and courage that they were, saw me through my weaker moments of despondency, anguish, and guilt.

I resolved also during that time that I would build a monument to my friend so that he would never be forgotten. Both Gretchen and Matthew agreed that it was a fitting gesture for Charlie, but I think they saw it also as an opportunity for me to heal the hurt of my own heart.

Therefore, more for my sake than that of Charlie, I had come to believe, they lent both their encouragement and support for the project throughout the day, even going so far as to help design the monument in a way befitting Charlie's cheeky manner. I can only imagine what Charlie would have said had he been able to preside over his own memorial service. It would surely have ended in laughter, no doubt.

I already missed his jollity and jesting.

In the evil face of the storm, as it pressed

onward, I looked for some comedic relief, and not finding it in Charlie's irreverent regard for anything of a serious nature, I confess to you that I fell into a slight mental depression for a time.

During the second night of this monstrous tempest, I did not sleep once again. I was tired, mind you. Exhausted, really, but I dared not sleep for fear that I, in my sleep, be swept up and dashed against rocks on the other side of the island as Charlie must have been. Being alert and ready, should it happen, I might have some control over the final event, perhaps preventing it altogether.

I know what you must be thinking at this very moment. If the storm, being as truly evil as I describe, wished to take me and dash me against rocks, I would be powerless to prevent it. Begrudgingly, I must admit that you are correct. Still, it calmed me to know that if I remained awake, I would not be tossed about so helplessly as in my sleep. I would rather be aware of my frightful fate than be killed without even knowing that I had died. I should very much prefer to know the manner and form in which I might suffer my end.

Chapter 7

During mid-evening of the second night, the storm winds began dying down. Within an hour or two more, all that remained of that awful monster were light breezes gently fluttering the canvas of the tent, illuminated by the light of the full moon and still standing.

I stuck my head out into the night and saw, to my great delight, a firmament of brightly shining stars overhead in spite of a full moon.

I know that this may sound quite trite, but I felt that we had actually fought a war against the monster and we had won. We were alive! Pressed as we were, the storm could not take our lives. After all was done, we stood, thereafter, as victors over evil itself.

Upon some later reassessment of the aforementioned conflict, I came to a different conclusion. It is not so much that we achieved victory over that evil thing, for if we had been truly victorious, dear Charlie would still be with us. No, then, not victorious were we; rather, we were not defeated.

You might regard this statement as splitting hairs, but I submit that the storm could have killed us all and it did not. And I believe that my preparations helped distinguish us from the dead. Yes, we lost poor Charlie, but we three survived. We may have not defeated the storm, but neither had the storm defeated us. Thus I considered it to be a measured victory of sorts.

For the first time in two days, I slept deeply and awoke rested that third morning, my 263rd day on the island. The awakening was a muted one, with no Charlie to douse me with cold water or teasingly inundate me with taunting words. Sweet Gretchen slept soundly next to me, and that gave me some comfort, but I shed many tears for poor Charlie that morning before arising.

I moved gently away from Gretchen so as not to awaken her. I barely had enough time to get outside and to the fire pit before the real floodgates opened, and I wept bitterly for quite some time. I hadn't known Charlie long, but he had become as dear a friend as I had ever known. He was more than a friend; he was family, and I missed him terribly.

After a time, my head buried in my hand weeping, I felt a gentle touch upon my shoulder. I looked up with swollen eyes to see Gretchen's beautiful face before me. Her sweet, understanding smile eased my pain.

"Charlie's gone, Gretchen," I said.

"But he is not forgotten, my love. We still have

a memorial to build in his honor, do we not?"

"Yes, we do, but I wish not to begin it today. Today I wish to mourn my good friend."

"Then today we shall set aside all tasks, that we might mourn dear Charlie."

"Thank you, my sweet."

Matthew then made his appearance from the cave and glanced about him, surveying the damage left by the beast.

"We have much to do, Thomas, if we are to resurrect our campsite. We shall need to rebuild the bird pen and recapture the fowl, but look, our tent survived—a testament to our being bent but not broken. Come, Thomas, let us begin to restore our home and build Charlie's monument."

"Not today, Matthew. Today we shall mourn."

"For Charlie?" he asked.

"Of course for Charlie. Who else is there to mourn?"

"Why would you mourn him?"

I looked up at Matthew and could hardly believe my ears. "Why would I *not* mourn him, Matthew?"

"Because, dear boy, one mourns only the dead."

"Your words confuse me, Matthew."

"Only the dearly departed should be mourned, Thomas."

"Is Charlie with us? Look about you, Matthew. Do you see him anywhere?"

"I see him everywhere, lad. Take that log over

there. I see him sitting on it even now, wearing that silly grin on his face. Do you not see him there?"

I looked to the log, but I did not see Charlie.

"I also see him over there by the tree. The one that he always slept under following our midday meal. Do you not see him there, Thomas?"

I looked to the tree, but I did not see Charlie there either.

"And there, Thomas, by your side. I see him there also, poking you in the ribs and giggling away. Do you not see him there?"

The swirling mist of grief in my brain finally cleared, and I understood what Matthew was saying. "Yes, Matthew. I see him now. I see him all around. Thank you."

"Excellent, my boy! So, where shall we begin to build his monument?"

I felt suddenly reenergized. Matthew was correct. Charlie was everywhere I looked now. He was not dead. He was alive in my heart, and he was present in most everything around the camp. Thanks once again to Matthew, still ever perfect in his advice and counseling, Charlie was not dead. He would never be dead so long as we kept him alive within us— within our hearts and minds.

I leapt excitedly to my feet and pulled Gretchen to hers. "There, Matthew. Under that tree. We shall build it there!"

"Excellent place, my boy. I think he would have liked it there."

We spent most of that morning building Charlie's monument by dragging and carrying basalt rocks to the front of the tree and placing them in a conical formation—a cairn for Charlie McShane.

Afterward, we gathered in front of it and Matthew, the best orator among the three of us, offered some kind words to the memory of our friend.

"To whomever may be listening out there somewhere in the great beyond, I would introduce you to our dear friend who may have just arrived. Please know Charlie McShane, of late an island dweller somewhere in the South Pacific last residing on this unnamed island."

"Wait," I said. "Introduce him as being from McShane Island, for that shall be the island's name from now on."

"Excellent choice, lad. I say, then, allow me to introduce you to Charlie McShane, who last resided here on McShane Island. Accept him, please, as he was, a trickster and a jolly fellow to be around. Please do not hold him to any serious end, for our Charlie took no care for anything serious. Life to our Charlie was full of humor and joy. Even in his demise did he find joy, for on the day of his death he did learn to fly. We heard him fly away with laughter on his lips. He was a kindly soul as well, although he would never admit to it if it meant that someone might take him for a serious thinker. Charlie will bring joy to the place where he dwells now, and for that, whoever you are, it is *you* who should be giving thanks now. Be kind to our friend and let him never know a single day from here on out without laughter."

"Thank you, Matthew," I said.

"That was lovely," offered Gretchen.

A voice from behind startled me.

"That's a lovely cairn. Who are we eulogizing? Somebody I know?"

We all turned as one to see our Charlie standing behind us, appearing perfectly well after his unexpected flight and wearing that wide grin of his.

"Charlie!" I bellowed. "You're alive!"

"Of course I am, silly man. Why wouldn't I be?"

I ran, nay, I absolutely raced to grasp my dear friend in a great bear hug. And if the truth be told, I wept openly, for there was no way to contain all the joy I felt.

Gretchen rushed to Charlie and hugged him as well, and Matthew walked over casually and placed a hand on Charlie's shoulder.

"Welcome back, lad," said Matthew. "Thomas, does this mean that we must dismantle the cairn now?"

I laughed as I hugged Charlie, then I reached out and grabbed Matthew, pulling him near to include him in the hug. He could only eke out a nervous smile. Matthew had much too restrained a personality to allow his emotions to burst forth in an uncontrollable manner.

Charlie just giggled as usual as we hugged him

tightly for what seemed like hours but was really only minutes.

Finally, I pushed a little away from Charlie, but still held fast to his shoulders as I now scowled. "What were you thinking, Charlie? Why didn't you come inside the cave? You caused me great stress the last few days, thinking you dead."

"Dead? No, no, silly man. I told you I would learn to fly, and I did. Well, not really, but the wind carried me a goodly distance before it dropped me on me bum. It was quite fun! That is, until those nasty men came ashore and tried to spoil it all."

"What nasty men?" I asked, now alarmed.

Charlie chortled. "The pirates. You should have seen them gag and choke in the ocean. It was a riotous event to behold, they swimming to shore and crawling out onto the sand. It was delightful."

"Pirates, Charlie? You mean there are pirates on the island? Right now?"

"Of course. The storm sank their ship and they washed ashore. And they are an argumentative bunch! All the fighting, the swordplay—though it looked rather fun. The swordplay, I mean," he said, pretending a sword fight.

"How many, Charlie? How many pirates came ashore?"

"Six came ashore."

"Six pirates are on the island?"

"Yes. Six pirates...until two were done in."

"Two of the pirates are dead? So there are four

pirates?"

"Yes. Until the other four arrived."

"The others? So there are eight pirates on the island? Is that correct?"

Charlie fiddled with a long piece of wood that had suddenly captured his attention.

"Charlie!" I said loudly in order to recapture his awareness. "Are there eight pirates on the island?"

"There were eight."

"There *were* eight? How many are on the island right now?"

"Four."

"Four. Where are the other four, Charlie?"

"They are quite dead, I expect."

"Dead? Why are they dead?"

"They were killed by the others. I think I could whittle a sword from this wood if I tried."

"Charlie," I said, more forcefully this time, grabbing him by the shoulders and staring straight into his eyes, "concentrate. Tell me what happened and tell me the full story, please."

"Must I? It really isn't much fun."

"Yes, Charlie. Tell me all of it."

"Very well. The six who first came ashore killed two of their own. Then four more tried to swim ashore, but the original four killed them before they made it onto sand. Are you satisfied?"

"Then there are four pirates on the island?"

"Yes, but they lack all sense of humor."

I became very serious.

"Charlie, listen carefully to me. Are you saying that the pirates are on this island at this very moment?"

Charlie reached up his hand and slapped me lightly across the cheek, grinning as usual. "Are you listening, old man, or are you still daft? I just told you that they are."

"On the eastern end?" I inquired.

"Of course," answered Charlie matter-of-factly.

"The pirates are, at this very moment, on the eastern end of the island?"

He grabbed my head, turning it to the side, attempting to look into my ear. "Are your ears full of sand?" He giggled once again.

"Dear me!" I exclaimed. "We have pirates on the island! We are in serious trouble!"

"What are we to do now, my love?" asked Gretchen, a worried expression replacing her usual smile.

"I don't know just yet, but we must not panic. Not yet at least."

At that point, I felt the stirring of a new fear arise yet again within me—fear of being murdered by cutthroat rogues. With what rationality remained, I reasoned that we were safe so long as the pirates remained on the eastern end of the island, but I knew they would not remain there long. Sooner or later they would necessarily need to search the island for both food and water. Their search would surely bring them to our camp, for we occupied the ground where the only source of sweet water was to be found.

"When did they come ashore, Charlie?"

"I told you already. After the storm."

"I mean to ask, did they come ashore last night or this morning? When exactly did you see them come ashore?

"Very early this morning. About sunrise."

"They came ashore on bits of wood, correct?"

"Yes, yes, old man. They came ashore hugging bits of wood."

"They floated in, then?"

"Some paddled in. I had quite a bit of fun watching them come ashore. It was hilarious."

"I'm sure it was, Charlie, but you're certain they arrived around sunrise?"

"I know what sunrise looks like, old man. They started coming ashore around then. Why?"

"That's good," I answered with some relief. "Well, it is not a good thing that they are here at all, but the timing of their arrival should give us some time to prepare."

"For a party?" Charlie asked excitedly.

"No, Charlie. Not a party. If they have just arrived, then they might not yet be ready to search the island."

"And this is a good thing?" asked Matthew.

"Yes. If they had been here a while already, then they would have grown thirsty and hungry and would already be exploring the island." I turned to Charlie. "So, there are four pirates on the island?"

"Yes, yes," he responded with irritation in his voice.

"Forgive me, Charlie. I'm just trying to be certain of our situation. Four against four, then. Well, four against three. I will not have Gretchen be a part of this."

"But Thomas," Gretchen protested.

"My love. Hand-to-hand combat is not suitable for a young woman."

"Neither is it suitable for an accountant, Thomas."

"This is true, but more suitable for me than for you, my dear."

Gretchen pouted, but I believe I made the correct decision. I could not bear it if she were to be injured in the coming battle. "Our odds are good then," I continued, "and we have the element of surprise on our side. This could be manageable. That is most fortuitous."

"May be, my boy," said Matthew, "but we presently have no means of defending ourselves."

"I know, Matthew. We must make preparations for the attack that is certain to come."

"Why would they kill their own?" asked Gretchen.

"I would assume that to be a question of resources," I stated. "Feeding four men is easier than feeding ten."

"This island could easily care for fifty people without any problem, Thomas," insisted Gretchen.

"They have no sense of loyalty, the brutes," added Matthew.

"They're pirates, Matthew. Their only loyalty is to themselves individually."

"Well, it seems a very barbaric way to go about deciding such issues, that's all I can say," said Gretchen.

"Yes, my dear, it does, and I must also assume that they are as yet unaware of the abundance of our resources here. Their need for water could well herald our undoing, though. They will eventually find the spring, and after that, they will then most certainly find us. We must prepare for battle."

Charlie giggled. "Battle? Whatever for?"

"Charlie. Do you have no memory of your own undoing? They slaughtered you and Matthew."

"Really? They slaughtered me? When was this?"

"Don't you remember? That is how you came to be on this island."

"I have no memory of that, silly man. Why would anyone want to kill me? I'm no threat to anyone."

Matthew struck a confused pose. I noticed his expression.

"I know this is a poor time for the start of such a discussion, Matthew, but do you recall your own execution?"

"I do not, lad."

"You don't remember rowing to shore during

the battle?"

"There was a battle?"

"Yes. A great battle between ships. The pirates. You have no memory at all of coming to the island?"

"I'm afraid not, Thomas."

"This is very strange. I do not understand any of this myself, but to be sure, the pirates are now once again on the island and they have just killed their own, probably out of concern that this island could not adequately sustain more than four men."

"How do you know such things?" asked Matthew.

"I don't. I'm only reasoning, but if they find us seemingly in control of the only source of sweet water, do you think they would hesitate to kill us?"

"I don't fight, Thomas," declared Charlie. "You know that. I am not a warrior, I'm a funster. Why not just make friends with them? I'm sure they have some wonderfully entertaining stories to tell."

"Dear Charlie," I said, "you care about very little, it seems."

"I care about having a good time."

"These men murdered you. They beheaded you and Matthew. I saw it happen right before my eyes. If not these exact men, then others from the same ship. Do you not think that they will do so again if they find us?"

"If they did murder me as you say," replied Charlie, "then it was only a mild inconvenience. Because here I am, my neck whole and feeling wonderful. Why do you worry so, old man? It will hasten wrinkles."

"He will be of no help at all, Thomas," inserted Matthew.

"Matthew, you truly do not recall what they did to you?"

Matthew thought a few seconds before answering. "I have no memory of such an event, my boy, but it matters not. I believe they will do us harm now if they are able to do so. I think it best, though, not to count on young Charlie should any adverse contact with those pirates be initiated."

Matthew was correct, of course. Charlie was not a fighter. As for Matthew, I was not sure. "And what about you, Matthew? Can I count on you to help defend our camp should the need arise?"

"I would prefer to negotiate, lad. Failing that, however, I would proudly stand by your side in battle. I should confess, however, that I was not trained for battle. I was a cargo master."

"And I, Matthew, was merely an accountant who worked in a comfortable office. Circumstances have changed, my friend. The question standing before us is this, can we successfully defend ourselves should there be a battle?"

"Well put, my boy. I would have to answer thusly: we shall see, shall we not?"

I did not ask Gretchen the same question. She also was not a warrior. And, as I stated before, I would not allow her to become one. Battling pirates in any fashion was not a task well suited to a proper young lady.

"I think we have time to build up our defenses. They may not be organized yet to explore. Let us make ready, then, for war," I ordered, now considering myself the leader of the defensive team.

"Well put, sir," responded Matthew, coming to the proper erect stance of a soldier before his commanding officer.

I immediately set for us the task of collecting wooden poles six feet in length. We collected nearly twenty. I then set about sharpening one end of each pole into a very sharp point. Within only an hour, we had twenty deadly spears in our new arsenal.

I next set out to find the right tree branches to make bows. Arrows would not be a problem. There were thickets of small trees with perfect branches that we cut into two-foot lengths for our arrows. Because of the lack of time, I was forced to fashion the arrows without fletching, knowing full well that the lack of fletching would make the arrows less stable in flight, but it couldn't be helped. This simple task took a full hour and a half as it was. In the end, though, we added six new bows and thirty arrows to the weapons cache.

Next, I chose our field of battle. It would not be wise to face them head on. In sheer numbers of fighting men alone, we already faced a two-to-one disadvantage. Just Matthew and I would face four beasts who held further advantage over the two of us in fighting experience and the ability to fight. I decided that we should take refuge in amongst the boulders and make our stand there.

My plan of attack was simple. We would wait until they came out into the open area of our camp. If we implemented our tactics correctly, the first volley of arrows would incapacitate two of them, leaving two to battle into the second round. We would then draw them into the rocks and finish them quickly. At least that was my hope. Not being trained in the art of warfare, however, this was only a guess as to how the fight would go.

I divided our stash of weapons into two lots, one more forward and one more rearward. My thought was to establish first contact and then retreat to our first stash, where we would use the weapons there. If the battle continued and our first line of defense were breached, we would then retreat rearward to our second line of defense. It was my fervent hope that we would not need a third, for there was nowhere else to fall back to.

I had no idea whether this was the correct strategy. As I had told Matthew, I was not a military man, but as an accountant who advised investors, I knew that putting all one's resources into a single investment was not a wise thing to do. So I guessed it was also in battle. We would find out soon enough if it was the correct strategy.

We moved a substantial amount of fruit and several gourds of water to each position, not knowing just when such a battle might begin nor how long it might last once begun, having never before been in a battle. Prudence dictated, however, that we prepare enough drinking water and food in each location in the event that we faced a protracted siege.

I placed Charlie, Gretchen, and Abigail into the final defensive position. This way Matthew and I could fight and move about without worrying if they might come to be in the line of fire.

I believed that there was about to be much blood spilled in the coming conflict. I did not want a single drop of it to be ours.

Chapter 8

After another hour, I felt that we were as prepared as possible. Matthew and I remained hidden behind a large rock and waited. Just then, I remembered that I had left one of the hatchets near the fire pit after making the spear points. I did not want it to fall into the hands of our enemy and possibly end up being used against us, so I laid down my bow and ran to the fire pit to retrieve it.

As I neared it, I heard voices off into the underbrush quickly approaching, so I grabbed my hatchet and dashed behind some nearby smaller boulders. In my haste, I forgot to erase my footprints, which could lead the pirates directly to me, so I grabbed a few branches from a nearby bush and erased the marks as best as I could.

As I turned to join Matthew, the voices grew much louder. They were nearly upon me. One of the pirates then popped out from the underbrush, almost spotting me. I ducked behind a large boulder of basalt just in the nick of time and remained very still. I heard another pirate shout out to the others that he had found the spring, and the pirate near to me turned around and noisily disappeared back into the underbrush. Moments later, hearing the sound of splashing water, I used the opportunity to crawl back toward Matthew.

As they seemed most interested in the water and had not yet noticed my campsite, I had plenty of time to get back into position and take up my bow.

My heart beat so loudly in my own ears that I thought everyone else would soon hear it plainly enough, giving our position away. My hands and knees began trembling violently, and I questioned whether I would be steady enough to fire an arrow with any degree of accuracy. My mouth dried until it felt stuffed with cotton. So much sweat poured forth from my pores and down my face that it felt as if Charlie had dumped a gourd of water over my head.

Matthew, however, remained calm and patient. How he did so I could not say, but I supposed it was his nature to never panic. What I wouldn't have given for just an ounce more of his strength and courage at that moment.

The splashing went on for a while longer, and possessing a small measure of daring, I peeked over the rock and looked down upon the pirates from our elevated position and saw them making good use of our spring some twenty yards beyond the thicket. They had not yet seen the path through the thicket from the spring to our campsite, but it would only be a matter of time before they did.

In my limited observance of the beasts, they being nearly forty yards from our position, I could see that most were massive men. They looked like fighting men, men completely unafraid of anyone. I glanced at Matthew for a comparison. There he sat, properly dressed, his posture straight and perfect, his hands on his knees and quite calm, his eyes staring straight ahead, as if he were a statue. In stark contrast to Matthew, I was sweating profusely, trembling uncontrollably, and obviously very frightened.

I turned my attention back to the pirates. One of them finally stood up and turned to his right. His saber glistened in the sun, and I was shocked to see how big it was. Even across the distance that separated us, it looked as if it could lop off a man's head with the slightest effort of the arm that wielded it. I became dizzy with the thought of such a blade falling down upon my neck as one such had beheaded my friends. Bile suddenly rose in my throat, tasting hot and bitter. I forced it back down into my stomach, but the taste of it lingered on.

I turned once again to Matthew. "I'm frightened, Matthew." I whispered.

"As I am also, my boy."

I heard him say it, but I did not believe him. It was as if he were at the theatre casually awaiting the start of a performance. He exhibited no fear or concern whatsoever.

I then caught movement out of the corner of my eye. I turned my head and watched as the other pirates moved about round the spring. It was then that I noticed their number. I counted them in my head. *Eight!*

I tell you, dear reader, I was not at all prepared for that bit of information.

"Eight, Matthew! There are *eight* of them, not four!"

"Ahh, it seems a bit more than we planned for."

Again, his voice was steady and calm. It was all the same to Matthew, one pirate or one hundred. It made no apparent difference to him. He was not the kind to react emotionally to any situation, and his courage remained equal to any task.

"What shall we do, Matthew? There are too many of them!"

"Steady, my boy. You have planned well, and your strategy still seems sound. Let us see how events unfold."

"Matthew! Are you insane? They are four times our number. We stand no chance against these cutthroats."

At that moment I heard one of them call out that he had spotted my tent. I could not believe how rapidly they gathered just outside it, their swords drawn and ready to spill blood as one of them, the officer, I presumed, drew his sword and entered. Seconds later, he stepped out and turned his head left and right, apparently looking for the occupant.

"Keep a sharp eye," I heard him order. "It appears that we are not alone. Find whoever it might be!"

From our elevated position overlooking the entire area, I peeked around the boulders now and then to see them milling about the campsite.

I watched them spread out and begin looking

about the area. One squatted next to the fire pit and placed his hand over the ashes.

"Still warm, Lieutenant," he announced. "They must be near."

One pirate walked away from the tent and toward the boulder field and spotted our partial foot tracks in the sand leading in our direction. He looked up toward the rocks where Matthew and I were hiding. I drew back around the rock before he saw me. I was shaking so badly that I could not fit the nock of the arrow to the bowstring.

"Whatever are we going to do?" I whispered to Matthew. "I think he's found our tracks."

"We do what we set out to do, my boy. We fight."

Without another word, Matthew nocked his unfletched arrow, stood up fully, aimed, and let it fly. I jumped to my feet just in time to see the arrow pierce the heart of the pirate walking toward us. His eyes opened wide in startled amazement, and he died before striking the ground, without uttering a single word.

Matthew and I dropped down behind the rock again.

"That was amazing, Matthew!" I whispered. "You struck a perfect blow, and did so without fletching! I thought you were not a warrior."

"That I am not, my lad, but I was a champion archer before becoming a cargo master."

What was most curious was the matter-of-fact

manner in which he made the statement. There was no boasting in his tone. He was simply stating a fact.

This gave me great confidence. I nocked my arrow and then peeked over the rock just as another pirate discovered his dead mate. Before he could call out, I aimed and let my arrow fly. I missed, the lack of fletching causing the arrow to wobble uncontrollably from its intended path, but Matthew rose up again and pierced the wretch's heart a second later. And just like that, two of the beasts had been taken out of the fight, improving our odds.

Another pirate approached our position from the left. Admitting my lack of skill with the bow, I dropped it to the ground and picked up a spear and charged him. He called out a warning, but for him it was too late. I ran the spear straight through his heart and out his back.

The warning sounded, the true fight was on. Two pirates quickly ran toward me with their sabers drawn and raised. In a coward's dash, I ran back toward Matthew.

"Drop down, lad," he shouted.

I did so, and an arrow whooshed over my head. I heard the thud of the strike and then the shriek. I did not look behind me. Instead, I jumped back up to my feet and ran back behind the rock. I grabbed my next spear, turned, and with all my might I flung it at the second pirate, now only yards away. He parried it away from him with his sword, but by then Matthew had nocked another arrow and let it fly straight at him, piercing his neck. The man went down immediately, clutching at his throat, unable to speak.

"Retreat, Matthew!" I screamed, running toward the pirate with the arrow in his throat. I picked up my spear and thrust it into his heart, killing him instantly.

I turned and ran past Matthew in a mad dash. He simply trotted, his posture still perfect and his demeanor apparently still unfettered by the dangerous nature of the fight.

I could hear the frightful screams of the other pirates as they gave chase. Their angry battle cries sent shivers up my spine. Still trembling with fright, I made it to our second position, picked up my bow, nocked my arrow, turned, and let it fly. And missed.

As one brute drew closer, I spotted a rock lying at my feet and picked it up and hurled it with all my might. Miraculously, it struck him straight in the nose, and he collapsed to the ground, clutching at his nose in great pain.

Five out of the fight, I thought.

We were doing superbly well, I reflected, for an accountant and a cargo master. Still, three angry pirates were three too many. Matthew reached the second position with another pirate on his tail. Without thinking about it, I picked up a spear and made a charge at the man, screaming like one possessed of pure evil. He stopped dead in his tracks, shocked to see me so vicious but still managing a slight sneer. Two other pirates were quickly approaching and would be fully upon us within seconds.

I made lunging stabs at the pirate, but missed each time. He swung his saber at me, narrowly missing. Just as it struck me that I was about to die, Matthew appeared at my side with his spear in hand. A split second later we were surrounded. Even the pirate with a bloody nose joined the ring around us. I could not even look to Matthew for strength, for he had shifted his position and now stood with his back to me. The pirate with the bloody nose gritted his teeth and growled.

"I'm going to gut you like a pig, boy. I'm going to feast on your heart and liver tonight."

"I'll eat his kidneys," said another.

"I intend to mix your brains with a little fowl and mango myself," added a third.

The officer said nothing. He only scowled at me.

"And how about you, sir?" I challenged in a defiant tone. "Is there no part of me that you would like to dine on this evening?"

"I'll roast your ribs over a nice fire. How's that?" he answered just for spite.

"I know who you are," I said.

"And just how would that be possible?"

"We shall discuss the issue this evening when you are tied up and begging for your life," I responded with a glare of my own.

One of the pirates laughed. "He's got spunk, I'll

give him that, Lieutenant."

"I'll give him a sword on his neck. That's what I'll give him," said another.

"Well, gentlemen," I stated, "you have us at great disadvantage, yet you do not charge at us. Is it fear, then, that stops you?"

At the time, being as frightened as I was, I did not realize the words of such boldness that came flying from my mouth. I was meeting their challenge with my own and speaking to pirates with a courage I had no idea I possessed. But know this, gentle reader: though my mouth moved with courage, my heart was beating like a drum in terror and my legs trembled below me like small twigs shuddering in the wind.

I remembered wondering why they did not suddenly rush us and slaughter us. It would not have been difficult for them. We were just two frightened, poorly trained fellows. They were battle-hardened and fierce men who had killed often. What was preventing them from attacking us?

Then I considered that they might perceive us as being more skilled than they knew, for we had, in fact, dispatched four of their number very quickly. And although we held only simple wooden spears, I had run a man clean through with one and plunged another into the heart of another, not to mention the precise aim of Matthew's arrows. Perhaps, I thought, we had earned a modicum of respect from these vicious men. Perhaps they recognized us as fierce warriors also and were a bit intimidated by our success thus far.

"Well?" I challenged again. "Are you going to just stand there trembling like children, or shall we finish this like men?"

The officer blinked, and I saw a slight hint of fear showing in his eyes. "Well, man," I then shouted more loudly, with a tone of anger and intolerance in my voice, "do you have nothing to say? Are you frightened to silence, you whimpering coward? Attack! Attack and let me be finished with you. I have supper to prepare. I would waste no more time on you, sir."

At that moment, I finally understood the unpredictable nature of both fear and courage. Fear is a fickle thing. It presents itself at a time of its own choosing and departs in like manner. Fear is never small; it is always a grand thing. It is absolute and final, and at times it can even be fatal to possess.

Courage is born from fear and can exist only where there was once fear. It relies on fear to show it the way.

This is what did it for me. After I shouted, I saw each of the fiends tremble slightly. It was then that I realized they were more frightened of me than I was of them, frightened almost to paralysis. They did not attack us because they feared we would prevail.

"If you do not have the stomach for it," I again bellowed, "lay down your weapons and surrender!"

"What shall we do, Lieutenant?" asked one pirate.

"They'll kill us if we do," said another.

"It seems they'll kill us even if we don't," said the third.

"Tell us, Lieutenant. What shall we do?" asked the first pirate again.

"Would you spare our lives, sir, if we surrender?" the officer asked, a definite tremble on his lips.

"I would spare your lives, but if you press me to battle, sir, I will have your heads on stakes around my fire tonight. Make your decision. I have no more patience with you."

I saw them tremble even greater, still frozen in their stances.

"That's it. I've had it!" I shouted in anger, firming my grip around my spear while gritting my teeth and putting a frightful sneer upon my face. "Matthew! You slaughter the two pigs in front of you. I'll take these cowards here."

The officer visibly shook. Then a miracle happened. He dropped to one knee and presented his sword to me as a conquered warrior would, laid out in his outstretched hands, his head bowed. I immediately stepped forward and took the sword from him.

I turned toward the other pirates, and two of them let their swords fall and dropped to their knees immediately in full capitulation.

"And you, sir!" I barked to the third, the one with the bloody nose, standing next to the lieutenant and still clutching his sword, perspiration running off his chin in small rivulets mixing with the blood still flowing from his wounded nose. "Do you still wish to make war on me? Is it your wish that I spill more of your blood, sir? If so, then step forward and let's have at it, *now*!"

"N–no, sir," he said. "I surrender to you, sir."

"Then drop your sword immediately or I shall run you through here and now!" I shouted, stepping toward the man as a crazed beast ready to slaughter its prey, now brandishing the officer's sword.

His sword immediately dropped to the sand, followed by the man dropping to his knees also.

Our battle was won.

I directed Matthew to bind their hands behind them and guide them over to the fire, where he then lined them up and sat each of them down into the sand. They continued to tremble in fear as I paraded past them slapping the flat side of my newfound saber into my palm, an intimidating scowl stretched across my face.

I finally turned back toward the rock positions and called out to Gretchen and Charlie, who then walked slowly toward us, Gretchen cradling Abigail in her arms.

As Gretchen came to a stop next to me, I stared at the officer. "Lieutenant, I hold you personally responsible for the actions of your men. This is my lady, Gretchen. Should one hair be harmed on her head by any of your men, I will have yours on a pike in the center of this camp. Are we clear on this, sir?"

"Y–yes, sir," he responded with remaining fear. "It is clear, sir."

"The bird is also under my protection. The same applies to it. Understand?"

"Of course, sir."

"Your name?"

"Malcolm, sir. Malcolm Jennings, Lieutenant and First Mate of the merchant vessel BOSTON BOUNTY, sir."

"Lieutenant Jennings? Merchant vessel? You are lying, sir. Speak the truth, man, or I will feast on your tongue tonight before your very eyes."

I heard the words bolt from my own lips, but I was at a loss as to how they formed in the first place. I could not believe such words could be spoken by me. I was both shocked and delighted that I possessed such a fierce vocabulary, but I was careful not to let them see my surprise.

"Lieutenant Jennings, sir," he then repeated. "That's the truth. First Mate of the BOSTON BOUNTY. These men were part of my crew. This man to my immediate left is Seaman Andrew Simmons, and then there is Seaman Samuel Crutcher, and on the end is Seaman Richard Barnaby. We served on the same vessel, sir. It is the truth I speak, sir. I swear to you."

"Do you think me a fool? You are pirates, sir. Some of your shipmates were on this very island only a short time ago. They murdered my two friends here and then left."

I could see confusion rise in his eyes regarding

my assertion that Charlie and Matthew had been murdered, but he said nothing about it. "I assure you, sir," he began again, "we are not pirates. It was not we who came ashore before. We were captured by them just over three months ago and forced into service until the storm sank the ship. We landed here only this morning, very early, a liberated crew. I swear this to you."

Now it was my turn to be confused. "You say you are not pirates, but only minutes ago you were threatening to eat me and acting as such."

"Yes, sir. Great apologies regarding that. We only meant to put a strong face on to hold you off. You are a fierce-looking man, and you frightened us. We learned to use that pose from the pirates. It worked to perfection before, but obviously failed us in this case. I can see that you are a man much experienced in warfare, sir. We are only humble merchantmen. I regret my words now, sir, and I beg your forgiveness."

I almost burst into laughter when he asserted that I was an experienced fighter. I fought back my urge to break into an imbecilic giggle. I also saw in his eyes that he was telling me the truth. His manner was that of an educated man, not a beast. A gentleman could pass for a pirate, at least for a short while, but there was no way a pirate could pass for a gentleman, not even for a second. As I looked at him further, and then to each of the others, they did not appear as pirates. Their demeanor was not one of challenge or bloodthirstiness. They were meek and frightened.

I then could no longer contain my mirth. I burst out laughing as I realized that we all were playing the role of fierce warrior and yet none of us were. They looked at me, still frightened, for they did not understand that my laughter was not founded on any evil intent, but instead was one of relief and joy.

"Matthew, please untie the lieutenant and stand him up."

Matthew moved immediately and did as I asked.

"Please, sir. I beg you. I'm a merchant man, not a pirate. Please, sir, spare me. I beg your forgiveness for my earlier outburst."

"Silence, friend," I said, holding up an empty hand, palm outward, "and fear no more. No one is going to harm anyone." I moved toward him and reached out my hand, and we shook hands. His expression was one of utter confusion and woe. I laughed again. "You thought me a fierce warrior, friend? Well, I thought *you* a despicable pirate. It seems we have both formed wrong opinions each of the other. I am no warrior. I am an accountant who was shipwrecked here over two hundred sixty-three days ago."

"You don't say!" Jennings finally laughed. "You should be on stage, sir. It was a performance worthy of note. I think I speak for all of us when I say you convinced us that you were about to slay us without hesitation or mercy."

The other three simply nodded in agreement as Matthew untied them.

"My apologies for the four dead men. Were they also of your crew?"

"No, sir. As fortune would have it, they were men who were also captured, but I believe they were born of an ill-formed inspiration. To be honest, sir, I am glad they are gone. Containing an evil disposition, as they did, I think a similar end would have befallen them sooner or later."

"Then I am relieved they fell so quickly, for I do not believe I could have sustained my act for very much longer. Please forgive my poor manners, Lieutenant. I am Thomas Bartholomew Cantfield, originally from New York City but now a marooned resident of McShane Island, the island upon which you presently find yourselves also. Welcome, friends."

Everyone politely introduced themselves.

"Charlie McShane, did you say?" inquired the lieutenant.

"Yes, sir, 'tis I," Charlie grinned.

"As in McShane Island?"

"Yes," I said. "And it is an interesting story."

"I can't wait."

We then all sat down and broke open fruit and coconut, sharing a meal together as we each exchanged wonderful stories about our lives.

By the end of the day, I realized that Charlie had been correct when he'd said that we should have made friends and that they must have had great stories to tell, for they did. Wonderful stories.

I think it important to pause my account here for a moment and point out the following. The wild events over the past months—the shipwreck, the storm, and the pirate attack—have given me a chance to study both fear and courage from a personal perspective. During my examination of both, I have come to some better understanding of them.

Fear represents a completely irrational state, and it seems to be absent or, at the very least, detached from any conscious state. It is a reactive emotion, not a proactive one.

Courage, on the other hand, is based on hope, and hope requires conscious thought. Courage may also then be likened to a lighted pathway through fear.

While fear lives, it seems to me, there is no possibility for courage to exist, for the mind is turned only to what can go wrong. In that state, therefore, the mind is absent any hope.

Perhaps, then, when all is said and done, that is what defines courage: the presence of conscious thought, the hope for a better outcome than if left to fear.

I am certainly no expert in battling the consequences of fear, but I see that, at least for me, there was a direct correlation between fear and courage in the relationship of conscious and unconscious thought.

As I am able to look back upon the events now through clearer vision, I have come to the understanding that courage comes not *through* fear, but *in spite of* it, through the simple act of having hope.

I have come also to understand that when faced with distress, so many opportunities for courage rise up if the mind is kept in proper perspective, and yet there are few who are able to reason it through when so confronted.

I made another important discovery that night after the attack. Conscious thought and proper preparation can minimize the most debilitating effects of fear, for if one considers most aspects of a coming stressful event rationally and suitably prepares for it, then fear does not have a chance to seed itself into one's brain. I believe that is the reason Matthew and I fared so well during the battle. It was our clear thinking and preparation that made us strong. Fear had no chance to infect us. It did infect our foes, however, for they were not prepared to do battle and had not given conscious thought as to how they might defend themselves. Thus they were defeated despite their superior numbers. They succumbed to fear while we did not allow it to take root.

I stand perplexed, however, for if I give the issue even more thought, I find that thinking one can consciously overcome irrational fear every time is the thinking of a true fool. Sometimes it is simply not possible.

Still, I shall never stop seeking how to defeat fear. I shall never accept the consequences of what fear can achieve, for it can achieve only what I allow it to achieve and nothing more.

It may come down to an internal battle, a battle that I might lose in the end, but it would not be for the lack of trying to overcome it. After all, what is it that I would lose in at least trying?

Since that time I have given much thought to the brothers fear and courage. I cannot say that my study is yet complete, nor can I say that I have come to any great conclusion regarding their character. I can say only that I have come to the point upon which I now stand with firm conviction, believing this: fear is the catalyst by which courage is born. And if fear be a necessary component of the whole, then it follows that courage requires that there first be fear, yet fear requires only that it be accepted. Therefore, I encourage you to fear not. Do not yield to fear. Stand up against fear. Battle it even unto the end, your end or the end of *it*. Never capitulate to fear, for fear is not an end but only a path walked by the unenlightened. Seek instead courage, for it lights the path guiding you through fear's obstacles to a higher and better place. And if these sentiments hold a favorable place in your brain, consider this also, dear one. Success requires courage. Failure requires only surrender.

Chapter 9

So as not to overwhelm you with so many varied stories all at once, let me sum up most of what was done and said over the course of that afternoon and evening after the battle, still my 263rd day on the island.

After we all took a few moments acquainting the others with the story of our lives, we were then confronted with the dreadful task of burying the dead.

I must tell you that I had a great struggle with this—not with the physical task involved, but with the fact that it was by my hand that two men lay dead, their blood staining the sand very near where I lived and had to pass by each and every day thereafter.

I had never before taken a man's life, and while one could argue that these were hardly men anymore at the time of their deaths, men in the definition of being kindly souls, but had taken on the likes of bloodthirsty animals in need of destruction, it still haunted me that I knowingly had been the instrument of their obliteration.

As I dug the hole in the sand, I found it difficult to involve myself in the idle chatter that some of the others seemed to have little problem with. It was I, Matthew, Lieutenant Jennings, and Seaman Samuel Crutcher who dug the graves.

Charlie, taking none of this seriously, of course,

made silly with Andrew and Richard, being very much of the same mirthful spirit as Charlie. Samuel was the quiet one of our four new friends. He was a listener, that one. As others spoke, I could see that his mind was absorbing everything being said, to be considered later as to how it all fit in with what he already knew or suspected.

But more on him and his mates later.

As I dug the grave for one of the men slain by my hand, the first one, the one whom I had pierced completely through, I could not help but wonder if he had anyone back home awaiting his return. I realized that he had changed from what he once had been, but still, he may have had a wife, children, or parents who anxiously awaited his return from the sea. They would never know that I had stabbed him to death in a heated brawl. I would never be able to tell his loved ones how he had died. As with me, I presumed, they would one day simply stop wondering and move on with their lives. While the others tugged and yanked the bodies into their graves, I took great care, gently moving him into his.

Did he note my gentle and kind thoughts regarding him? Of course not; he was dead. But I knew, and that was cause enough to render a measure of respect to his corpse.

Abigail waddled back and forth from grave to grave, wondering, I believe, what all the commotion was about. She stopped at my grave and stared at me for several seconds.

148

"They were wicked men," I announced. "But they deserve to be put away with some respect. Do you understand?"

I received the look.

Later that evening, seated once again around the fire, Lieutenant Jennings told us about how he and his three shipmates were on their vessel heading back home after a two-and-a-half-year journey to the South Seas when they were attacked by the pirates. Apparently, there was quite a battle and the pirate crew was deeply diminished from the fight. The pirate captain spared their lives because of the loss of his own men of equal rank and skill, but forced them to accept conscription in return for their lives. They worked during the day or night, depending on their shift, but were held in chains and irons when not on duty. The pirate captain held several men in that fashion on board the ship.

Jennings explained that when the pirate captain saw the approach of such a large storm, he knew instantly that he would be unable to outrun it and that his ship would not survive the full fury of such a heinous tempest. The captain then recalled the island and ordered his helmsman to immediately make for its coast, hoping to get ashore before the storm struck. They had almost made it, too.

He became rather emotional when he told me that it was only by way of good fortune for them that they were on duty when the ship went down during the last evening of the storm. It seems that many good and decent men drowned while still chained like animals down in the hold as the ship went under— abandoned like rats.

Jennings and his mates managed to swim to a large piece of the ship's shattered hull that was adrift after the sinking. They were joined by two pirate crewman. Together they paddled through the night, reaching the island just after daybreak.

Knowing a second group of castaways following them on another bit of floating wood to be a part of the fearsome pirate crew, and that they were an evil group of men and would, no doubt, do in him and his mates at first opportunity, Jennings decided quickly to dispatch all the pirates as soon as he could. Immediately upon getting a good foothold in the sand, he drew his saber and, due to their weakened condition he easily dispatched both pirates on his piece of wood. Then he ordered his men to kill the next group as they gagged and choked in the surf just off the shoreline. Jennings had acted first to save his life and the lives of his men, but he deeply regretted his action. Knowing full well that it was a simple matter of self-preservation, he claimed no pride for what he had done.

The second group of pirates, being fully armed and even fiercer than the first group, arrived much later, paddling in on still another large portion of the shattered hull. Charlie had missed their arrival by coming to tell us of the advent of the first two groups of castaways.

The pirates that Matthew and I slaughtered, being well armed and of a very cruel nature, frightened Jennings and his men, so Jennings had decided to act peaceably and wait for a better time to send that lot into the next world. Then they happened upon our camp and we dispatched the scoundrels for them.

I casually looked around for Abigail. Facing away from us, she squatted on the grave I had dug. She was still, so still that she looked stuffed. I was mesmerized by her and wondered what she was thinking.

Did she know the man? Had she seen him before? It was odd that of the four graves, she picked that one to sit upon.

She finally turned her head and looked straight at me. It was then that I knew for certain.

Lieutenant Jennings then took note of me staring at Abigail.

"Dear God," he said. "It's the bird! I didn't recognize it before, but I'm certain that it is same bird."

Seaman Andrew gasped. "Aye, sir. 'Tis the same bird. I'm sure of it now."

They piqued my full interest. "Tell me," I asked, "how do you know the bird?"

"It is the same bird that Benjamin was feeding on the ship not but a few days ago."

"Are you certain of this?" I asked.

"Yes. Very certain."

"So that is where you went during your absence here," I said loudly in Abigail's direction.

The look.

"Benjamin? Did you say Benjamin?" I inquired.

"The man in the grave, the man you killed. His name was Benjamin Hartford, Seaman First Class. And a most wicked man he was, too."

My heart skipped a beat. Suddenly this slaughtered cur had a name, and it was a good name, Benjamin Hartford. His death then took on a much different meaning. I had not killed just a nameless and despicable pirate, I had killed a man, a man who had a life and now a name. I had killed Seaman First Class Benjamin Hartford. I had run a wooden spear straight through his heart with such force that it exited his back. I could now put a name to the face of my victim.

"Benjamin Hartford, Seaman First Class, you say?"

"Yes," said Jennings.

"Lieutenant, can you tell me anything about him?"

"Not much. I know that he hailed from Charleston. His family, it was said, are good people, but I was told nothing more about them. He was a good sailor, I know. He performed his duties adequately enough. It was the bird, though. It was the bird that made him stand out in my mind.

"He said the bird had landed on the ship one

night a month or so ago. It appeared wounded, so he fed it and kept it out of the night air until morning. He released it, but it hesitated to fly away. It just roosted on the yardarms and only descended to the deck when Benjamin brought it some food.

"He and the bird sat together for a while each night. He would talk to it as if it understood his every word. Many crewmen took it as an bad omen and urged him to shoo it away. He tried, but the bird would just fly up and land on the yardarms.

One day Benjamin fired a pistol at it, intending it no harm, but merely to chase it away, as the crew was beginning to consider eating it. The bird rose into the air, then landed next to Benjamin, who brought his face down to the bird as if to speak to it. The bird immediately snatched some hair off his head and flew away. Over the next few days it returned briefly from time to time. Then the storm hit, and you know the rest."

"You're certain it is the same bird?" I asked.

"Yes, sir," answered Jennings, "I'm certain of it. Look how it has settled over poor Benjamin's grave. I think it knows he is dead."

I stared back at Abigail, who simply stared back at me, frozen on the spot.

"She knows," I replied. "I'm certain of it now."

"So she has adopted you then instead, eh?" asked Jennings.

"It would seem so," I responded. And then it struck me full force. I had killed a man who had a life, a name, and even a story. For a man whose heart was seemingly filled with evil, he had shown compassion for a wounded bird. I concluded that even men of evil hearts own some compassion.

I realized then that Abigail was mourning his loss. She turned to me once again. I smiled at her, but she turned away and stared out into the night a while longer and then flew away into the darkness.

I took strong note of the three young seaman seated across the fire circle and studied them more closely. My victim was near to their age, I guessed, perhaps a few years older.

"Young seaman, tell me. Whence do you hail?"

"I am from Virginia, sir," answered Andrew.

"I'm from North Carolina, sir," said Richard.

"I hail from New York, sir. Same as you," said Samuel.

I nodded in acknowledgement and appreciation that these young men also had names. They also had stories.

They seemed nearer to Charlie's age. They were kindhearted men and also of a joyful and mischievous spirit. Charlie was overjoyed that there were now other mates to share in more mirthful pursuits.

It seemed that Andrew's father was a farmer. He grew tobacco in his fields. Andrew was a restless sort and apparently a pitiful farmer, and it was his father who had suggested that he might find some happiness in going to sea.

Young Richard, like his apparently famous father before him, was a man bred to the sea. His father, I learned, was a cannoneer officer who died during the War of 1812, perishing from the blast of British cannons during the sea battle of Lake Erie on September 10, 1813, under the direct command of Commodore Oliver Hazard Perry. Richard's father was one of the acknowledged heroes of the battle, a man mentioned by Perry himself in eulogy. Those seemed to be awfully big shoes for this particular young man to fill, and thus, I learned also, that he preferred to have people think him of a more mirthful spirit than he might have genuinely been. I believed his immature manner to be a ruse, therefore. He was a very fine young man.

Samuel, as I have stated earlier, was unique. He was a quiet man, a very bright lad, and not one who shied away from responsibility. He usually remained so quiet that sometimes I didn't know he was there at all.

I liked Lieutenant Jennings from the very start. He was from Boston, like Matthew, and from a very noble family. He was a gentle thinking man, and he possessed many excellent skills which would later prove themselves very valuable to our blossoming community.

"Well, Lieutenant," I said, "we don't have much use for titles around here. As you can see, we are far from any ship. Do you mind if we dispense with formalities?"

"Absolutely, sir."

"Wonderful. Would you then allow me to simply call you Malcolm?"

"I would be honored, sir."

"Thomas, Malcolm. Thomas, please."

"Then Thomas it is."

"Well, Malcolm, the storm tore apart my fowl pen. I think we should attend to repairing it at first light and begin gathering a new stock of birds. What do you say to that?"

"It is your island, Thomas, and we your grateful guests. Set the tasks and we shall comply."

"I would prefer to think of us as a team, Malcolm, and dispense with any hierarchy."

"As you wish."

"As for the fowl, I shall have to point out which of them are the best-eating fowl. Luckily, they are a dimwitted species and easy to snare. I would think that within a few days we should once again be well stocked. We have many more mouths to feed."

That evening, I was stunned to see Samuel and Richard coming through the thicket, each with a large armful of wood for the fire.

"Thank you, gentlemen."

"No thanks necessary, Thomas. Just doing our part," said Samuel.

Within a short time, a blazing fire's light

flickered on each face. As we sat around the flames, bellies again full of fruit and refreshing water, I glanced skyward once more and sent another gracious nod for the arrival of my new friends.

Just then Abigail landed near to us, waddled over to where I sat, and laid her head down upon my thigh, as was her customary pose. All was complete. All was well. All was as it should be.

We were now a growing family.

Five days later, on my 268th day on the island, we finished capturing the final birds we required to suitably repopulate the menagerie for our expanded needs. Malcolm, Matthew, Andrew, and I took the primary responsibility of building the pen while Charlie and Richard gathered the necessary materials, although it took them a good long while to do so. It seems they found plenty of time for merriment and jest, but somehow they were able to complete their duties between all the bouts of frivolity.

With everyone's help, but especially with Andrew's knowledge of building pens on the farm and even Abigail's assistance, through her simple accompaniment, we managed to build it much sturdier than I had built it originally, and substantially larger. The pen now measured ten feet in length, six feet in width and remained four feet high. Seeing that we had need for many more birds, it seemed the proper thing to do.

Gretchen took a particular liking to young Samuel. He apparently reminded her of her younger brother, whom I had never met. They became very close, those two, and I was very happy that she had someone else to share time with while I was busy performing the chores necessary to maintain a large camp such as ours.

Malcolm, Andrew, and I took the opportunity to lay out an area appropriate to accommodate separate huts for those who wished for more privacy. Over the following twelve days, we managed to put up two very large huts of wood and grass thatch. Gretchen and I, of course, remained in the cave, while Malcolm and Matthew shared the tent, Charlie and Richard shared one hut, and Samuel and Andrew shared the other.

From a short distance, I thought, it looked like a burgeoning community, complete with all the accommodations necessary to establish a civilization.

By nightfall, the end of my 280th day, while we lay around the fire together, young Samuel suggested that we were our own nation now, the nation of McShane Island, and therefore its charter citizens. Richard then recommended that we should call ourselves McShanians instead of Americans from now on. My dear Gretchen suggested that if we had the cloth, we should create a flag for our new nation. I thought it a wonderful idea, but alas, we had no extra cloth with which to make one. The only cloth we owned was already hanging on us.

We ended the evening, we few, new, and proud citizens of McShane Island, with a group declaration of allegiance to both our new nation and to each other. It was an amazing thing for me to witness how quickly strangers had become friends, and how friends then had become family. I adored my new family. It was a rather glorious moment for me.

On the morning, that being my 281st day there, sitting against the great log by the fire and writing words into my journal, I looked out at our little village, as we had then started calling it. I couldn't help thinking that with only a few more of us we would become a town.

In that moment, I could not imagine ever being alone again. And even if rescued, I could not envision us ever going our separate ways, to never see each other again. It just did not seem possible at the time.

It had been an exciting and adventurous several days. We had accomplished much in a very short time, working together as a team. We had come together and created a new village, a new way of life, and even a new nation.

Quite an accomplishment for castaways, I think.

On the afternoon of the 298th day, seventeen days since I had last entered anything into my journal, I finally managed to find some time to sit down and write.

I should remind you that it had been my initial intent to note nearly each day's accomplishments into my journal, but as you have no doubt concluded, things happened there sometimes very quickly. I tried updating the journal as often as I could, but unfortunately, the time needed and the time available were not always synchronous.

Let me say that since I had written last, our new family had become very much more bonded. Most of our days were spent roaming the island together, taking our meals near the coast or up on the mountain trails. For the most part, the previous several days had been peaceful and quiet. If I do say so myself, the days had been rather mundane and uneventful. No evil forces had attacked the island, no storms had struck, no new family members had washed ashore.

In fact, I had not seen a single ship on any horizon since the original pirate attack. This troubled me greatly. Was it that ships had stopped sailing or was it that the island was far away from the normal shipping lanes?

According to Malcolm, the island was not charted on any maps of which he was aware. He reasoned it out, same as I, that the island was far outside the standard shipping channels.

None of us could say whether the island was northward or southward of the standard shipping routes. As you know, I'm an accountant and not a mariner, certainly not one who could successfully navigate my way back to the shipping lanes. For all we knew, dozens of ships sailed past our island every day just beyond the horizon, with never a need to come any closer. Thus I gave up any hope that we should be rescued anytime soon.

In our discussion of the matter, we came to the conclusion that should we see another vessel, it was the prudent choice to be wary. Merchant vessels would stay in the channel lanes for reasons of both security and expediency. Therefore, any ship seen was either a ship of exploration or up to no good. It would be hard to distinguish their intent until they would be well upon us. We concluded with the decision that unless we could clearly identify any ship happening toward us as non-hostile, we would be better served to remain hidden.

And so it was that many of our nightly discussions revolved around our potential rescue. While engaged in such repartee, however, we knew that it was highly unlikely we would ever be rescued. Still, it did make for lively discussions.

As I have already stated on several occasions, life on the island was not difficult. Rather, at times it had become exceedingly boring. With the lack of exciting challenges such as attacking pirates or sudden storms, we found ourselves becoming quite complacent and indolent.

It was only because of my training as an accountant that I maintained my calendar, as it were, scratching marks on a parchment page denoting the passing of days. I don't really know why I continued doing it with so much accuracy, but perhaps it was out of some need to know my fate, or simply the need of an accountant to record something. I couldn't really say then, nor can I say why even today. It had become a morning ritual for me. Rise up, ink a mark on the page, shave my face, and then go about my day. Whether for well or ill, it was just one of the many things done in their proper order each and every morning regardless—accomplished almost unconsciously.

Odd, the way such trivial things find their place and priority in the ordinary lives of simple people.

It was then I realized that it was a real possibility we could all perish from boredom before anything violent or frightening would ever occur again.

And there it was, conceivable that on one particular morning we might just see no need to wake up and would all perish in our sleep because there was nothing else to do but die. Well, I reasoned, at least that might cease the boredom.

I lay about for several days thereafter, contemplating my life. Gretchen was always near and always of a positive demeanor, her smile evermore on her lips. I don't think she knew what an unhappy moment was like.

On the 305th day, after having ample time to think calmly and quietly, I had come to entertain the idea of what I would do with the rest of my life should I ever be liberated from this island. It was foolish to think such thoughts, but it gave me a slight reprieve from the tedium.

I imagined where we all would settle and what opportunities would make themselves available to us. I supposed that in the short while, we would be celebrities, traveling and speaking about our life as castaways. I even imagined that, for a time, we would attract large crowds wishing to hear about the exciting events of our lives. But our stories would be short and few, given the lack of excitement.

Nevertheless, in time, the stories all told, I guessed that our lives would become less and less encumbered, our presence at events of high society no longer desired.

At some point, we would have to get on with our lives as just ordinary people, although we clearly were not common people. I would have to find some manner of employment once again, as would the others. I wondered if that simple necessity would eventually separate us, or if would we find a way to stay together.

During those languid days of thinking such thoughts, I conjured up ways to stay together, but I had to concede the possibility that in the reality of a normal life, we would in all likelihood, in order to secure our futures, end up going in different directions. It was a sobering thought, and a distressing one, but it was realistic. How would it be possible for a cargo master and a first mate to find work on the shore? Moreover, how would it be possible for an accountant to find gainful employment aboard a ship? How would it be possible for a fine woman, used to living in high society, to follow the simple accountant to sea?

At times I dreaded thinking at all, for the foolishness of such thoughts was hard to ignore.

On the 310th day, Gretchen came to me as I was on my back under a tree, thinking my usual deep thoughts, and bade me to give her my full attention. In her own words, she was feeling a bit troubled.

I was shocked to hear such disquieted comments coming from her, of all people.

When I asked her to explain herself, she became quite forlorn and confided in me that she wished to be married.

My response, however, that for all intents and purposes, we *were* married, was not greeted joyously. And seeing that there was no magistrate to perform the ceremony, I didn't see how we could formalize our relationship without such a person.

She expressed disappointment in such reasoning and felt that she was living in shame. I explained that I could not think of a resolution, to which she made an excellent suggestion: that I consider myself the magistrate, this being its own country and all. I thought for a bit, and it seemed quite a reasonable position for me to assume. "Magistrate Cantfield," I mused.

It did have a certain ring to it.

I thought it an inspired idea. Therefore, that afternoon, I declared myself magistrate. No one objected at all. In fact, everyone voiced the opinion that I was befitting the title.

Being now in the position to formalize such events, I beseeched Matthew to be my best man. Having no other female on the island, Gretchen implored Charlie to wear a bonnet of leaves and act as bridesmaid. For the sheer silliness of it all, he was only too happy to participate in this way. I fashioned a ring from tiny vines in the trees, and thus on that evening, with the rest of my family singing an off-key rendition of the bridal march and Malcolm giving the bride away, I slipped the ring upon sweet Gretchen's finger and made her my wife.

In celebration of the glorious event, we all made a party of it on the far westerly end of the island until late into the night.

The next morning, the 311th day, having awakened to yet another cloudless sky, we decided to stay where we were for most of the day, returning to our camp only in time to cook a few fowl for supper.

You may think me a callous fellow because I do not write with more depth and excitement about my marriage, but it was just another event like so many others, without any real challenge or adverse consequence.

Gretchen was calmed and returned to her joyous disposition once again, and other than that, I could see no changes from what had always been, though perhaps that observation comes only from a man's perspective.

That evening found me once more seated under my favorite tree, lost again in the wonderment of what I would do if I were ever to leave the island.

Adding to my previous thoughts on this matter, I would say that I would very much like to travel. I would like to see all the great cities that I have heard so much about but never even dreamed that I would one day be able to visit.

I would like to walk the streets of Paris, Rome, London, Prague, Warsaw, and Moscow with Gretchen on my arm, our eyes hungrily devouring every wonderful sight of those great cities. I heard once about the great pyramids of Egypt and how they rise majestically over the Egyptian plains. I would like to behold their wonderful image as well.

I would, if I am ever able to do so, like to travel to all points of the earth, but being marooned here, it is doubtful that I will ever see another landscape other than this.

Chapter 10

Where do I begin?

Let me first announce that it has been thirty-seven days since we were liberated from the island.

That is such a poor way to start an exciting tale.

Allow me to begin again and first ask your forgiveness for not keeping you abreast of all that has transpired since last I entered my notes here into this journal.

With so much excitement and so much to record, I had to take pause and sort it all out in my own mind before I could properly write it down. Still, I hardly know where to begin.

As you are already aware, life on the island was rather mundane. We all got along wonderfully. There was never any strife or argument. Food and water remained widely plentiful. No more treacherous storms came to cause us grief and angst, no more unwanted visitors arrived to threaten the security of our new nation. In short, there was absent any excitement whatsoever.

That is, until my 340th day on the island had passed.

Early the next morning, Gretchen and I were walking along the beach as we had begun doing every morning since the 315th day. It had become a ritual now, our alone time, and something she had orchestrated. It allowed us the time we needed as a couple, away from the others, whom we loved very much but not the same way that we loved each other. As Gretchen put it, it was "our time to reconfirm each day that our love is special."

Over the past several weeks, I had grown very fond of this special time together and I eagerly looked forward to our early morning walks along the shoreline.

On the day in question, as we walked along the northwestern shore and talked, I spied a dark object on the very distant horizon to the west. I pointed it out to Gretchen, but she as well could not make it out clearly.

We sat down on the beach and watched the growing object with great interest until I could finally make out the topsail.

"A ship!" I yelled.

"Yes!"

"We are saved!" I screamed loudly.

I wondered how we could attract their attention and let them know of our presence, then remembered my signal fire built on the opposite side of the island. It had been so long since I had seen a ship, I had forgotten to maintain the pile of wood.

"It looks to be heading straight at us, Gretchen! We need to get to the signal logs and set them ablaze."

I hugged Gretchen with all my might. "We're saved, my darling! We are rescued!"

We hugged and jumped as one. She laughed with glee.

"Come," I said, "we need to get to the other side of the island and light the pile. With luck, they will spot our smoke and come to our aid. Quickly, my dear, we must dash."

With that, we ran down the beach toward the path that would lead us through our camp and out toward the signal pile. The steeply upward trail leading toward the camp nearly exhausted both of us, but with our liberator ship in sight, we discovered new strength to scale the mountainside without slowing.

At the top of the path, I stopped and turned back to see a most frightening sight. It appeared to me that the ship was in the midst of making a starboard turn, which would take it back over the horizon in a short while.

"Come, my love," I shouted, "we must run even faster!"

I dashed along the trail. I did not look back for Gretchen, but I heard her panting and that was confirmation enough that she was behind me.

When I got to camp, the boys were lazing around a nearly extinguished fire. I noticed a stick still red hot in the dying embers. I scooped it up without slowing and continued on the trail toward the signal pile.

"Why the rush, old man?" asked Charlie drowsily.

"A ship!" I answered without slowing.

I dashed through the underbrush as if I had wings on my feet, hardly feeling the ground beneath me as I ran.

Within minutes I reached the signal pile. It was still stacked as I had left it, but the kindling in the center was gone. I searched around the area for any dried sticks. There were none.

As the others caught up with me, I asked them to find dried leaves and weeds to help set the blaze alight. They each did their best, and soon we had enough dried material set into the center of the pile.

I blew on the stick in an attempt to spark a flame. I tried for several minutes, but the ember was nearly at its end.

"Curse you!" I screamed.

"There, there, my boy," I heard Matthew say in his usual calm voice.

I looked up to see him walking slowly toward me, a stick in his hand with a bright flame licking the end of it.

"Matthew!" I shouted. "Bless you, Matthew."

"Thank you, lad. Thank you so very much."

Matthew bent low and held the flame under the dried twigs and leaves, and an instant later a bright flame burst forth in the center of the mass.

Moments later the fire was scorching hot as it raced up toward the top of the pile.

I searched the western horizon to see if the ship was still in sight. It wasn't. From this spot on the island it could not be seen. My joy sank to a place deep within me, swallowed by the beginnings of despair.

The fire roared and danced high into the air.

"Green leaves!" I shouted. "Lay green leaves upon the fire. That should create more smoke. Hurry! Hurry!"

Everyone did as I asked.

"I'm going to the west end to see if I can spot the ship. Please keep the fire going strong, Matthew."

"Certainly, my boy."

I galloped westward down the beach, toward the westerly point where I had first seen the ship. Gretchen ran along behind me.

Minutes later, reaching the end, I gasped at the sight of the ship now only partially above the horizon. I turned to see a large billowing column of dark smoke rising over the island. I then looked back toward the ship, hoping to see it making a turn.

It did not.

Gretchen then caught up to me and stopped alongside. Abigail, having taken flight earlier, landed near us.

"Do you think they see the smoke, Thomas?"

"It appears dark enough, but I just don't know."

Together we stood watching the ship as it continued its track away from us for several more minutes.

"I don't think they saw it, my love," Gretchen said.

"It appears not," I answered, deep dejection

obvious in my tone.

Minutes later the ship was gone, having disappeared over the same horizon whence it came.

I fell on my buttocks to the sand and stared mournfully out over the ocean. Gretchen promptly sat down next to me and gently rubbed the palm of her hand across my forehead and then pulled my head to her shoulder. I closed my eyes tightly, not wanting to see an empty ocean. Abigail cuddled near and laid her head upon my thigh.

"I'm sorry, Thomas. I know you must be disappointed."

I tried to respond, but I could not find the strength to speak. Instead, I sat leaning my head against her shoulder in utter and disconsolate silence. My hand dropped down onto Abigail's soft back. I stroked her feathers.

This was a good thing, I would later reason. The silence, that is, for I feared that if I had found any words to speak, they would have surely been ill chosen and harshly spoken. There was no reason Gretchen needed to hear such drivel from a man so full of shame, anger, and self-loathing. So it was to my great relief that I could find no words to speak.

Then the impact of the moment, soundly striking both my heart and my soul with a permanence that I had been denying all this time, made everything finally clear and without question. We would never be found, and although it was a congenial place to be stranded, we would never be liberated from this island.

We were going to die here, forgotten by all who had ever known us, loved us, or even hated us. They would never learn of our fate, and we would never again see any shoreline but our own.

I felt the birthing pains of a new rage growing inside me.

It was not a question of being rescued as much as it was the lack of choice that I had in the whole matter. I wanted the choice of whether or not I would remain here to be mine. But I was without that choice, I felt exiled, having been adjudged for some great crime and sentenced now to be forever banished from all civilized society, without the opportunity ever to have spoken up in my own defense. The choice was torn from me by force, willed so by some malevolent entity, and I had never been given a voice to object to either the verdict or the sentence. I suddenly felt abandoned by all that I had ever judged to be good in this world.

I fell swiftly and deeply into hopelessness and remained there mightily so for a good long time. And while there, I began a hard questioning of myself in all forms and manner. Each question was as a dagger thrust into my heart, for I immediately and correctly knew the answer to each question.

As I saw it, I was at fault for everything. I blamed myself for this missed opportunity. I was in charge. I was responsible for being prepared for the moment now passed and perhaps lost forever.

Was the fire not large enough? Should I have taken more time when I built the pile to make it larger, higher? Could I have done something more, something different? Should I have built a signal fire on both sides of the island? Question after question pounded upon me with no quarter offered, no mercy shown. They each fell incessantly upon my shoulders as weighty yokes, reminding me of my failure—my disastrous response to the only opportunity to escape this damnable island in all these many months.

What will the others say? I questioned myself further. *Will they hold me fully responsible for my failure to properly plan for this event? Will they now lose all faith and trust in me and my judgment? How am I going to face any of them?*

They had put their reliance and confidence into my decisions up until now. Was I about to lose the assurance of my family?

I could go on and on about how each question raised in my head sent me deeper into the abyss of melancholy, but you have, no doubt, being as bright as you are, reasoned it out already, that it was a deep and dark place that I suddenly found myself living in.

Gretchen, the wonderful and understanding wife that she was, offered no words of criticism, and I needed to hear none from her, for I had blasted myself with enough self-scorn. No. Instead, she sat patiently and understandingly, continued stroking the back of my neck and kissing my forehead, allowing me the time I needed within to afflict myself until I found the acceptance I so desperately searched for, for my failure.

Had this moment been a fistfight, I would have looked a bloody pulp, for I was ruthlessly hard on myself. But in my own mind, it was well deserved. I had let everyone down with my unpreparedness. And, given the fact that it had been a long while between sightings, I surmised that we would have to endure at least as long again before another opportunity would present itself, if indeed any should do so.

After a time, I finally managed to stand up. I turned promptly away from the ocean so as to forget the vision of my failure, the empty blue ocean, and began walking back toward the others, choosing to remain in the deathly silence of my disconcertment, fearing the terrible words with which they, no doubt, would greet me.

Abigail took once more to the air and circled above us. She was lucky. She could fly far away from the expected wrath, while I, lacking the means for such an escape and with my feet evermore cemented to the sand, would have to endure it all, the full of it, the complete ruinous end that I so well deserved.

Gretchen remained affixed to me, her head now resting on my shoulder as we slowly made our way back to the fully billowing smoke column continuing its wasted journey into the otherwise cloudless sky.

As we neared the group, I could see them running toward me. Abigail remained skyward in a small circle directly overhead.

I think even she was frightened of the approaching horde.

The mob appeared most angry, rushing to pummel me, no doubt, but they were family, and being so, they had a right to take out their disappointment on me. I would not flinch or try to escape their wrath. I, alone, was responsible for this lack of success. If I was to receive a beating for this, then it was my obligation to take it as well as I was able to do so.

As they neared me, I heard them hollering as one. They seemed a fuming lot, and for a moment I forgot that they were family and I feared them. I closed my eyes and pushed Gretchen away from me, fearing that she would be innocently struck by the others as they went for me.

They were then upon me, but it was not what I expected. Their touch was neither harsh nor violent. Instead, I was met by warm embraces and playful slaps upon my head and shoulders. Their shouts, which I had initially perceived as angry, were actually screams of joy and laughter.

I opened my eyes to smiling and grinning faces. Then I saw Matthew standing off from the others, his hands folded in front of him, a gentle smile on his face.

"Well done, my boy. Well done."

I admit to you that I was at a complete loss as to why I would have received such a warm greeting from those whom I had let down so disastrously.

"Why is everyone so joyous, Matthew?" I asked in earnest. "The ship is gone, it disappeared over the horizon. We are not to be rescued. I have failed you all."

"If this is failure, lad, then you should do it more often."

"What are you talking about?"

"Look, my boy. Look behind you."

I turned and saw the ship, now in large silhouette against the far horizon, its full sails billowing in the wind, growing closer with each passing minute.

They had seen my signal after all and were coming to our rescue. It would be yet several more hours before their arrival, but release from our captivity drew nigh.

Upon seeing the ship approaching, I fell to my knees as tears flowed in great abundance. I did not attempt to remain brave and stoic. I let it all flow out of me in a great rush. I yearned, at that moment, to feel the full joy of my relief all at once.

During this event, I had completely forgotten about our decision to remain hidden until we knew exactly what kind of ship we were about to signal. In all honesty, at the time, I simply did not think about it.

A sinking feeling then washed over me. *What if they are pirates? What if pirates have seen my signal?*

"What have I done?" I asked in worried astonishment.

"You have saved us, dear boy," responded Matthew.

"Are you certain of that, Matthew? What if they are pirates? What if I just signaled the means to our destruction?"

Everyone stopped smiling instantly.

"Good thought, Thomas," said Malcolm. "I hadn't considered that."

"Can anyone see them well enough to know?" I asked.

All eyes strained to see the ship more clearly. No one, it seemed, could make out the type of ship any better than anyone else, thus no one offered an opinion.

"Dear God," I cried, still not believing that there was such a deity, "I may have killed us all." I stood up and stared out at the approaching ship.

Worry washed over me.

"Now, now, Thomas," urged Matthew, "let us not rush to call upon the Devil so soon."

"I'm sorry," I said to all. "I saw the ship and did not take the time to think through my excitement."

"All is not yet lost, Thomas," encouraged Malcolm. "It just may be our salvation."

"Not if they are pirates," I answered. "Why didn't I take the time to be certain?"

"From the looks of it, dear boy, you did not have the opportunity to consider all avenues of possibility," said Matthew.

"I did not, Matthew, but still I acted in haste. I didn't think before I acted. I was just so excited to see a ship at all. Perhaps we should make preparations for the possibility that they intend to do us harm."

"Calm yourself, Thomas," added Samuel. "The ship is too heavily masted to be anything other than a merchant vessel. And see how large the vessel is. It cannot have the same maneuvering ability as a ship built for war. I believe you have saved us, Thomas. I believe it is a merchant vessel come to rescue us."

Whether Samuel's words were merely intended to calm us or were an accurate assessment of the ship's design, none could be certain. What was certain, however, was that they considerably lightened the mood of all.

I tried to turn my mind more toward the positive aspects of our immediate situation. I acknowledged, at least inwardly, that Samuel's evaluation made good sense. It was a great tall ship, and it did appear to be constructed for transporting heavy cargo and not for tactical maneuvering.

An hour later, we received our glorious answer when the ship turned to starboard to maneuver around the reef and we saw only small and few gun ports on her side. She was, indeed, a beautiful merchant ship.

I immediately fell once again to my knees, in either exhausted relief or pious gratitude, I am still not certain for which.

Gretchen knelt in front of me and smiled. I

reached out to her and hugged her tightly.

"We are saved," I stated tearfully. "Dear good God, we are saved."

"We are, my husband. Our future together begins soon."

"It will be wondrous, Gretchen. Of that I am positive."

I hugged her even more tightly as I watched the ship bobbing about in the ocean and making its way toward our signal.

After a time, I stood and hugged each of my family again. Then a new thought filled my head.

"I need help to bring personal things from the camp to the shore here. Who will help me?"

"We all will, of course," said Malcolm. "Let us dash there now and make ready together our exodus from this boorish hell."

Upon our return to the camp, I immediately tossed the manuscript into the chest, along with the quill pen and what ink bottles remained viable, and shut it tight.

Malcolm and Charlie lifted it and walked it back toward the shore as I stood gazing about me at the village we had constructed. I had made a mental note that on that day, the 341st day on this tiresome rock, or March 6, 1831, by my calculation, we were, finally, to escape.

Having plenty of time before the ship's arrival, I took a solitary walk to the gravesites of my friends. I knew they were alive and that such a trip was unnecessary, but I felt compelled to visit their former resting places just to be certain in my own mind.

I found them exactly as I had left them, the grave markers untouched.

Abigail landed nearby, but she chose to keep her distance. I knelt into the sand on one knee between the markers and laid a hand on each of them. "We are homeward bound, dear friends," I declared. "I don't know what I would have done without your help and guidance, and I certainly don't know how you achieved your resurrection as you did, but I needed to make this one last visit for reasons that are my own."

I stood up and set my right foot against Matthew's marker. I forced my leg outward and tipped over the marker into the sand. I then did the same to Charlie's marker. "You have no need for these markers, boys. You have a long life ahead of you. As you said, Matthew, the need for mournful remembrances are only for the dead."

I then left the empty graves and made my way back to the camp with Abigail again taken to flight. I walked into the tent one last time and looked around. I then went to the cave and sat at my desk. I ran my hands over the top of it and smiled. "You have served me well also. I shall leave you in peace."

I then stepped out of the cave and moved to the bird pen. I loosened the hinge to my menagerie and drove the birds out from it.

"You also are liberated this day," I decreed.

"Enjoy what life you have left, and thank you for your part in sustaining me and my friends." Many of them stayed nearby, however, having never known another home but the pen. In time, they would learn that they could go where they pleased, and so I did not worry for them.

I moved to the three empty wooden poles that had once held my grass friends and laid my hands on each of them. They were still firmly planted in the ground just outside the tent. I thanked them as well.

I turned then toward the shore and walked out of my village, hopefully forever, not looking again behind me, wishing instead to go forth into my new future absent any thoughts of my unfortunate past. This was my new beginning, and thus I turned my mind and thoughts to only that.

A little more than three hours later, we stood side by side upon the deck of our rescue ship, the ANNABELLE LEE, named after the ship owner's daughter, I would later learn, staring back at the sandy shoreline that was our island nation as it slipped slowly away. I tried not to look, but its ability to draw my attention kept me yet a prisoner for a little longer still.

A young seaman approached and touched my shoulder.

"Mr. Cantfield. Beg your pardon, sir, but the captain would like to see you when you are finished observing the retreat of your island."

I suddenly felt renewed and turned immediately away from the railing. "I am finished, sir, and I have no need to see it ever again. Please show me to the captain's quarters, if you will."

"Certainly, sir. Follow me, please."

Opening the door, I found the captain seated at his desk. Before stepping into the room, I spoke. "With your permission, Captain, may I enter?"

The captain rose immediately, moving around his desk to greet me warmly. "Of course, Mr. Cantfield, of course. We have much to discuss. Please have a seat."

"Thank you, Captain, for giving me time along the railing with the others."

"Certainly, sir. I can only imagine what trauma you are experiencing, leaving a place that has been home for so long. Are you feeling well? Is there anything you would like? A glass of brandy, perhaps?"

"Brandy," I replied incredulously. "That, sir, would be an absolute delight. Thank you."

"Not at all."

The benevolent captain moved to a small table fastened to the floor boards and poured a snifter of his finest brandy, presenting it then to me. I lifted the glass to my nose and took in the exquisite aroma of the brandy.

"Dear me," I announced, "I thought I would never smell again a bouquet so sweet." I took a sip of the golden liquid and let it slide slowly down my throat. "Unbelievable, Captain."

Forgive me once again, but I have regrettably jumped ahead, leaving you to only guess at the circumstances surrounding our liberation.

Allow me, then, to state that it was the captain and his first mate, along with his rowing seamen, who first came ashore in the small launch and greeted me. As their boat slid into the sand, but before stepping out onto my shoreline, the good captain looked me square in the eyes. "Permission to come ashore, sir?"

I laughed. "Permission granted, dear sir."

As the captain stepped from the boat, our hands instantly met in a hearty handshake.

"I am Captain Amos Quigley, sir. And this is my first officer, Benjamin Ostrander, and Seaman Johnson and Seaman McDever."

"Pleased to make your acquaintance, Captain Quigley, Mr. Ostrander, gentlemen. I am Thomas Bartholomew Cantfield, originally from New York City, but as you can see, I am lately of this small island nation and am the marooned wretch you see before you now. May I present my wife, Gretchen. And these fine gentlemen, Matthew, Charlie, Malcolm, Andrew, Richard, and Samuel. Welcome, gentlemen, to McShane Island. I don't know how yet to thank you for coming to our rescue, but I shall surely find a way."

"It is our pleasure, Mr. Cantfield," said the captain. "Well, sir, you look fit enough. Are you well?"

"Remarkably so, Captain. We are fit as fiddles. Life here has not been difficult, just endlessly boring and restrictive."

"Excellent! Then who shall come aboard first?"

"Please take my wife and these gentlemen first. I shall be last."

"Well spoken, lad," said the captain. "Like the leader I expected you to be."

Within a short time, my wife and friends were safely on board. The two seamen rowed back toward me. I watched them draw nearer and I suddenly felt the urge to look back onto my island one last time. I stared at all I could see. A tear formed in my left eye, and I did not attempt to wipe it away. The light breeze, to which I had become so accustomed over the last several months, caused the leaves and branches of the surrounding trees to flutter lightly. For all its entrapments, it was a kindly island to me. I laid my hand upon the sand, thanked my sister for taking good care of us, gave her then a good thought and wished her well.

Abigail landed near me and waddled to my side. I kneeled into the sand and took her head into my hands. I leaned forward and put my forehead to her head.

"Come, Abigail. Come to the ship with us. You

shall never be without kinship." I kissed her on the top of her head and let her go. She came immediately forward and laid her head upon my thigh, and for several seconds she remained still. I stroked her back for that time and then she pulled some strands of hair from my head, stepped back, and buried the hair in the sand. She then took to the air.

"You are a strange bird, Abigail. I'll give you that," I yelled up at her with a smile, rubbing the spot on my head from where she had plucked my hair.

She circled overhead for several minutes, then turned inland and disappeared over the island. I waited to see if she would return, but she did not.

The young seamen came ashore and helped put my chest into the launch.

"Begging your pardon, sir," said Seaman Johnson, "but that was a unique bird, was it not?"

"Yes, Mr. Johnson. A unique bird she was, indeed."

I climbed into the launch, and away we went. I did note that it was the first time my feet had left the island in the past 341 days. It was a glorious feeling, but at the same time a very emotional moment for me.

Somehow, someone, from somewhere, be it either a sympathetic deity or just the attentive seaman in the crow's nest who spotted the plume of rising smoke, had granted me a pardon for whatever sin I had committed. My sentence had either been completed or commuted, I did not care which it was. I was finally free—free to make the choices best for me. Free to stumble or free to walk. Free to remain grounded or free to take wing, if I so chose to do so. Whatever lay ahead of me in my restored future, it was now my choice to make that determination.

Chapter 11

As I said, the brandy slid down my throat easily.

The captain returned to his chair. "I'm very curious to hear about your adventures on that island. I have no doubt that the crew would like to hear them as well."

"Certainly," I answered. "It is the least I can do to begin to repay you for your rescue and to earn my keep on the voyage home. You should know that I'm no sailor. I am a rather experienced accountant, but I don't suspect you have need of my services in that regard."

"A rescue does not require payment, sir, but if you are offering, I could use your knowledge and assistance when we make calls to port and trade. Your accounting experience could prove most valuable to me at those times."

"I will do my best for you, sir." After a considered pause, I looked him square in the eyes. "Captain, I do have a peculiar question for you that I have wanted to ask you from the very first."

"Please. Ask. I shall answer if I am able," replied the good captain.

"We have long assumed the position of our island to be well off the standard shipping lanes. Am I correct in that assumption?"

"You are indeed, sir. A long way off the typical

routes. Your island lies well north by almost a full two degrees."

"Then, captain, how is it that you happened near us?"

"Ahh," the captain smiled. "I might say that destiny has played a hand in it all. We had been substantially delayed in Tonga for needed repairs to our mainsail. My helmsman, having navigated through the area some years ago on another vessel, assured me that the route we were on was the fastest way to Bora Bora, but he warned me of certain high reefs along the route. When you first made sight of us, we were in the midst of circumventing one of those reefs."

"I don't know which it is, captain, destiny or just good fortune, but I'm utterly delighted you found us."

"Indeed, it was fortunate I had my best seaman in the crow's nest."

"I would like to thank him personally, if you would allow me to do so."

"Of course. I shall make introductions later."

"To reiterate, captain, I shall be honored to help you in any way I can when we reach Bora Bora. Additionally, I would be happy to offer myself toward any menial tasks that you might find for me in the meantime."

"It is most kind of you to offer your help. I may have some light tasks you can help me with. Tell me, Mr. Cantfield—"

"Thomas, Captain. Please call me Thomas."

"Thank you. Thomas, then. Can you tell me a little about the rest of your group, Thomas? Some of them look to be able seamen."

"A keen eye you have, Captain. Yes. Four of the men, the younger ones, are seamen from merchant vessels similar to yours. Three of the seamen are off the BOSTON BOUNTY, which was attacked and scuttled quite a few months ago by pirates. Lieutenant Malcolm Jennings was first mate on that ship."

"First mate, you say?"

"Yes."

"That's an extraordinary find, Thomas. I will have need of a first mate very soon. My first mate disembarks when we reach Otaheite in about nine days. I would like to meet this Lieutenant Jennings. How fortuitous for both of us, it would appear."

"Clearly, Captain. Would you have also a need for a cargo master?"

"Why, yes, I do, also needed after Otaheite. Is one of your men a cargo master?"

"Yes. Matthew Bodine was the cargo master of the AMERICAN DESTINY, also of Boston registry, along with young Seaman Charlie McShane."

"McShane? As in McShane Island?"

"Yes. An interesting story in itself. I will introduce you to both gentlemen this evening."

"Wonderful!" exclaimed Captain Quigley. "I feel blessed that we turned around."

"Most assuredly, sir, it is we who have been

blessed that you did so."

The captain pulled a string hanging from the ceiling next to him as we continued chatting. A few moments later, a knock on the door stopped my speech.

"Enter," called the captain.

The door opened and a young man walked in. "Yes, sir, Captain," he said, standing at attention.

"Thomas. This is Sebastian, my cabin boy. Sebastian, this is Mr. Cantfield. See to it that he and his mates get proper accommodations. Show Mr. Cantfield and his wife to the guest quarters, and make certain that his chest is promptly delivered to him without disturbing its contents." Then he turned again to me. "I assume it contains some valuables, Thomas?"

"Only a manuscript of my adventures, Captain. Nothing more."

"A manuscript? I would so enjoy reading it if you would allow me to do so."

"Of course, sir. It would be my honor. I would appreciate a keen eye and your opinion."

I finished my brandy. Sebastian immediately took the empty glass from my hand and placed it back on the captain's table.

"Of course all of you are invited to my dining quarters for dinner tonight, Thomas. We'll sort out the seamen from the officers later, perhaps while we are in Bora Bora. Tonight, however, you are all welcomed guests. Go now and rest until then. We shall have supper soon, and in about fourteen hours we should be tied to the dock in Bora Bora. Meanwhile, Sebastian will see to it that you all have a change of clothing. I'm afraid, though, we will surely come up short of proper clothing for your wife."

"Thank you, Captain. Gretchen is a woman of little vanity and will be most appreciative of any change at all. I'm afraid that we came aboard with all the clothing we own, and there is precious little of that."

"Think nothing of it. I believe we shall all get along splendidly, Thomas. All of us." The captain then stood up, and I followed suit. He moved around his desk and extended his hand, and we shook. "Captain Quigley, I cannot say thank you enough, but once again, thank you, kind sir."

"You are quite welcome, Thomas. I hope we shall become rather well acquainted during our journey back to America. I should warn you, however, the voyage will take yet well over four months to complete, and our home port is Charleston, not Boston or New York."

"Captain. I care not which part of the United States I first touch my foot upon, just so long as it is my homeland where I finally come to stand."

"Excellent attitude, Thomas! Until supper, then."

Suppertime that first evening of our liberation proved to be unique, for after we had finished eating, we continued sitting and chatting for quite some time more, disclosing in some detail the manner in which each of us had gotten to the island. One part of my story most intrigued the captain.

"So you say that Matthew and Charlie were chased onto the island by pirates. Is that correct?"

"Yes, Captain. That is what happened."

"Then the pirates came ashore and slaughtered both men. And yet they live."

"I saw the entire thing, Captain. They were murdered and left lying in the sand. After the pirates left, I buried them both with my own two hands."

"And yet they came back to life within a few days? Did I understand you correctly?"

"You did indeed, and I am at a complete loss to explain it."

"Perhaps they only seemed dead at the time."

"Captain, they were summarily beheaded."

"I find it then impossible to believe that they were able to put their heads back on and come back to life, Thomas. Have you listened to yourself?"

"I have, and I am still at a loss to explain it. I made images of them out of twigs, leaves, and grass and placed them on poles outside my tent, as make-believe companions, you know, something that my mind could relate to so that I would not go completely insane."

"That makes good sense to me."

"Indeed. Well, the next morning I awoke to Charlie's jest and discovered Matthew sitting next to the fire as real as you and me. Later that afternoon, Gretchen also came to life. I know how it sounds, but here they are. How else am I to explain their existence?"

The captain sat back in his chair and was then lost in deep reflection. Finally, after a few moments, he looked into my eyes. "Well, Thomas, I cannot guess how it is possible, except that the good Lord must have intervened, seeing how lonely you must have been. Who knows the mind of the Lord?"

"That's just it, Captain. I'm not a religious man. I don't believe in a god the way you do."

"Perhaps what you believe does not matter to God, Thomas. Perhaps it matters only that He believes in *you*."

"I am forced to concede that point to you, Captain, for it is the only explanation that makes any sense at all. But again, as you can plainly see, they are of flesh and blood now. In the end, I believe, it doesn't really matter how they came into being; here they are. And I, sir, am better for them. I love them all, and I would never have it any other way."

"Yes. Here they are."

The captain stood up and raised his glass in front of him. "To each of you. No matter how you came to be here, I am very glad to make your acquaintance. May the rest of your lives be as wondrous as they have been thus far."

We all stood and raised our glasses as well, then sipped from them. Reseating ourselves, the captain then asked what my plans were once I returned home.

"I would expect that I should go back to my work in Mr. Jenkins's shipping office and continue on as an accountant. I'm not trained in any other manner and have no other serious aspirations for doing anything else."

"You appear to be a rock-steady man, Thomas."

"Aye, sir, I fear that I am. Despite all that has happened, I was not born of an adventurous spirit. I prefer the mundane over the wild and unanticipated thrill of the unknown. Only not so much as I have experienced thus far," I answered with a chuckle.

"From my point of view, I see you as extremely adventurous or you would not have undertaken such a journey to begin with."

"I assure you, Captain, the journey was not planned to be so audacious. It was intended only so that I might enjoy a promotion to an upgraded position within the firm well ahead of my contemporaries. It was never my intention to become elevated to the status of a celebrity castaway."

"Well, Thomas, intended or not, you are so labeled, and I would expect there to be great crowds soon gathered in some hall or theatre comprising those who shall pay good money to have you recount your adventures in detail. I consider myself fortunate to hear them first hand and in such great advance."

"Perhaps, Captain, but I must warn you, there were but few moments that were noteworthy. The rest of the time was exceedingly boring and trite. If there are bookings to be had in the future, I suspect that they shall be few and brief."

"Of course, you may be correct, but I'm sure of one thing, Thomas. Tonight, under the eager gaze of such a naïve crew, your stories are sure to dazzle the lot of them. For them, Thomas, your simple rescue was an adventure that will stay with them for a long, long time. To be granted a personal audience with the castaways, yet so fresh from their ordeal, and to hear tales of their desperate battles for survival will, I believe, become etched into their memories, quite possibly forever."

"We shall do our very best to entertain them, then."

Later that evening, as the ship rocked gently in the undulating ocean swells, now only about seven hours out from Bora Bora, we imparted our tales to the excited crew. As Captain Quigley had suggested, our tales were accepted as great acts of theatre, and it did my heart good to give voice to our rich experiences and to such a warm reception.

As we all shared our experiences, a great burden suddenly lifted off my shoulders. I can best describe it as the weight of all my fears, hopes, and beliefs suddenly and no longer pressing down upon me. At that moment, I felt twice liberated: once from the island, no doubt, but then also from the uncertainty that had plagued me for such a great long time.

What uncertainty? you might ask.

For a long time, I had wondered if what I had experienced on the island was real or just a fabrication in my head. I admit that I was never quite sure of anything there. I had never known miracles to occur; I had never seen one, at any rate. And so you might understand when I say that I had never experienced grass people suddenly becoming live beings.

I have always supposed that miracles were possible, but I have also believed that they were reserved for the wholly righteous among us, those of a stoutly devout religious nature, those of a deeply pious character. And yet the woman who now lies beside me is of flesh and bone. I can reach out my hand and touch her warm skin. When it happened, I merely accepted it, but upon my rescue, I began to wonder how such a thing became possible.

Please understand that I am not complaining, but how am I to explain it all? The captain was surely acting most gracious when he so easily accepted my word of it. But does he truly believe me, or is he somehow exhibiting restraint for the sake of a desperate mind so long removed from anything sane? And if so, will I then come to remembrance of what is the truth?

Were my straw friends real all along and it was just that I was not able to receive them as such for some unknown malady that affected my reason for a time? Were they actually survivors of the sinking ship, as I was? I tried to recall my time on the ship. When I remembered it, though, their faces were not a part of any memory I could draw upon.

And since my rescue, I had been plagued by what was real and what was not, but during our story session I was released from any doubt. The solution was a simple one. It did not matter how they came to be on the island with me, they were there. That was all that was important to me at that time.

I will tell you now that I slept very soundly that evening, and in the morning, Gretchen lying still by my side, I again thanked whomever I needed to thank for my sanity being fully confirmed.

I arose that next morning, singularly aware and grateful to be on my way home.

Matthew and Malcolm were interviewed by the captain very early that morning, and when they all came out onto the deck later, smiles stretched across all faces.

Matthew was given his place as cargo master and Malcolm was awarded his rightful place as first mate, each by virtue of their righteous experience, all positions to be initiated upon our departure from Papeete.

A part of me was exceedingly glad, but I held a

bit of sadness within as well, for I wondered if they were going to choose to stay on the ship when we arrived in America. Would they resume their lives? Would I lose my family once again to the sea? I realized that they had lives before we all met, but I hoped that perhaps our new life as a family might outweigh any need they might have to move on with their own lives now that they had the opportunity to do so. Then again, perhaps it was just the fact that they'd had no choice, just as I'd had none, which accounted for our unification, and now, with their lives resumed, they would move on without me. It would be fitting, I believed.

But being a good four months away from any decisions having to be made, I put away my concern for another time. My new family was together for now, and for that I remained grateful.

It was when we docked in Bora Bora, at near nine o'clock that morning, that I truly felt liberated from the island. As I stepped off the dock and onto the ground of another island for the first time in more than eleven months, I felt my heart swell with relief.

I helped the captain negotiate for the needed goods and services and entered all trades into the ledgers as if I had never been away from my accounting duties. I was shrewd in my negotiations and assisted the captain in receiving a maximum number of the ship's supplies for the least cost. This act alone elevated my status, in the eyes of Captain Quigley, to a position of substantial worth. The captain was exceedingly pleased with my fiscal abilities, and when he went to negotiate for the sale of his on-board cargo on behalf of the shipping company that owned the ship and its wares, I was again by his side, giving him sound fiscal counsel. Because of my keen education and sound fiduciary skills, I was able to negotiate the new cargo rates greatly to Captain Quigley's favor. The captain was most gracious and offered me a wonderful commission for my efforts.

Thus, while on the island, Gretchen and I were able to afford new clothing and other articles appropriate to our needs and wants.

After six glorious days on Bora Bora, our holds now full of fresh cargo, under full billowing sails and clear skies, we began our way toward Otaheite.

Andrew, Richard, Samuel, and Charlie, delighted to be so easily absorbed into the crew, were most usually responsible for the ship's entertainment. Charlie, of course, full of his natural merriment along with his genuinely affable personality, quickly became a favorite among the officers and crew. I believe he single-handedly became the ship's unofficial entertainment mate. Captain Quigley was certainly delighted with his unique ability to keep the crew gleefully uplifted and spirited.

Normally, under typical nautical procedures for a ship's operation, the seamen would not be allowed to fraternize with the ship's officers. Because of my relationship with my family, however, the captain magnanimously set aside those protocols for our sake.

In so doing, he was thrilled to see that there was neither any breakdown in discipline nor any loss in the effectiveness of the crew. Quite to the contrary, he saw that the crew bonded even more strongly. The efficiency of the crew rose substantially, and the entire crew's general deportment was elevated to levels he had never before witnessed on his past voyages with them.

In sum, the whole crew was one happy lot. And so each night soon became rum-and-story night—the captain's daily reward for efficiency and sound effort. Thus, with a half tin of rum for each man and new exciting stories from a different crewman each night, I daresay that this ship operated more efficiently than any ship afloat at that time.

Three days later, we happy crew sailed proudly into the Otaheitean docks of Papeete.

As we disembarked, our cheerful ways must have attracted the attention of other crews. Our crew sang and whistled as the very difficult work of unloading all the cargo began, each man performing his duty without being ordered to do so by the officers.

In an amazingly short time all the cargo was off-loaded, and the crew was given leave to do as they pleased for two whole days. We bid a fond farewell to our first officer and cargo master, them being Mister Ormsby and Mister Janis, respectively, and celebrated the promotion of Malcolm and Matthew to their new duties.

We literally stopped the show, as crewmen working on other ships watched in utter shock the intermingling of our crew and officers as they milled about and later drank together and enjoyed each other's company, being much more than crewmates. I took great joy in this, for I had witnessed the birth of yet another family.

This crew was tightly gathered, and other crewmen found it impossible to break into our ranks. We were a crew firmly bonded one to the other through trust, respect, and genuine friendship. We, being a crazily happy lot, were quickly the envy of everyone on the docks.

During that time, Captain Quigley and I negotiated better cargo rates than anyone else. It was very soon recognized that there was something finely unique about the ANNABELLE LEE and her special crew.

Once again, the captain, being a very generous man, parceled out a handsome commission for my efforts. I began setting a good deal of it aside for when we landed in Charleston, for we would need many supplies and suitable transportation up to New York.

By the time we left Otaheite for South American waters, the captain and I had become close friends and trusted colleagues. I maintained the ship's log and accounts along the way. Malcolm and Matthew were delighted with their new positions and served the ship very well. Charlie, Andrew, Richard, and Samuel were treated with great respect, and they in turn handled their duties with great skill. All in all, we were a very happy and effective group sailing the seas together.

Gretchen was treated extremely well, and I think just her being there, as beautiful and kind as she was, helped calm the crew immensely. She busied herself during the day by offering to mend the crew's torn clothing. I'd had no idea that she was such a skilled seamstress. Even the captain utilized her services, for which he compensated her well.

Sometimes, at night, after most of the crew had bedded down and all was quiet except for the waves breaking against the ship's hull, Gretchen and I would sit out on the bow and stare at the stars while talking. I was a very lucky man to have a wife such as Gretchen. She was an easy woman to be with.

Between Otaheite and the United States, much the same occurred. I continued to earn good commissions on my work with the captain. He remarked several times that his future journeys without my assistance would most likely not be as profitable. He asked me to stay, but I insisted that I needed to return home to see my parents and establish a solid home for Gretchen. He reluctantly understood and agreed not to press me again on the subject. As I stated before, he was an excellent captain and a wonderful gentleman.

Our dealings together made us both wealthy men, he much more than I, of course, but I was able to save enough to make my journey back to New York with no concern and then some.

The weather, being highly favorable, made the trip around the horn a simple and uneventful one, but as we began our homeward leg, I began to feel nervous.

After several discussions with my family, I learned that they wanted to stay with the ship when we docked in Charleston. I tearfully understood their wanting to get back to living the life they had previously chosen for themselves. I recognized their need to reestablish their careers, and it gave me much comfort to know that they would serve together on the ANNABELLE LEE. I was the one who was out of sorts on the ship; I was an accountant who belonged on the land, in an office, going home to my wife each night. With reason, all seemed right and just, and yet I knew that I would miss each of them exceedingly.

Chapter 12

In the late morning of the 26th of June 1831, I first viewed the American landscape rising up out of the sea, but it was initially spotted by a young seaman in the crow's nest, of course. Her shoreline was yet still only a dark mass on the distant horizon, but I smelled the land. It smelled wonderful, and my heart was joyful that I was very near to stepping onto my homeland for the first time in well over two years.

I sent for Gretchen, and she soon appeared at my side, excited to see our home shores again.

"We draw near, my love. How long before we can actually set foot upon her soil?" she asked.

"In about four hours, I should guess."

"Are you excited, Thomas?"

"Much so. I have longed for this for many months now."

"Your parents, Thomas. Will you send word straightaway, or are you intending to surprise them?"

"I think I shall surprise them."

"I must have a new dress. When I meet them, I want to look my best."

"When we reach Charleston, my dear, you shall have all that you desire and so much more."

"You are a kind man, my love. My parents would have loved you also."

"Would have loved? Of what do you speak?

Your parents yet live."

"No, Thomas. My parents have passed on."

"Your father was still headmaster just before I left on my voyage."

"Yes, but sadly he passed. It was about two years ago now."

"I had no idea, my love. I'm truly sorry. You said nothing about it."

"There was nothing that needed to be said."

"And your mother?"

"She died with my father. Their carriage was washed off the road during a flash flood, the road next to the creek. Do you remember it?"

"Yes, I do. I'm so very sorry, my love."

"It is nothing you need concern yourself about, Thomas. I have you. It is all I need."

"And you are all I truly need, Gretchen. Without you, I would not have survived my time on the island. I think I would have slid into complete madness and would now be nothing more than bleached bones in the sun."

"I'm happy you found the courage to live, Thomas. I have no idea how it all happened; perhaps we may never know the truth of it. But here we are together, and within a few hours we shall once again be on home soil. Within weeks, we shall be standing in our home city, ready to begin our life together in earnest."

"I must admit I'm still perplexed how you came to the island. It almost makes me want to believe in

God, but a loving God would not have put me on the island in the first place."

"Thomas, you know that I would never attempt to influence you, one way or another, but it seems to me that He saved you by placing you on the island. He could have let you drown in the sea, but He did not. He provided a good island for you. He provided food and water for your survival. He brought to you loving company so that you should not be alone or feel forsaken. It seems that there is a God, a very kind and gentle God, Thomas. Please consider the possibility at least. Think on it longer, and if you still believe that there is no God, then I shall speak of it no more."

"I want to believe in something, Gretchen. Truly I do, but if there is a God and if He be loving and kind, then why did He not save all the others? I have tried to reason that out, but all answers continue to elude me."

"I have no answers either, but perhaps it was their time. Perhaps He has other plans for you. Perhaps your work is not finished."

"Perhaps, my wife. Perhaps. I don't think I shall ever know for certain, until the very end."

"Maybe we all receive our answers just before we close our eyes for the final time. May I offer a suggestion?"

"Of course. Anything."

"When we arrive on the homeland, let us move forward in life and never be ungrateful for anything that comes our way."

"Let us do that then."

I returned my stare toward the rising landscape.

"This evening, Gretchen, we shall sleep on American soil again. I will be in deep gratitude for that simple delight alone."

"I shall be pleased also, Thomas."

Malcolm and Matthew approached us.

"There we are, brothers, near to our home shores," I said.

"Yes, Thomas," replied Matthew. "Near to the end of a marvelous journey for all of us."

"A celebratory dinner tonight? All of us, one last time?"

"Absolutely, Thomas," said Malcolm. "Absolutely."

In only moments, the others joined us.

"Well, silly man," teased Charlie as he came up behind me, "you think you can survive without me?"

I laughed. "I don't know, Charlie. I'll have to think seriously on it."

"Ah, serious thoughts are for troubled men, silly man. I pray you don't take up the mantle of a serious thinker anytime soon. It will permanently crease your brow."

"And you. Whatever you do, never stop laughing. Your face could not handle such an untwisted state."

Charlie slapped me on the shoulder playfully. "'Tis not likely to happen, I assure you, old man."

I saw, for just an instant, something very unusual in Charlie's eyes. It was there only briefly, but I saw it nonetheless. I made no remark concerning it, however. Charlie would have denied it or laughed it off anyway, but it could best be described as concern. Our eyes met for only a split second, but there was a communication regarding it.

I think Matthew saw it as well, but as usual, he remained still and quiet.

"May we come to visit you in New York?" asked Samuel.

"If you do not, I shall be most disappointed in you, my little brother," said Gretchen. She then reached out and hugged him tightly.

"Then I shall make it a priority, sister."

"See that you do."

"And so you both will leave me here with this insane man?" said Andrew of Charlie. "Thank you so very much."

We all laughed. "I don't know which of you is unluckiest," I replied.

"I object," said Charlie jokingly. "Clearly, it is I who shall suffer most. Andrew is the one separated from sanity. Not I."

"I think it is I who shall suffer most, being required to listen to both of you," offered Richard.

"We shall have to discuss the matter more tonight. One last dinner before we shall part ways, then," I said.

"Yes," said Charlie, "before you go off to fail

without me."

We all laughed.

The captain walked up behind us and tapped me on the shoulder.

"Forgive my interruption, but I have need to speak with Thomas. Thomas, may I have a word with you in my cabin?"

"Certainly, Captain. Straightaway." I turned and took Gretchen's hand and kissed it. "I shall not be long, my darling. Remain here and give me your thoughts as we draw near to shore when I return."

I shall," she answered.

"As for you others," I jested, "don't you have duties to perform?"

They all laughed.

"Get on with you, man. The captain awaits," teased Charlie.

"Enough, lads," said Malcolm. "Let us get back to work. Soon enough we shall be on shore and well deep into trouble, I fear." He smiled.

The captain and I returned to his cabin to discuss the final documents and accounting entries. As I prepared the final entries, we entertained ourselves with a light chat.

"We draw near to the end of our voyage together, Thomas. I shall miss your company and sound counsel very much."

"I will never be able to thank you enough for our rescue, Captain."

"You have already done so many times over. I

have wonderful additions to my crew. You made the voyage very profitable for both the company and myself. It is I who remain in your debt. Upon landing, what do you intend to do?"

"I'm afraid I know nothing about Charleston, except that it exists. This will be my first time in your fair city."

"Ah. Well, after we arrive, I shall point out proper accommodations and services to you. I would ask that you come with me to meet the ship's owner. I would expect that he will want to thank you personally. With your lovely wife, of course."

"Thank you, Captain. I shall be honored to do so."

I finished making the entries into the accounts ledger and closed the book with a firm slap. "There you be, Captain. I'm certain all is correct and accurate."

The captain rose from his desk and poured two glasses of brandy. Handing me one, he clinked his to mine.

"Just a quick salute to our time together."

"Hear, hear, sir. To our time together, then." I drank the brandy down in one gulp. "Forgive me, Captain, but I would like to join my wife on the bow as we sail into the harbor. Would you excuse me?"

"Certainly, Thomas. I must head to the bridge myself in a short while. I shall see you on deck."

"Excellent, sir." We shook hands, and I departed his cabin.

I returned to Gretchen, whereupon she immediately slid her arm through mine as I joined her to stare out over the sea.

"You seem nervous, Thomas. Are you all right?" she asked.

"Not so much nervous as desperately longing to see my homeland rise up full out of the ocean to greet me. How about you?"

"No, not nervous. Only excited."

"We shall rest a day or so before departing Charleston. It will take me some time to arrange our transportation up to New York anyway."

"As you see fit, husband. I would like to buy some things for our trip."

"As I said, my love: whatever you desire. Give it voice and see it be made manifest."

"I am already nervous about meeting your parents. Do you think they'll like me?"

"No, my dear. They won't like you."

I saw the pout beginning on her lips and smiled.

"No, my darling," I continued, "they'll adore you, as I do."

A relieved smile formed and her face began to glow. She playfully punched me in the arm.

"You have a cruel and evil way about you, Thomas Bartholomew Cantfield, but I love you anyway."

I chortled, kissed her on the mouth, and then wrapped my right arm around her shoulders. We both stared out over the rolling waves for quite a while.

I can't say for certain, of course, but I think that during the next great while as she stared out over the ocean, she was contemplating what our life would be like once we finally landed and returned to New York.

That certainly was what I was thinking.

I tried to imagine what arriving in New York would be like, the look of shock on my parents' faces when they opened the door to see us standing there. I wondered what all my friends would say now that I was standing in front of them in the flesh, resurrected from the dead, as it were.

I also imagined how exhausted Gretchen and I would be after attending all the welcoming parties. I expected there to be many parties, and I also expected there to be much teasing from my friends as they all learned that I was actually married to my fantasy woman—the woman who had all but ignored me during my school years.

It would be difficult to explain to them how she came to be on the island, but they were my best friends. They would believe me, and all would be well in the end.

It was fully three hours and more before the lines were secured to the dock and the gangplank was set into place. Gretchen and I were the first to step off the ship, followed by several seamen carrying our belongings to a waiting carriage owned by the ship's owner.

The carriage driver looked at us oddly.

"Captain Quigley's orders, sir," announced one of the young seamen.

The carriage driver then smiled and nodded his head.

"Welcome aboard, madam, sir."

We both nodded politely and climbed aboard.

The captain stepped onto the plank and turned toward Malcolm. "Begin the off-loading procedures, Mr. Jennings. I shall return in a while."

"Aye, aye, sir," said Malcolm, who then waved to us.

"Dinner tonight," I yelled to Malcolm. "All of us."

He waved his acknowledgement and then turned away cheerfully to begin his duties.

Minutes later, having arrived at the shipping office, I helped Gretchen to the ground. "Thomas," she said, "I hardly look presentable, dear."

"Begging your pardon, Mrs. Cantfield," said the captain. You look wonderful."

"But I feel unclean and poorly dressed."

"Trust me when I say there are few women in this city who have ever looked better than you do presently, and they have had longer to prepare. You will do just fine. Besides, it will be only a short meeting and then I'll have the driver take you to a proper inn."

"Very well, Captain. If you say so."

"You look beautiful, my dear," I added.

"Thank you, husband. I think perhaps you're just being sweet."

"Not at all, my dear."

We walked through the doors and were immediately greeted by the ship owner's personal secretary, a Mr. Connelly. The captain introduced us, and we were instantly shown into the owner's office. He stood up at once and rounded his desk to greet us. His name was Jason O'Grady, a stout, well-dressed man of near fifty years of age. He was very well groomed and manicured, and his manner was most congenial and engaging.

After introductions, we sat at a great table and discussed some of the events of my past year.

"My, my," O'Grady stated in awe. "That was quite a story, Mr. Cantfield. I must say, you appear fit and well adjusted after such a challenging ordeal."

"Yes, sir. I can truly say that I am pleased to be on home soil once again, however."

"And the others just appeared out of thin air, you say?"

"Not all, sir. Just Matthew, Charlie, and Gretchen. But as I have said, I am at a complete loss to explain it and I cannot say any more about that."

"Unbelievable! I will say that, Mr. Cantfield. Just utterly unbelievable."

"And yet they exist. Here sits my wife as real as you or I, sir."

"Quite so, I must admit it," O'Grady said,

scratching at his chin.

"The Lord does work in mysterious ways, it seems," offered the captain.

"I cannot say whether it was of divine intervention or not, gentlemen. I can only say with certainty, here she sits."

"And you, Mrs. Cantfield. Can you explain your sudden appearance?"

"I cannot, sir," responded Gretchen. "I was suddenly there on the island and walking on a dirt path, to where I did not know, until I saw Thomas. But when our eyes met, I was instantly convinced of my purpose to be there with him."

"A miracle, I say," said O'Grady. "A bloody miracle is what it was."

"Miracle or not, sir," I said, "here we are, and I, for one, am in need of being refreshed. Captain, you said you had a suggestion of an inn. Could we go? I should like Gretchen to rest while I seek out our means of transportation to New York. I am growing anxious to see my home and parents once again."

"Of course, Thomas. Straightaway, then."

As we all rose from our chairs, Mr. O'Grady thrust out his hand, and we shook.

"Mr. Cantfield, these accounts are splendidly done. I cannot thank you enough for all your efforts. You, sir, have a job awaiting you anytime you want. If things do not turn out well for you in New York, please consider my offer here. Your services would be keenly appreciated."

"Thank you, Mr. O'Grady. It is most kind of you. Only time will determine where I am to settle, but I shall keep your kind offer well in my mind."

After we arrived at the Traveler's Inn and had checked into our room, I bid farewell to Captain Quigley, but not before he suggested some stores to buy supplies and where I might go to make transportation arrangements.

"Captain, forgive me, but there is one last favor I would ask of you."

"Certainly, Thomas. Anything."

"I have need of a special merchant."

I left Gretchen to freshen up in the room while I wandered about Charleston seeking the things that we would need on our trip home.

In a short time, I had purchased a fine enclosed carriage and two horses for an equitable sum. I also located a driver who had need of going to New York, so I offered him the position at a fair wage.

With such a sturdy rig, we could arrive comfortably in New York within seven to ten days from the time we set out. I then, with great delight, discovered the special merchant that I had been seeking.

I walked into our room just as Gretchen was finishing putting a pin through her hat. She looked beautiful.

I opened a sack and withdrew a wonderfully embroidered handkerchief and handed it to her.

"Oh, Thomas," she declared, beaming. "How beautiful, my darling. Thank you."

"I fear that you shall have need of it, my dear."

I received her confused glance.

"Why, Thomas?"

I put my hand into my breast pocket and then withdrew it, presenting my closed fist to her. A perplexed smile formed on her face. She turned my hand over and fought to force my hand open.

"What is it, Thomas? Open your hand, please."

I took great joy in struggling to keep my hand tightly closed while she battled to open it. Finally, I allowed her to pull my fingers open, revealing what I had kept hidden.

She halted her excited struggle and stared in shock at what lay in my now opened palm.

"Thomas!" she said softly.

"Yes, my love."

She looked up into my eyes in utter disbelief. Then I saw her eyes fill with tears until they overflowed and streaked down her cheeks.

"Good thing you have a handkerchief," I teased.

"Thomas!" she repeated, snatching the handkerchief from my hand and dabbing her moistened eyes.

I rolled the diamond and gold ring in my hand and then, cradling her left hand with my left hand, I placed the ring on her finger. All the time she simply stared at it and cried.

"A perfect fit, too," I declared confidently.

She stared at the ring on her finger for several seconds and then hugged me tightly.

"Thank you, Thomas. Thank you. Thank you. It is so wonderful to be your wife."

"I am the one so very lucky."

I took her handkerchief from her hand and dabbed her cheeks dry. Finally, she smiled at me.

"It is wonderful, my love. You have stunned me to silence."

"It is not your words that I seek. Only your approving smile."

"Then you shall have it. Broadly and bright."

Chapter 13

We all gathered that evening at the inn's dining facilities. It was a merry event, and dinner was wonderfully prepared by an excellent chef.

Conversation was as lively as ever, until I brought up the matter of Benjamin Hartford, the young pirate whose life I had taken back on the island. Everyone ceased speaking and drifted inward, into their own hearts and minds, seeking whatever it was each needed to find.

"I want to find his parents or family and explain what happened to him."

"Is that wise, Thomas?" asked Malcolm.

"Perhaps it is wise. Perhaps it is not, my brother, I feel that I owe his loved ones an explanation that can come from me only. For without my words, they will never know what befell him. They would go on never knowing anything about him. I cannot live with that. It is what is right for me to do."

"Well said, lad," said Matthew. "I shall go with you."

"That is not necessary, Matthew. It is my task to bear. I am the one who ran him through."

"And I was there with you. I shall go and stand by your side."

"As you wish, Matthew. Thank you for your support."

"I shall go with you as well, Thomas," said Malcolm. "I served with him. They should hear what became of him from me also."

"And I," offered Samuel.

"We'll all go," said Charlie.

"Charlie, thank you, but I don't feel that humor would be appreciated by his loved ones. And I know that you take nothing seriously."

"Then I shall remain silent, Thomas, but you shall not go without me. Besides, silly man, you need me there. You know that you do."

It was there once again. Only for a brief moment, but Charlie's eyes flashed into mine. There was a part of him that felt compassion deeply. It was a constrained and hidden part of him that I felt he would, of course, never admit to anyone, including me. But I saw it. As before, however, I let it go and made nothing of it.

"Of course, Charlie. You'd be most welcome, brother."

Andrew and Richard nodded their heads in agreement.

"Well. There it is," said Matthew. "We shall all lend you our support. All we have to do now is find his loved ones. Does anyone know where to begin?"

"With the constable's office, I presume. Who better to know the people than he?" I remarked.

"Well said, lad. Of course you are correct as usual," said Matthew, continuing as always to be the voice of reason, compromise, and support.

When this time with my family was done, I concluded then, it would be Matthew that I would come to miss the most. As I look back upon it now, this reasoning was confirmed. A tear forms even now in my eye as I fondly recall his image.

The next morning we all gathered at the office of the town constable and introduced ourselves. I presented my inquiry as to the whereabouts of the Hartford family. The constable asked the nature of our need to speak with his family, to which I answered only that it was a matter concerning their son and could not say more at that time. I, of course, held back the true purpose of our visit.

My intent was not to hide our purpose but rather to honor the parents by presenting them with the information first. I felt it to be a matter of respect.

The constable, being an honorable man, pressed no further and even was kind enough to offer to escort us to the home of Benjamin's parents and make our introduction.

I gladly accepted.

While Gretchen, Matthew, the constable, and I rode in one carriage, with one of the constable's men driving, the others rode along behind in another carriage which I had hired. Along the way, I learned that Benjamin was an only child and was unmarried. The constable also informed us that Benjamin was a popular lad in the town and that many knew him well as a kindly young man, even a genuine hero.

I listened to all that was said about young Benjamin Hartford, yet the man described was a man I had never met.

I did not know the child who played so gleefully with the other children and did so well in school. I had never met the lad who selflessly pushed an old woman out of the way of a runaway steed just in the nick of time, injuring himself in the process. I had never heard of the young man who never missed a single day of singing in the church choir. Certainly this was not the young man whose heart I had pierced through with a wooden spear.

I admit that the more I came to know about young Benjamin, the more nervous I became.

Along the way, I began trembling slightly for fear of having to reveal what had become of the well-known and well-liked lad. I began to regret starting this horrible journey to destroy the reputation of a young man so obviously loved in this town.

What right did I have to tell parents that the child they knew and loved so deeply had so terribly fallen into the abyss of evil? How could I tell them that his body lay rotting now in a sand grave on some forgotten island in the South Seas? What right did I have to tell them that their child had died a despicable and hated cur?

How does a man of good conscience and gentle intent break news of that nature to loving parents?

How would I, nay, how could I tell them that their child, whom they thought was joyously traveling about on the oceans seeing things he had never seen before, experiencing wonders he could never experience by staying on land in his hometown, would nevermore return to their loving embraces? *How could I tell them, I thought? How could I break it to them that they would never be able to visit his grave and lay flowers of gentle remembrance on a headstone that had neither been made nor set to mark his place of eternal rest?* I felt as despicable a man as ever.

I think Gretchen sensed my unease, for she tightened her grip upon my arm. As I listened to the constable reciting stories concerning Benjamin's cheerful ways as he remembered them, I felt even more keenly the pain of what I had done.

I knew that I had had no choice in the matter. It was a battle for life. I was being attacked and I had to defend myself. I understood all of the outward reasoning behind such an act. Still, it was my hand that had stilled young Benjamin's heart. Now I was on my way to the home of his parents with the evil purpose of presenting myself to them as his slayer.

We had arrived upon the front porch of the stately mansion. The constable knocked on the door, and a genteel butler answered and escorted us into the receiving parlor as he announced our arrival.

Several minutes later, he returned to escort us all into the expansive living room, whereupon I was introduced. I then proceeded to introduce the rest of my entourage.

"Please be seated," said Mr. Hartford, a distinguished and gentle-looking man, somewhere in his mid-fifties, finely dressed and graced with impeccable manners. He was obviously a well-educated man and well-placed in upper society.

Mrs. Hartford was fine lady, dressed immaculately. Her hair, put up in a perfect bun, was of a beautiful light brown. The necklace she wore was distinctively high fashion and appeared very expensive, its diamonds and blue sapphires twinkling brightly even in the diminished light of the candles. She was a most refined and pleasant-looking woman.

My heart quaked in my chest as I pictured this majestic lady falling to pieces when I broke the news to her. At that moment I felt even more a horrible wretch.

Mr. Hartford offered fine brandy to us all, but we each refused.

"Gentlefolk," I began, "thank you kindly for receiving us so magnificently. I do wish we could have met under different circumstances."

"I was told that you have news of my son," said Mr. Hartford.

"Yes, sir," I said. "I met him only briefly, but these gentlemen here," pointing to Malcolm, Andrew, Richard, and Samuel, "actually served with Benjamin aboard a certain ship."

"How wonderful," Mr. Hartford said. "I'm not

surprised that he made such wonderful friends. He was always such a fine and friendly lad. Did you get on well with him?"

"I was an officer on the ship," said Malcolm. "I can tell you that he served very well. He was a good and fine sailor when I knew him. These lads here served directly with him."

"I knew him quite well, sir," said Samuel. "He was indeed an able seaman. He served the ship with distinction."

"I see," said Mr. Hartford. "I am not surprised to hear that. He was always a lad who so enjoyed pleasing others. But tell me, please. What news have you of him? I am anxious to hear how he is doing."

"Dear," said Mrs. Hartford woefully, "I fear these fine people are not here to give us good news of Benjamin."

"Oh, my. Well, then, please tell me. What has happened to our Benjamin?"

Malcolm looked to me. I nodded.

"Well, sir," Malcolm began hesitantly, "some time ago, our ship was attacked by pirates. It was a fierce battle, and…"

He looked to me for support. I nodded once again. I then noticed Mrs. Hartford bracing herself for bad news, stiffening slightly while trying hard to remain stoically brave and strong.

"As I said," said Malcolm, "we were viciously attacked. One of the attacking pirates, sir, and I do apologize for this, one of the attacking pirates was your son, sir."

I saw both confusion and shock fill Mr. Hartford's face, but he remained still and silent.

"My crewmates were eventually defeated and taken captive. It was because of the vicious nature of the battle that many of the pirate crew were killed. Thus, the pirate captain had need of replacements. We each here were spared, but we were required to swear allegiance to the pirate captain and work on his ship."

"You're saying that my son is now a pirate?"

"Sir," I interrupted, "what Malcolm is saying is that your son *was* a pirate."

"Was a pirate? Then he is no longer a pirate?"

"No, sir," I responded. "He is no longer a pirate, but I'm afraid there is more to the story. Mr. and Mrs. Hartford, I wish I could find a kindly way to tell you what I'm about to tell you. And I assure you, if there were any way possible to avoid this altogether, I would do so."

"My son is dead, isn't he?" stated Mrs. Hartford.

"Yes, ma'am. Your son, Benjamin, is dead. But there is still more yet to it than that."

I saw her shudder slightly. She was an amazingly strong woman. She sat with her hands folded on her lap, clutching a handkerchief, and she remained so during the entire telling of my story as I related what I observed before the storm and after.

As I told them both of what happened after the storm and how I was confronted by the pirate attackers on the island, they remained proudly serene. But I had yet to tell them of the final disposition.

"The battle was brief," I continued. "I am not trained as a warrior. As I said, I am a simple accountant. We were two against eight of them at the start. During the heat of the battle, your son came straight at me with his saber at the ready to strike. I was frightened beyond words and acting solely out of instinct by then. I picked up a wooden spear and charged at Benjamin, thrusting it through his heart. He died instantly and with little pain, I believe. I am so very sorry to have to relate this to you."

"So, Mr. Cantfield. You are telling us that our son died as a despicable and shameful pirate and it was by your hand that he so died?"

"Yes, sir. I'm afraid that the man you so graciously accepted into your home this morning is, in fact, the slayer of your son. I so apologize for my action. I have regretted such ever since I came to know his name. I dug his grave with my own two hands and I spoke gentle words of his life and passing later. I realize that I have wounded you both deeply by reciting this tragic event, but I wanted to come and face you with this difficult news so that you no longer wondered where your son was or what he was doing."

"Sir," added Malcolm, "we all bore witness to what Thomas has told you. I tell you, sir and madam, what he has said is the truth. Every word of it. I knew your son only after he had given himself over to the pirate ways; I never knew him before that. I also am very sorry for your loss, and I'm certain that I speak for every man here who served with him as well."

Everyone nodded. Then we all fell into utter and regretful silence.

After a few tenuous seconds, Mrs. Hartford reached out to her husband. He took her hand in his and then stared straight into my eyes.

"I can see, sir, that you are a man of honor and forthrightness. It took great courage for all of you to come here and tell us what you had to say. You have no reason to regret anything. It is we who owe you an apology for our son's actions. I am at a loss to explain how our son could become such a terrible thing."

"Sir," said Malcolm, "take heart in knowing this. There was great pressure put upon us all by the pirates. It was a matter of survival, I think. We had to adapt to their ways or be put to the sword. It was as simple as that. If it means anything to you at all, let me say that while I served with Benjamin, he performed his duties extremely well and to the admiration of all the officers. He was a fine sailor in every way. I believe that if his ship had not been attacked and he had not been taken captive and treated so ruthlessly, he would still be the lad you raised and sent off to sea."

"Thank you, sir. Your words are kind and reassuring. It is most caring of you to speak about our son in that way. We will never know what he could have become if he had not been put through such an ordeal. All we have is our memory of who he once was."

"Sir," I said, "we have put you both through too much already. We shall take our leave now and only say this one final time. We all share in your sorrow, but no one more than I. I shall not insult you by asking for your forgiveness, but I just wanted you to know how much I regret it."

"Whether you ask for it or not, kind sir, you have our forgiveness. We do not hold you responsible."

"Thank you both so very kindly. Good day to you."

I nodded respectfully, and we all departed.

That terrible task completed, we took the carriage directly to the ship, first dropping off the constable at his office along the way and thanking him for his assistance.

Arriving at the docks became another tearful moment, for Gretchen and I had to finally say good-bye to the rest of our family.

Matthew handed me a sealed letter, previously written, which I promised to put into the hands of his wife when I first had the opportunity to do so.

Each of the others also gave me sealed letters for their families, also previously written in preparation for my departure.

We openly and tearfully wished each other well. I gave Samuel the address to my parents' home, and he promised to come and visit us when and if he should ever set foot again in New York.

Thus, with hugs rendered and kind words warmly exchanged, Gretchen and I started on our journey to New York.

It took us fully ten days to reach the city limits of New York, having driven our team of horses nearly 750 miles. Along the way, of course, we stopped by the families of our family and brought them the letters and updated them as to the status of their sons.

Our first stop was in Raleigh, North Carolina, to visit with Richard's parents. Next, we visited Andrew's parents in Richmond, Virginia. Both families were thankful for our visit and our news. We planned to visit Boston at our first opportunity, but it would take some time to arrange to travel there. In the meantime, we held the letters of Matthew and Malcolm in security. As for Samuel's parents, we would make time to visit them once we were settled in.

When we finally arrived outside my parents' home, I was shocked to see chains on the front door.

"Perhaps they have gone away on holiday," I mumbled.

"Perhaps, my love. Is there someone we can ask?"

"The neighbors. I'll inquire with them."

I walked up to the home of Mr. and Mrs. Whitman. They had been neighbors since I was but a sprout of a lad. I knocked on the door, and Mrs. Whitman answered promptly.

"Hello, Mrs. Whitman. Do you remember me?"

She stared at me, but I could see that she did not recognize my face.

"I'm Thomas Cantfield. I grew up next door."

Sudden recall then filled her face, followed by a delighted smile of full recognition and then a sorrowful frown.

"Young Thomas Cantfield. Come in, please, Thomas. Follow me to the living room. It is so good to see you, Thomas. I heard tell that you were lost in a terrible storm some time ago."

"Yes, ma'am. 'Tis a true tale, but I have returned and am perplexed as to the whereabouts of my parents. Have they gone on holiday? The door is secured with chains."

"Have a seat, Thomas, and I shall explain. Who is this lovely young woman?"

"This is my wife, Mrs. Whitman. Gretchen, Mrs. Whitman."

"Hello, Mrs. Whitman. Pleased to make your acquaintance."

"Charmed, my dear."

We sat on the divan, and Mrs. Whitman sat across from us in a high-backed chair.

"May I offer you some tea?" she asked politely.

"No, thank you. Please tell me where my parents have gone. I'm eager to let them know that I am well and have returned."

"Thomas, please forgive me for having to speak

of this, but both of your parents have passed, my dear. They passed nearly two months ago. The house has been sealed ever since. I'm so sorry."

I sat completely stunned and found it impossible to speak immediately. I turned my face to Gretchen and saw the tears flowing from her eyes. I moved my mouth to speak, but no words filled the void. I then looked back at Mrs. Whitman. Her eyes were becoming wet as well.

I finally gathered myself.

"H—how did they die?"

"I fear it was from a broken heart, Thomas. They heard that you had perished at sea, and they did not take it well. Your mother succumbed first with a sudden stroke. It was only a matter of weeks before your father suffered a heart attack. I believe it was the stress of it all, first thinking you had died and then your mother's death. I think that is what did it."

"I see," I answered, trying to remain brave.

"They held onto hope for quite a while, but I guess it was too much for them to bear. Please accept my condolences for your loss, Thomas."

"Thank you, Mrs. Whitman. I appreciate your telling me. Where have they been buried? I wish to visit them."

"In the Sacred Heart Cemetery, Thomas. On the south end, in the middle of the last row nearest the fencing."

We again thanked her and we left her home, driving our team immediately to the cemetery.

Chapter 14

I stood over the gravesite, tears of woeful despair streaking unabashedly down my cheeks. Gretchen, on my arm, held her tongue still, allowing me the latitude to mourn without prosaic and unnecessary remarks, allowing me to feel deeply my bitter loss. My parents were dead, never to know that I had returned home safe and sound.

Once again, I felt that I was to blame for their passing, for had I not embarked upon my selfish journey, they might still be alive and living a robust life and I would not be standing here faithless and mired in an unhealthy regret.

"It's my fault," I said in a low and quiet tone. "In my self-centered desire to expand my own worth, I have caused these good people to surrender all of their desire to live. I am a louse, my dear—a worthless and heartless brute—a destroyer of lives. I deserve no blessings at all in this life, for I have sought to serve only myself, and I am at fault for any losses I now suffer. I am a damaged and useless soul who can find no way to save either myself or anyone else from the vile grief of knowing me. Whosoever I touch, I demolish. My only regret now is that I still live."

Gretchen maintained her stilled tongue, giving me opportunity to exorcise my demons in the only way I knew how. And demons they were. Anger and self-loathing are vicious spirits if left unchecked, free to strike out against one's self. After a while, if free to grow untethered and untamed, they also can seek out ways to harm others.

I have found over the years that giving these fiends an unmolested voice, at least for a time, assuages an even greater outburst later. I think Gretchen understood that as well. She allowed me to speak out, and in so doing I soon exhausted myself and retreated once again into silence.

I remained in that terrible stillness for some time thereafter.

"It broke their hearts when they learned that you were lost," a voice from behind us spoke.

I turned to see my childhood friend Angus McGready standing behind me. I rushed to him and hugged him tightly.

"Welcome back, old man," he said. "It is so very good to see you again."

"It is good to see you also, Angus. I've missed everyone so very much. How did you know that I was here?"

"I just saw Mrs. Whitman sitting on her porch. She told me as I walked by. You look well for a dead man, Thomas."

"I am well, Angus. Well enough as can be expected under the circumstances, that is."

"My condolences, Thomas. And who is this lovely creature?" he asked.

"This is Gretchen. My wife." Gretchen stretched her hand toward Angus. He took it and kissed the back of it.

"Your wife? My, my. It seems it was to your good fortune, then, to be lost at sea."

"Yes, except that I caused my parents such grief and torment."

"Yes. Except for that, of course. I am truly sorry for your loss, Thomas."

"Thank you, Angus." I recovered and put on a brave smile. "Will you join us for lunch?"

"Forgive me, Thomas, but I cannot. I am to leave for Europe this very day on an extended trip. Perhaps when I return next year."

"I see. And what news do you have of the rest of our little gang? How about Susan, Tommy, Bertrand, and all the rest?"

"Gone, Thomas. All gone. Some to other parts of the world, some off to the rest of their lives. I am the last one to leave our fair city. I'm sorry to have to leave you alone, but I am committed."

"Gone? All of them?"

"Yes, Thomas. All of them."

"Well, then, so be it. Tomorrow I plan to return to the office."

"That is unlikely, Thomas."

"How is that?"

"The company is closed. Mr. Jenkins died of a heart attack immediately upon receiving the news that his ship had gone down in the hurricane. I heard that he clutched his chest and was dead before he hit the floor."

"Oh, dear God."

"The company was not able to sustain itself, and it closed about three months ago. I'm afraid there is no job to go back to, Thomas. I regret being the bearer of all this tragic news."

"Take heart, dear friend, it is not your fault, but here I am, without my parents, without my friends, and without my employment. Dear me, what shall I do now? Perhaps I was better off on the island."

"There is a bit of light in the darkness, old man. Your father's attorney holds the assets of your father's estate. You would do well to visit him as soon as you can. Perhaps today even. You will not have your parents, but you will have what they left for you to get started, now that you have returned, and make no mistake about it, Thomas. Your father knew that you would return."

"And yet he died?"

"I think it was the shock of your mother passing that did him in. He never accepted that you were dead. He believed you would return right up to the day his heart burst."

"Thank you, Angus, for such kind words. I shall visit the attorneys straightaway and settle my father's estate."

"Well, Thomas, I hate to do this to you, but I must be off for the wharf. The ship leaves in two hours."

"It was good of you to search me out, my friend. Best wishes to you on your voyage."

"Thank you, Thomas. I'm happy that you survived to make it home, and so sorry that your return was not such a happy one. I shall think about you, dear friend, and we shall get together immediately upon my return. And to you, Gretchen, my congratulations. Thomas, here, is a fine man. You have chosen well."

"You are most gracious, sir," replied Gretchen.

"Travel safely, Angus," I added.

Angus nodded, then turned and walked away, leaving Gretchen and me standing over my parents' gravesite. Knowing but a soul or two now in the great city of my upbringing and having no idea of what our life would be like from here on out, I struggled to find any gratitude in my heart.

I was thankful that we had each other to depend upon, for without my Gretchen, I would have felt completely lost and abandoned. I hugged her tightly.

"It seems that we have only each other, my dear. I don't know what else we will have in the future, but for now we have at least that," I whispered.

"We will do quite well, Thomas. Take heart, husband. All of this shall pass, and we will find our joy soon enough."

"I think it wise to make our way directly to my father's lawyers and see what they might have for me."

Rather than trouble you with so many dull details, let me say that it was good fortune that Angus had told me about the lawyers, for they still held my father's estate in escrow. In a short time, however, had I not returned to claim my inheritance, it would have been turned over to the state and I would have had nothing with which to begin our new life.

But fate smiled kindly upon me that day, and money would not immediately be a matter of concern for us. My father had left me a small fortune, enough to live comfortably, although not lavishly, and a fine home.

In a considered effort to manage my newfound finances more competently and with so many public carriages available for hire and so easily accessible, I sold my carriage and horses to a boarding stable operator, not wishing to endure the overly expensive and continuous upkeep of two horses. After all, I was back in New York and a gentleman once more. I intended to live as one and make sensible use of all public services available.

Gretchen and I returned to my parents' home, and it was as if I had never left. Everything I remembered about the house was exactly in its place, as if awaiting my return.

Within a few weeks, and after hiring new house staff, a man and his wife named Albert and Mildred, our home was running smoothly and on a normal schedule, although much emptier without my parents' presence.

Through my extended knowledge of finance and accounting, I was able to make several initial investments over the following months that began to pay back a modest monthly return, enough so that I was able to avoid dipping into the principle sums. As I stated, we did not live a lavish life, but it was one of comfort.

We had not the excess funds to travel about as I would have liked, but we were never pressed hard to find money enough for a nice meal out or to enjoy an occasional evening at the theatre.

Gretchen was a fine wife, and while high society was very fond of us both, it was she who found the most attention. I was extremely proud of her.

As I stated, not having money enough to travel, I mailed the remaining letters to the families of Matthew and Malcolm in Boston and let them speak for themselves. As for Samuel's family, they were not at home when we visited them. We left the letter with a neighbor instead in the hopes that that should suffice.

I made it a point to write of such events and happenings in my journal, at least a little, nearly every night. It may have been only a paragraph or two, but it gave me some comfort to do so.

No longer was having enough light an issue, as it had been on the island, for I had nearly a dozen candles burning brightly any night I wished. Nor was comfort a concern, for I had at my disposal a very fine desk to write upon. I also had possession of several excellent quill pens and bottles of black ink aplenty, and blank parchment enough for several books.

In a relatively short time, we completed our triumphant return. Because of new acquaintances made through my business dealings, more and more people learned of my time marooned. I became a topic of much interest and subsequent discussions among the dinner parties we attended in the early days and was often asked to recite some of the events of my time on the island.

I admit that at first most of those in the audience scoffed at the very idea of grass people coming to life, but they were also unable to explain the presence of Gretchen on the island. Some suggested that she must have been on the ship with me, but then they could not explain why she would have arrived nearly six months later.

I should say at this point that in all the discussions on the matter, I never once tried to explain or defend my stories. I simply stated the truth as I knew it to be and let each audience member choose whether to accept or reject my statements as fact. For the most part, my statements were believed, and thus was I spared the label of an eccentric or a liar.

Of particular interest to all the audiences was the story of the pirate battle and their landing on the island. Again, I never debated anyone wishing to think my story a fabrication or an exaggeration. I simply directed them to make their own inquiries with my brothers on the ANNABELLE LEE and left the subject at that.

On Friday, February 3, 1832, I was contacted by a representative of a rather large publishing house. It seemed that my stories had attracted the attention of a Mr. Wilfred Housing, the owner of the firm, who was well known and well respected in New York society. He wished an audience with me to discuss a book addressing the events of my time on the island—an autobiography, as it were.

Thus, on Wednesday of the following week, that day being the eighth, I met with Mr. Housing. He was a delightful man and well interested in my story at first. We discussed the structure of the book in some depth. He had asked me to bring in some of my parchment pages for him. I did so, and he spent some time reading the selected parts of several pages.

After about an hour, he looked at me and asked a most curious question.

"Where is the conflict?"

"Conflict?" I asked, completely perplexed.

"Yes. Every story has three major components to it: the Setup, the Conflict, and the Resolution. I don't see any real conflict here."

"There really wasn't any conflict, sir."

"I don't see any struggle here, no battle to survive, no tenuous moment where you might have died. No substance to your struggle, Mr. Cantfield, nothing to draw the reader into the story. There seems to be little harrowing adventure to your adventure. In fact, there seems to be little adventure here at all. Did you not have to battle any cannibals or ferocious animals?"

"No, sir. From day one, I discovered plenty of food and water. Within days of the shipwreck, I had canvas and chests containing everything I needed. There was very little struggle involved. If I had to be marooned on an island, I was glad it was that one."

He fell silent and remained so for a good long while. Finally, he adjusted himself in his chair and stared me straight in the eye. "Can you devise some other tragedies or struggles, something monumental, some near catastrophe, some mind-numbing events that will excite the readers?"

"I could invent anything, Mr. Housing, but if it is an autobiographical account of my life on the island, then such inventions would be disingenuous, would they not?"

"I'm a publisher, sir. I don't care for truth; I want to print a good story. My readers want a fascinating tale, a tale to take their breath away, something that takes them on a fantastical journey, a story that makes them dream and fantasize about a life they will never know. Quite frankly, Mr. Cantfield, your story lacks any real intrigue. It seems to me you had a fine vacation, and that is all."

"I see. Well, if you are looking for a tale of excitement, danger, and intrigue, Mr. Housing, I'm sure that my story is of little interest to you or to anyone else like you. I shall take my leave of you, sir. Thank you for seeing me."

I gathered up my things and left his office feeling a bit disillusioned. He was right, of course; little had happened to me that would hold the interest of any reader. In fact, as I considered it myself, with the exception of a few noteworthy events, nothing of any critical interest had occurred at all.

The carriage ride home was less than I had hoped for. Mr. Housing was correct in his assessment: I'd had little more than an extended vacation while on the island, which was now past. It was time to move on.

Upon returning to my home, I gathered up my journal pages, had my manservant, Albert, put them back into the chest in the attic, and dismissed from my mind writing in my journal ever again.

Over the next several months, I concentrated on both and only Gretchen and my investments. We attended parties and eventually settled into a normal life. Requests for my island recounts finally ceased altogether, and within a short time, even I no longer considered them of any real interest.

Gretchen and I began to settle into yet another mundane life of little struggle and littler intrigue.

Perhaps, I thought on occasion, this is my lot in life. A blessed life, really. I had found no real challenges to face. All seemed to go, for the most part, rather easy and well. And so, in the face of such diminished trials and tribulations, I moved onward into my future with no expectations for anything different anytime soon.

I recall now that nearly eight months later, on one particular night, I was awakened by a strange sound that seemed to be coming from somewhere downstairs. I eased myself from the bed so as not to awaken my wife. Putting on my robe, I then lit a candle and stepped quietly down the stairs.

The sounds of someone stirring about continued as I tiptoed toward the front door to arm myself with my trusty cane and thence into the parlor, whereupon I was shocked to see a young child seated on the floor directly in front of the fireplace, her back to me, the glow of dying embers casting an eerie red hue about the room.

"Hello," I said nervously.

"Hello," she answered without turning around.

"Are you lost, child?" I asked, moving slowly around to sit in front of her.

"No."

"What are you doing here?"

"I came for you."

"For me?"

"Yes."

"Why?"

"I wanted to meet you before it's too late."

"I don't understand, child."

"I'll be coming soon, but we'll never meet. So I wanted to meet you now."

"Are you ill, child?"

"No. I'm well."

"How old are you?"

"I don't know. How old do I appear?"

"I would guess you are about seven or eight."

"That seems about right. I think I'm closer to eight. That feels right. About eight months old."

I chuckled lightly. "No, child. I meant you look about eight *years* old."

"Eight years?"

"Yes."

"I don't think so."

"This is all very strange. Where do you live?"

"Right now I live very far away."

"Perhaps you should come with me. My wife will know what to do with you."

"No. I want to know more about you. What is your name?"

"My name is Thomas. What's yours?"

"I don't know."

"You don't know your name?"

"No. What name do you like for a girl?"

"Of late, I have grown fond of Annabelle Lee."

"I like that name. Why do you like it?"

"Well, it's the name of the ship that rescued me after I was marooned on an island for almost a whole year."

"What is ma...ma...marooned?"

"It means that I was on an island with no way to get off until the ship found me and brought me back home."

"Were you afraid on the island all alone?" she asked.

"Not really afraid. Just very lonely."

"Are you lonely now?"

"No, no longer. This is very uncomfortable for me here on the floor. Would you care to sit in the chair?"

"May I sit in your lap?"

"I don't know if that would be appropriate since I hardly know you."

"Please. I want to sit in your lap."

"Well, all right, then. I think that would be acceptable for a short while. Perhaps you can tell me more about yourself."

"I'll try."

We arose from the floor. Before I sat in the large chair, I stoked the fire back to life and loaded more wood into the fireplace. Within minutes the fire was fully alive and giving the room a soothing warmth and a bright orange glow.

I sat down in the chair and the child sat in my lap, leaning up against my chest. I wrapped us both in a warm blanket.

"So, you don't know your name or how old you are. That's very odd."

"I like Annabelle. May I have that name?"

"If you would like. Very well, then. I shall call you Annabelle for now."

"I would like that."

"Wonderful, Annabelle. Can you tell me how you got into my home?"

"No. I just woke up on the floor where you found me."

"This is very, very odd indeed."

"Do you live here alone?"

"No, darling. I am married."

"What is her name?"

"My wife's name is Gretchen."

"I like that name, too."

"I think it is a very fine name. Are you warm enough, Annabelle?"

Yes, thank you. I feel fine."

"You don't perhaps live somewhere in the neighborhood, do you?"

"No. I'm sure that I live very far away."

I noticed that she was getting sleepy. I held her and rubbed the tips of my fingers across her forehead and soon noticed her eyes growing heavier.

"Are you getting sleepy?"

"Yes," she responded.

"Rest then, child. When you awake next, we will get this all sorted out. For now, sleep peacefully, little one. You are safe."

"I know I'm safe."

"How do you know that?"

"I just do. Can you tell me a story?"

"I can. Once upon a time there lived a young princess…"

I felt a soft hand against my face and opened my eyes to see Gretchen smiling down at me.

"You were asleep. Come to bed, my love."

I then remembered Annabelle. I sat up straight in the chair. "Annabelle," I called out. The child, however, was nowhere to be seen.

Gretchen looked at me very oddly. "Annabelle? Who is Annabelle, Thomas?"

"The little girl who was here earlier."

"Someone was in the house?"

"Yes," I answered, my head beginning to spin as I looked about for the mysterious child.

"It must have been a dream, Thomas. There is no one here."

"She was here."

"In your head only, you stupid fool," she said with a cold and acerbic tone.

I looked up at Gretchen in great bewilderment. I had never heard her address anyone in such a tone.

"You're insane, you wretched simpleton. Next you'll be seeing unicorns and tiny fairies. I don't know what I ever saw in you."

"Gretchen! Why do you speak to me in this manner and tone?"

"Because I'm sick of you!" she hollered. She

raised her hand high in the air and slapped me across the face. I bolted from my chair in both shock and anger.

I then felt a gentle hand against my face again and opened my eyes to see Gretchen's loving and tender face in front of me.

"My love," she said with a startled tone, "it's all right. You just had a bad dream." She then brought my head to her chest and rubbed the back of my neck. "It's done now, Thomas. Relax."

"Dear me," I uttered, still in some shock. "I had a horrible dream, Gretchen. Simply horrible!"

"I know, my love. As I approached you, I saw you tossing about in anguish. It has passed. Be calm now."

I sat still for several more minutes, sorting out the outlandish dream that continued on a conscious level in my head, although diminished in its intensity. Then the fear and terror of it quickly faded. Within a few more minutes, all emotional intensity of it was gone from my mind. What remained was only the memory of the anomalous visions.

Gretchen sensed my return to normalcy and released my head, but then caressed my face in both her hands and, drawing near, smiled warmly. "You gave me quite a fright, my dear. Are you better now?"

"Yes. I'm fine now. Thank you."

"Then come to bed. It is still quite early. I'll rub your back and soothe you to sleep."

"I think I would like that very much."

Just then my manservant approached, carrying a lighted candle.

"Is everything all right, sir?"

"Yes, Albert. Thank you. Go back to bed."

"You look distraught, sir. May I make you some tea or perhaps warm some milk?"

"I just fell asleep out here and succumbed to an odd dream. We're going back to bed now. Goodnight, Albert."

"Pleasant dreams, sir."

Gretchen and I walked together, arm and arm, up the stairs to our bedroom, leaving Albert standing at the foot of the stairs, his candle casting a dim light onto the stairway.

"What was the dream about?" asked Gretchen gently.

"It was bizarre and bewildering, my dear. Bizarre and greatly bewildering."

When I awoke later that morning, I thought of the dream once again, but I soon dismissed it as just the adverse reaction to something I had eaten the night before. I went about my day in the usual manner, roaming the streets on my morning stroll and chatting with some of my new acquaintances and neighbors.

In the evening, Gretchen and I attended the dinner party of one of my clients I had recently advised on a business matter. It was a splendid affair, and all was well until Gretchen clutched at her abdomen, doubling over in some pain. I escorted her out onto the balcony and sat her down to rest.

"Oh, Thomas," she said with a cringe, grasping my arm tightly.

Doctor Millstone came out onto the porch to examine her.

"It was fortunate for us, Doctor, that you also attended tonight's party," I said.

"Good fortune indeed, Thomas. Let's have a look here."

The good doctor took several minutes to examine my wife, carefully pushing and prodding her all over. He finally stood up straight and stepped back.

"Mrs. Cantfield, how long has it been since you experienced your last crimson flow?"

"A couple of months, Doctor. Do you think I'm with child?"

"That would be my guess. I'd like you to come to my office tomorrow for a full examination. I'll know more afterward. For tonight, however, I would prescribe rest and relaxation."

"Thank you, Doctor," I said, shaking his hand. "I'll have her in your office around ten. Will that be soon enough?"

"Yes, that will be fine. Goodnight, Mrs. Cantfield."

"Thank you, Doctor."

I sat with Gretchen for a while longer until she regained her composure, and then we made our apologies and bid our good-byes and left the party with the well wishes of everyone.

On the way home, she remained silent. Respecting her apparent wish not to discuss the matter, I also remained still. Once we returned home, Gretchen went straight to bed and fell immediately to sleep. I retired to the parlor to sit again in my chair and contemplate the changes that were coming by way of a child.

The more I thought about it, the more excited I became. I began wondering whether the child would be a son or a daughter. In my deliberation, I came to the conclusion that I wished only for the child to be healthy, strong, and of a kindly disposition. The sex of the child was unimportant to me.

I sat for a good long while, excitement building within me to a level that finally caused me to burst out of my chair and dash up to Gretchen. As she slept, I stood staring lovingly at her for several sweet moments, and then I bent over and kissed her on the forehead. I continued watching her sleep for several minutes thereafter and smiled at the delicate slumber of the mother of my growing child. I felt a truly blessed man at that moment.

I returned to the chair in the parlor and reseated myself in deep contemplation.

How could a man such as I continue to be so

richly blessed in so many ways, I wondered. It was not for my works, for I did not feel that I had done anything of particular note to warrant such rewards. It was certainly not the consequences of holding to a great faith in any divine intervention, for I still was not convinced that divinity, in any form, existed at all in this world. And it most assuredly was not the result of pure chance, for my life by then was clearly established well beyond the statistical probability of normalcy.

Nay, it could be none of these reasons, I surmised, for I was, in fact, a pure statistical anomaly for good fortune. It had fallen upon me in such great abundance as to make me think it all just one long charming dream, and I, for whatever it was worth to anyone, had no wish to awaken from such blissful repose.

Chapter 15

The next many sanctified months whisked by with such rapidity that I can hardly recall them clearly enough to set them to parchment herewith. I can only say that my blessings continued to flow unabated during this period.

I watched my wife's belly grow with enormous elation. She was near to delivery, but the pregnancy was not without its difficulties. On several occasions, Doctor Millstone expressed concern for the safety of both my wife and our child. It seemed that during her given time, her heart had begun to murmur slightly. It seemed that the child's heart also was of like condition. Thus, for the last three months prior to her coming to full term, Gretchen was confined to either the bed or the divan and was discouraged from needlessly walking about.

I will tell you now, as I have stated earlier, I was never a man who turned his face from challenge, but I lacked the necessary courage to face the possibility of losing either my wife or my child in such a way. It was unthinkable to me then, and I am finding it equally difficult to speak of it even now, these many years later.

To gaze upon my wife every day and be unable to diminish her worry and stress found me of little worth. My attempts to sport a strong and happy face were often met with a slight, understanding smile from her. My meager efforts to invoke positive comments regarding the coming birth were also met with gentle demeanor. Still, I knew that she harbored deep concerns for the child's well-being. And I will admit to you that despite my well-intended words and my brave front, I felt weak and ineffectual.

I remained virtually by her side all day and night. I read her stories, I engaged her in deep philosophical discussions regarding the most mundane issues. I even would sit for hours brushing her hair or rubbing her shoulders. I did anything and everything I could think of to offer reassurance to her that all would soon be well and in the very near future we would hold the small and loveable bundle of joy and laugh about all our concerns of the moment. I spoke only words of affirmation and never expressed any doubt. I purposely kept all conversations to light matter. And when I saw the beginning of a fearful tear, I would smile and present a joyful and bold countenance for her to see.

I was such a deceiver, or so I believed.

"We are only one month away from our child's entry into this world, my darling. I want the event to be without equal. I am making wonderful plans for a party to announce her official birth. Is there anything in particular that you would like me to arrange?"

"Only a quick and painless birth, Thomas," Gretchen smiled.

"If I could, my angel, I would arrange it so,

sparing no expense or effort toward such an end."

"I know you would, husband. I am so very fortunate to have such a man to comfort me and stay with me as you have these many months. I want to give you a healthy child."

"You shall, my love. All will be well. In the end, my dear, all will be well. You shall see."

"All difficultly will flee from my brain if only the child emerges in good health and possessing all parts working well."

"She will emerge so."

"Thomas?" she asked, a new thought suddenly spilling forth. "We should pick a name. What name shall we give if the child is a boy?"

"I should like him to be called Matthew Charles Cantfield, if it pleases you."

"Certainly so. I think it is a wonderful name. I can think of none better. And if it is a girl?"

"Annabelle Lee Cantfield," I answered without hesitation.

"Annabelle Lee? After the ship?"

"Yes. In special manner of speaking," I responded, the thought of my young ghostly visitor those many months ago now revisiting my mind.

"Is there another manner of speaking?"

"No. I believe it a special name for a special young child, for she is being sent to rescue me once more, I think."

"That is a beautiful thought, husband."

Just then a sharp pain struck Gretchen, and she

yelped loudly in response to its intensity. She reached for me. I took her hand, and she pulled herself to her feet and stared into my eyes with terror.

"No!" she exclaimed in fright. "It is too soon." She looked down at her expanded belly, rubbing her left hand in circles across it.

"Relax, Gretchen. Relax."

"Too late. The baby comes now. Run, Thomas, please. Fetch the doctor."

"Are you certain?"

"Yes. Please run quickly."

I shouted for our housekeeper, Mildred, who soon bolted into the room, both hands clutching her own face in horror.

"It's too soon, sir!"

"I know this. Take care of her. I'm going to get the doctor."

I kissed Gretchen on her mouth and stroked her pain-filled face. "Be calm, my love. I will run as if my feet had wings."

I raced out of the house and flew down the street well possessed of some unexplained stamina and speed, and although the doctor's house was some distance away, I completed my dash in what seemed to be no time at all.

Without realizing it, I beat so vigorously on his front door and screamed so loudly that I awakened several of the good doctor's neighbors.

The doctor, now fully awakened and rousted from his bed, opened the door and raised his hand to quiet me, but my desperate mind gave strong and loud voice to my worrisome thoughts.

"It is my wife, doctor! The child comes now, and there is great pain. Come quickly, please!"

"Very well. Calm yourself, Thomas. I'll be right with you."

"Hurry, please, doctor. She is in great pain."

The doctor shut his door, leaving me on his stoop in a nervous and excited state and prancing about in circles.

I saw people in their doorways staring at me.

"My wife is having a baby. I need the doctor."

"I hope she's quieter about it than you," came one man's response.

"Please forgive me," I replied, now realizing that I was even shouting about my wife's condition.

Then I saw many others with disturbed expressions, shaking their heads and closing their drapes.

It seemed to take the doctor forever, but he finally opened his door, dressed and carrying his medical bag, as I am certain he had done so many times before with other expectant fathers nearly out of their minds with worry.

He shut his door.

"Let us go, Doctor. She's in great pain," I said, starting to sprint away.

"Relax, Thomas."

I had gotten only a few yards away when I noticed that the doctor was walking in another direction.

"No, Doctor!" I shouted, caring not that my voice might disturb his sleeping neighbors. "This way!"

The doctor ignored my words and disappeared around the corner. By that time, I was very confused and desperate for him to follow, so I ran around the corner just in time to see him crawling up inside a waiting carriage. The driver readied to crack the whip over the horses' heads when the carriage door opened and the doctor waved me inside.

I crawled into the carriage, out of breath and perspiring heavily.

"I won't be running to your house, Thomas. Now relax."

He shut the door, and I heard the snap of the whip. The carriage launched forward.

"I'm sorry, Doctor, I didn't think. She's in great pain. She's not due for another month. I'm very worried."

"Sometimes babies decide to make their entrance a bit earlier, my boy. We'll be there soon."

I tried to relax into my seat, but I fear my body thought otherwise. I ended up rocking back and forth in my seat, wringing my hands in a nervous manner while the doctor sat calmly still.

Trotting along as we did, I began to shift more in my seat until I could take no more. "What is wrong with this driver?" I asked loudly. "Is the man lost?"

Just then the carriage came to an abrupt halt.

"What is it *now*, man?" I bellowed.

"Thomas. Please try to relax. We're here."

I tell you, I was in such a state that I had not realized the carriage was stopped directly in front of my home.

I dashed out of the carriage and flew toward the house, leaving the doctor behind. I burst through the door and up the steps, shouting for Gretchen while leaping up the stairway two steps at a time.

I was greeted by Albert, who took hold of me by the shoulders, preventing me from going into my bedroom.

"Sir," he said firmly but politely, "you need to stay out here. It is women's business in there."

"But I need to know that she is all right. Let me go!"

I struggled against his grasp, but he held me firm. "Let me go! I order you to let me go, Albert. I want to see my wife!"

Just then I felt a firm hand upon my shoulder. It was the doctor, still in his calm manner.

"Thomas, go out onto the porch. Gretchen does not need to see you in such a state. I'll send word when I know something. Do it now, my boy. You're not helping the situation."

I realized that he was correct. My wife was struggling to bring a new life into this world; she did not need to see me in such a shambles.

I turned and walked down the stairs. I didn't immediately realize that Albert was holding onto my left arm as he guided me down the steps.

Upon arriving at the bottom of the staircase, he let go of my arm.

"Go outside and sit on the porch, sir. I'll bring you some sherry to calm you."

"Yes, Albert. You're right, of course. Yes, I'll go outside."

Moments later, Albert brought out a tray with five glasses filled with sherry. I tossed three of them down immediately, taking up the fourth and rolling it in my hand.

"Tell me, Albert. Was she still in much pain after I left?"

"Yes, sir, but it is a common thing for women to be in pain during childbirth. I wouldn't worry about it."

"Of course," I replied, now calming down a bit. "Of course it is. Childbirth is very painful. Yes, of course. I understand." I downed the fourth glass of sherry and then rolled the empty glass between my hands.

Albert removed the glass from my hand and replaced it with the last full glass.

I sipped at the sherry now, its soothing effect slowly taking hold of me.

"Do you have children, Albert?"

"Yes, sir. Two. A son and a daughter. They are grown and have families of their own now."

"That's wonderful. So you're a grandfather, eh?"

"Yes, sir. Four times already now."

"Four grandchildren. I'm sorry I did not think to ask before now. You're a very lucky man."

"Yes, sir. I am a very lucky man, sir."

I sipped again and sat back into the rocking chair and rocked. After several minutes of silence, I asked, "Albert? Did your wife deliver before term?"

"No, sir. She went to full term and a few days beyond for the boy. My daughter was born just about on time."

"Did you know they were healthy and well immediately?"

"Yes, sir, but still I counted all their toes and fingers just to be sure."

I chuckled.

"I see the sherry is working now, sir."

"Yes. It certainly is. Thank you." I downed the fifth glass and handed it to Albert.

"Would you care for more, sir?"

"No, Albert. That was sufficient. I see that you know the correct amount of sherry to serve a man in my state."

"Only because I have been on the receiving end before," he smiled.

"Ah, indeed. There is nothing like experience, is there? Thank you, Albert. I'll be fine now."

"Very good, sir. I'll return in a few moments to keep you company."

"Thank you, Albert. Thank you for everything."

"You're welcome, sir."

He went back into the house, leaving me temporarily alone with my many thoughts.

The sherry had accomplished its task, and I sat calmly in the rocking chair. I was periodically visited by Albert, I think more than anything else to see if I was yet awake.

I heard the shrieks of severe birthing pains coming from inside the house, but I knew that I was powerless to ease them or to comfort my wife in any way. Thus, I sat alone on the front porch, anxiously rocking back and forth, doing what every expecting father has done before me, waiting for the birth of his child and knowing all the while that he can do little else.

It seemed as if hours and hours had passed, but in reality it was perhaps only three hours or so, before the shrieking ceased altogether. Several minutes of silence followed, and then Doctor Millstone stepped somberly through the door.

I stood immediately and excitedly awaited the good news, but his saddened eyes and forlorn frown took me immediately aback.

"No," I said. "No. It cannot be."

"I'm sorry, Thomas. There were complications. I did everything I could."

"No!" I screamed, pushing him aside, then roaring up the stairway and bursting into the room.

There, as if in silent slumber, lay my wife, my child lying as still next to her, both sets of eyes closed. I stared at them, my eyes shifting back and forth and seeing neither chest rise in rhythmic breathing.

I clearly remember teetering on my heels, my eyes fixed on their deceased forms and my head suddenly becoming light, my vision blurring, and then nothing at all.

I was told much later that I lay unconscious for several hours before I finally opened my eyes. Doctor Millstone was not present, but Mildred sat on the edge of my bed with a wet compress, dabbing my forehead.

"What happened?" I asked.

Mildred told me what had happened, although for the life of me, I could recall nothing after the darkness closed in upon me.

I do recall, though only glimpses now and then, of the burial services. And I also recall visiting their graves from time to time, their names carved into the granite headstones, one over the other: Gretchen Amber Cantfield and Annabelle Lee Cantfield. I have since stopped visiting their graves because I simply cannot see their names without breaking down and sobbing uncontrollably.

It is only recently, after so many years, that I am able to bring to memory the ghastly visions of seeing my dead wife and child lying upon bloodied bed sheeting without falling to pieces inside. I wish for a complete loss of such memories, yet every now and then they return to haunt me. Perhaps they always will.

It was months, they say, before I recovered sufficiently enough to venture out of my home unescorted, conscious of my steps and surroundings, a lost man searching for any signs of life once more out in the dreadfully darkened world.

For me, as I now recall it, I felt as if I again stood on the brink of dark oblivion, preparing to leap off the precipice and into the blackness of something unknown, uncaring about what would await me at the end of such a tumble.

Yet, holding onto just enough faith and hope, I wondered then, if only for a brief moment, if it were all just some horrible nightmare from which I would soon awaken.

But each time I returned home from visiting my cherished ones' graves, I found that it was all sadly true and I would then feel myself once again sliding down some slippery slope into a black abyss.

It seemed an endless cycle of constant fear and terror followed by spurts of hope and faith, and then back again. I felt forever pursued by a sinister force, some demonic will with the sole purpose of destroying me completely.

They say it was several more months until I was able to come to terms with the fact that my beloved wife and my beautiful child, never known to me, had perished and that I was alone once more, this time, I feared, to remain so until my own ingloriously deserved end.

Once again, therefore, I experienced the sadness of my empty heart, felt the tragedy of my empty mind, and felt completely lost within my empty soul.

It was some months later, late into the night, that I heard a rustling downstairs. It was not loud, but it had been sufficient to arouse me from my light sleep, a sleep neither restful nor deep enough to bring me peace.

I struck a match, lit a candle, and crept down the stairs. There once more, in the same spot, stood the young Annabelle from my dream before. Only this time she was adding wood to the fire.

"Annabelle?" I asked softly.

"It is I, Father. I'm warming the room for you."

She turned and smiled at me.

"Is it truly you, or am I yet fast asleep in my bed and this but a dream?"

"You're awake, Father, and I am here again."

I rubbed my eyes in disbelief, and yet when I removed my hand, she was still present before me. I sat in my large chair, and she arose off the floor and took her place again upon my lap, her head resting also again against my chest.

"How is this possible?" I asked.

"I was sent by Mother to speak to you."

"Your mother? May I see her?"

"No, Father. Not yet. She is still coming to terms with her new beginning. She is not ready to meet with you."

"Will I see her soon?"

"Not soon, but you will see her again."

"Would you tell her that I miss her so much?"

"I don't need to tell her, Father, she knows."

"I miss you also, yet we had never met. How is that possible?"

"I cannot say right now, Father, but I was sent here to tell you something of great importance."

"Tell me, then, my child."

"You must return to the island, Father, and it is very important that you return soon."

"Why? Why is it so important that I return?"

"I cannot answer that, Father. I was just sent to tell you this. Do not delay. You need to return to the island very soon. Before it is too late."

"Too late? Too late for what?"

"I'm not permitted to tell you the reason, Father. Only that it is extremely urgent that you do so."

She then jumped down off my lap and moved toward the fireplace.

"Wait!" I shouted. "Where are you going?"

"I must return, Father."

"Will I see you again?"

"Yes. You will see me again, but hurry, Father. Hurry back to the island."

"Why, child? Please tell me why."

"I cannot. Hurry, though."

A noise behind me forced me to look back. When I turned my head again toward my daughter, she had disappeared completely, leaving me alone in the parlor, drenched in whitish-orange light from the fire.

The sound was Albert walking into the room.

"She was here again, Albert. I saw her clearly. I spoke with her."

"With whom, sir?"

"My daughter, but she was much older than at her death."

"Your daughter, sir?"

"Yes, Albert. She was standing right there in front of the fireplace. I turned toward the sound of your approach. When I turned back, she was gone, vanished into thin air."

"I'll get you another sherry, sir."

"I don't want any sherry, Albert. I tell you, she was here tonight. I spoke with her."

"I understand, sir."

"No. You don't. You think I've gone mad again, but I assure you, she was here just as plain as you are now, speaking with me, urging me to return to the island."

"Are you saying you saw her ghost?"

"Ghost, spirit, whatever you call it, yes. She was here speaking to me, clear as a bell."

"I'm sorry, sir. Please try to understand it from my perspective. I saw no one. I heard no voice but yours, sir. Besides, she was just an infant, you understand, incapable of speaking."

"I know that, Albert. I'm not daft. But she appeared to me and she seemed much older, like before. She looked to be about eight years old. I can't explain it."

"She appeared to you before, sir?"

"Yes, before the birth."

"She appeared to you before she was born?"

"Yes! Are you deaf?"

"No, sir. I hear you quite well, but do you hear yourself? A child appears to her father *before* she is even born. Do you know what that sounds like, sir?"

I stopped and thought carefully about what Albert was saying. He was correct. Of course he was. Any rational man, hearing such nonsense being spoken by someone still grieving the loss of his loved ones, would also think him to be mad, or at the very least despondent and not thinking clearly, the grieving process continuing strongly.

"I know what it sounds like, Albert. Perhaps I was dreaming and only awoke before you arrived. Or it may have even been a manifestation of my own need to find some closure to the matter. In any event, it seemed so real."

"I'm sure it did, sir. Grief is a powerful force, and I think you have yet to fully accept your loss. It can be a great struggle for anyone. Why don't you go back to bed now? In the morning I'm certain all will seem much clearer to you."

"Yes, Albert. Thank you. You're right. I do need a good night's sleep. It has been so terribly long since I experienced the gentleness of a sound sleep."

Albert helped me back to bed and waited patiently by my side for sleep to take me.

Chapter 16

Several more agonizing months passed in like manner, the terror of it all arising and then falling. Soon the date of my birthday arrived once again.

Turning thirty-five years old should have been a celebratory day, but not for me. Instead, I remained at home and took no visits from acquaintances and other concerned parties. Albert greeted all at the door and simply told them that I was ill and unable to receive any guests.

For this empty and forsaken man, hidden away in my parlor, there was no reason for celebration. This date was merely a painful reminder that another year had passed and I was one more year yet misplaced within myself. At the time, I could not conceive of a more wretched soul bound to earth, more lost and confused, than I.

It was terribly difficult to imagine a life more wasted than mine, and so every day was a battle just to rise up out of bed. I had ostensibly, at least in my own mind, stored in a box by the bed, a brave face solely for the sake of Albert and Mildred, and each morning I would replace my woeful expression with a happy one. Despite the darkness of my stark reality, I saw that I was deceiving no one and soon thereafter I did not even bother with trying to hide my miserable moods.

Each day's battle was fought within my own head and heart, of course, but as each successive morning's contest raged deep within me, I found that I had greater and greater difficulty finding justification to continue struggling against my downward slip into the black abyss of my empty heart, born of my terrible sorrow and my horrible misery.

Each new day brought with it new reasons to simply lie down and surrender to the terrors haunting me. I found it almost soothing to think about closing my eyes and not opening them ever again. In those moments of deepest despair I could see my shattered life crumbling and falling down around me as if I were a detached observer witnessing the demise of a decrepit man, his vacant eyes staring back at me. I saw little reason for him to continue at all.

The task of venturing outdoors became overwhelming to me. So much so that I found, over time, little justification to even dress in the morning.

Some tried to check in on me, but I refused to see anyone. In fact, I became so isolated that there came a time when inquiries were made by those same people as to whether I was even still alive.

I will say that if it hadn't been for the care of Albert and Mildred, I would have perished, for I thought nothing about the simplest need to feed myself. I most certainly would have starved to death lying in my bed, and I would not have even known.

Here also, in this gloomy world that was now my life, challenges were no longer met with any determination or a will to overcome them. I felt quite content to surrender whatever life remained within my broken heart and confused brain.

On the day of my birthday I received a post, and thinking it was just another well-meaning but empty birthday wish from someone who knew of the day, I cast it unopened next to me on the bed, closed my eyes, and tried to discover how to stop breathing.

Albert came to my side, interrupting my attempt. He noticed the card and encouraged me to open it, citing the reason that it might cheer me up even just a bit.

I argued against wasting the time, but Albert was a persistent man, and I picked it up and tore it open.

"Tell me, sir. Which of your exciting well-wishers is identified therein?"

I read the letter silently and wished I had not opened it.

It was from the law offices of the attorneys representing Jason O'Grady, the shipowner located in Charleston, South Carolina, informing me that the ANNABELLE LEE had reportedly gone down in a storm off the tip of South America, in the infamous and perilous Cape Horn area, presumably with all hands on board.

I let the letter slip from my hands and wept bitterly and openly, my head falling back onto my pillow.

I recall Albert picking up the letter and reading

it. I also remember the sorrowful expression building on his face as he read.

"Sir! I'm so very sorry," he finally said, the words barely forming in his mouth and only now trickling from his trembling lips.

"They're gone, Albert," I replied through my sobs. "All of them. My family is gone."

"Is there anything I can do for you?"

"No. There is nothing anyone can do for me. I'm now completely alone. I am a man now completely devoid of hope, lost forever in the mire of broken and torn dreams. My only wish now is to fall fast asleep and nevermore awaken."

My wife and child dying ten and a half months before still seemed like a recent event, and my adopted brothers now had also been taken from me. I found myself in the midst of such blackness that I thought I would never see the light of day ever again.

It took me a long while of sobbing and moping about before I could resume any activities that remotely approached normal.

Seven weeks more passed, and I had finally achieved enough inner healing that I had taken to nightly strolls, in the brisk night air, as a means to prepare myself for sleep, for, although most of the terror had passed, I was still having great difficulty falling asleep at night. The walks relaxed me, and after such I found that I was able to fall asleep soon after crawling into bed, although my sleep was still troubled.

On one particular evening, that being May 20, 1835, as I walked along my usual path, I heard noises that sounded like a scuffle or a brawl. I picked up my pace and soon came upon two men in the dim light of gas lamps.

An old man lay helpless upon the ground as I approached. The thief hovering above him wielded a large knife and was threatening the old man.

"What gives here?" I questioned angrily. "Cease and desist immediately, you barbarian."

The thief then turned the large blade toward me and grinned a nearly toothless grin.

"Give me your wallet as well."

"And why would I do that?"

"Blessed is the hand that giveth," he said, cackling, the few teeth remaining in his mouth black and rotted.

"Aye," said I in return. "And cursed is the hand that attempts to steal from good people! You pathetic dullard! I see what you are, and I call you out, you vile and worthless creature."

"I am that, sir, and more too. Still, give me your wallet."

"I will not, but endure this, foul one. May you never find peace, in this life or the next, for I believe that even God, if he exists at all, has no need for the likes of you. I beseech you, then, to do everyone on earth a favor and depart from this life as soon as you are able to do so, and more so, do it by your own hand. Perhaps in that act, you might still do some good for humanity."

My dissertation initially stunned him, but he was not the sort of person who would ever feel remorse for anything ill conceived or ill gotten. He would only try to take more from good people and give more pain to all if he were left able to do so.

Thus, he grew angry at my words and made a foolish lunge at me with his knife. I parried it with my cane easily enough and struck a hard blow to the right side of his head. He staggered, and I stepped forward with immense resolve and struck him once more. This time he went down and did not rise up again, instead remaining on the ground with a guttural moan emanating from his lips.

I heard the familiar shrill of the constable's whistle. Soon enough he was upon us, pistol drawn and a wary look in his eye. He spotted the cur upon the ground and immediately took him into custody while I helped the old man to his feet and dusted him off.

"Thank you, young man," the old man said.

"Think nothing of it, sir. I could do no less."

"You can do no more here either, lad. That is why you must return to your island."

I was taken aback at his words, for I did not

know this man. "How do you know of my island, sir?"

"You speak of it often enough, but it is now time that you return. You can do nothing more here. Heed my advice, young man, and return."

"How do *you* know what I speak of?"

"You already know the answer to that question."

"I do not, sir. Whatever do you mean?"

"Think on it hard. Think on it, and it shall manifest itself well in your head soon enough. Suffice it to say that you need to go back."

I cannot go back. I do not wish to see that place ever again."

"It is not your choice to make, Thomas. You are being beckoned back for good reason."

"Tell me, sir. How do you know my name, and tell me, what is the reason?"

"You already know the answer to both those questions as well. Do not delay, Thomas. Time is running out. Only precious little of it yet remains."

I gazed deeply into his eyes, and they suddenly looked familiar.

"Do I know you, sir?" I asked.

"Of course you do, you dolt. And well, too, although at times you try to deny it. Go soon, Thomas. The time is nigh."

His calling me a dolt startled me, but before I could ask him another question, the old man turned and walked away, never looking back.

I thought hard on his face for some time afterward. He had looked very familiar, but I could not place him among any remembrances.

My good deed for the day now well accomplished, I strolled home, considering what the old man had said. Upon reaching my porch, I sat down in the rocking chair to give extended thought to what had been told me over recent months. Somehow, I *was* being called back to the island.

It was the disconcerting voice in my own head, however, that plagued me most, for even after the several years now well behind me, I could still hear the island's voice, haunting me, taunting me, beckoning me back. Resist as I might, the whispering voice was ever present in the back of my brain, never quiet, never still.

At that moment I finally understood that the voice would continue forever if I did not yield to it. It would never release me from its persistent call. It would remain as a disturbance in my head, preventing me from succeeding at anything more.

That very evening, then, I began to give initial thought to yielding to that coaxing siren.

Later that night, in the hallowed silence of sleep, I was sharply awakened by a deafening scream. So loud was it that it fully awakened me out of a dead-like sleep. I leapt from my bed to search out the source of such a horrible shriek. I looked out my window and could clearly see that the streets were empty. I walked through my home seeking a possible intruder, but found none.

The terrible screech sounded once again, this time as two different voices. So shrill were the voices that I was forced to cover my ears. Panic began to set in, for the shouts seemed so mournful and torturously painful. And then there were many more voices, howling as one.

I ran around the house seeking who it might be. There was not a soul anywhere.

I heard the shouts again, and this time I surely recognized the source. They were all within my own head. Then the wailings began, so woeful and so wretched that they made me ill. Nausea filled the pit of my stomach. I gagged impulsively.

"What do you want?" I said, pleading my question. "Why do you torment me so?"

No answer. Just continued bellowing.

I staggered back to my room and collapsed upon my bed. The wailing would not subside, but continued in ever-stronger intensity. I clutched at my head, trying to cover my ears, but it was to no avail. The voices grew louder and more insistent.

"What?!" I shrieked.

It was then that I heard the island's voice. It rose above the clamor, and this time it was no whisper. It was a deep old voice, rich in resonance and tone. "Come home," it said clearly.

"I'm afraid," I answered.

"Come home, Thomas," it beckoned once again.

"Please," I begged. "Molest me no more! You are *not* my home."

"Come back, Thomas. This is where you belong."

"Quiet!" I finally shouted in earnest.

All the voices ceased instantly. I waited a moment, and when they did not return, I unshielded my ears.

The house was still once more.

I lay upon my bed, troubled and unable to fall back to sleep. My head, although now silent within, throbbed. I finally yielded to my better sense and arose from the bed and went to the kitchen. I prepared some tea and sat in the parlor, choosing consciously not to light the lamps. I preferred to sit alone in the blackness of early morning and in the darkness of my own mind.

What was it about that damnable island that beckoned me so? Why, now more than four years past, did I yet feel so connected to that island? It was as if it were still trying to protect me, keep me hidden and safe from the world outside, as if it knew that I was not meant to live here in this great city, and trying to shield me against all the things that I was now battling against.

I thought of Gretchen and my child, both now fully given over to time but still often felt wandering within some secret part of my consciousness. I was again alone, not on an island this time but within the heart of the great city in which I had been raised.

If the island was not home, so, neither, was the city. I was orphaned from life itself, it seemed, not belonging in either world, neither there nor here. But when conscious thought was present, it did feel as if I had been more at home on the island. My needs there were simple. My life there was simple. The island had plentifully provided all that I needed...though it could provide me with nothing that I *wanted*. Here in this city, contrarily, I had been provided with most everything I'd wanted, but nothing that I needed. At least nothing that I truly needed.

Then I thought of just what it was that I wanted. I did not want to be so alone. I did not want to be so adverse to the world. I wanted peace, serenity, and harmony with all things and all people. Was I to find it here? The answer came upon me boldly: NO. I had not found any *real* peace or harmony since my return. My parents had died, my friends had all moved away, my wife and child were taken from me. And if that weren't enough for one man to endure, my adopted brothers had all perished. I lived utterly alone once again, and forevermore, it would seem.

So if peace and serenity were what I was searching for, I had certainly not found them here. Where, then, would such a search lead me? Where *would* peace and serenity be found? Where *could* they be found, if it were even possible?

Questions such as these plagued me through those wee hours of the dark morning, but in the stillness and darkness, no answers found their way into my mind.

Often enough that morning, my eyes would weep as an unexplained sadness suddenly swept over me. I knew it was precipitated by those empty, unanswered questions and mournful thoughts, but it seemed deeper than that. It was wretched sadness that was growing inside me, an overwhelming sense of all things forever lost to me.

A sudden realization then confronted me with clarity: I would not ever succeed at anything here in this city, or in this country, for that matter. This was not home, and it never had been. My life, in fact, was back on that island. Magic was there. Happiness was there. My *future* was there. I was not meant to return to my homeland. I was not meant to be rescued, and yet here I was.

I then remembered my manuscript tucked away up in the attic in the old chest. I heard it calling to me now, its needful bellowing, its deep yearning to become once more intrinsic to my life. I bounded up the stairs to the attic, to the chest, and thrust open the top. There inside, just as it had been laid there long ago, was my unfinished manuscript staring back at me.

I lifted it out of the chest and hauled it back down the stairs to my parlor. There, after lighting several candles, I began to read. Perhaps, I reasoned by way of some hopeful wish, some of my answers might lie within those scribbled pages.

Then I heard their voice. "Hearken unto me," they cried. "Your destiny lies within. Forsake us no more. For your sake, continue your writing. Give voice to your heart. Give us the blood of ink to sustain us. Give life to these pages."

I spent the next several hours reading all that I had written. It was a magnificent story about a simple man, living simply. And yet within the words lurked a much deeper man, a man of worth, a man of spirit, a man of determined will.

Turning the pages was like watching the passing of a grand event right before my eyes. The story was about me, about my life, but a life so unlike the one I lived now. This storybook life was a happy one. And yes, I saw the boredom as well in those pages, but I had my family then, we were together. And that alone was justification enough for me to consider returning to the island.

I must admit that the thought of what the island was capable of urged me forward. If I returned, I wondered, could the island bring back to life my family? *For that matter, might they even be waiting for me now?*

A resurgent feeling of hope again floated in my heart, causing it to flutter excitedly.

The old man was right; I could do no more here. I needed to return home, home to my island.

I stunned myself with the new thought that I

had finally placed the face of the old man. It was *my* face, the face of my older self. It was I, myself, urging me to return. I figured it all out in a flash of crystal-like clarity. It was my older, wiser self who urged me to go back to the island, and it all made sense. I would not have listened to a younger me. No, I had to come as an older and wiser man. And why not, I thought. If my daughter could come to me before she was even born, then would it not be possible for me to come to myself as an old man?

My heart leapt for joy within my chest. "Yes!" I declared aloud. "I am going home where I belong."

Just then Albert appeared in my chambers. I think he was surprised to see my smiling face looking back at him.

"Are you well, sir?"

"I am," I sparkled. "I am returning to the island, Albert. It is where all things will rectify themselves. It is where I shall find all the answers to all my questions. It is where my family awaits for my return. I am going home!"

I rushed to Albert and hugged him tightly.

"I am well, Albert. I'm better than well. I'm alive and filled with joy again."

Poor Albert did not know how to respond to my unbounded joy and stood unmoving as I hugged him tightly. I released him and began dancing around the room in unrestrained glee.

"Very good, sir." He stared at me, holding a lighted candlestick as I skipped lightly around the room.

I'm quite certain that he thought me finally descended into the abyss of total and forever madness, a man who had slid away down the slippery slope into some darkened place where no one could follow to rescue him.

I wanted to reassure him that I was again my happy, normal self, yet with so much joy bubbling forth from my lightened spirit in the form of a childlike dance, I had no way to assure him that I was not a madman, but only completing my journey back into the light of clarity and awareness. I had to keep moving or I felt I would simply explode from the joy of it all.

On June 10, 1835, precisely four years, nine months, and twenty-six days since I had left McShane Island, I was headed back, with the full expectation of reuniting with my family on that loving and magical rock—a paradise for those precious few harboring a sorely wounded heart who happened to find it.

I had closed up the house and left it to the attorneys to sell for me. I bid a fond good-bye to Albert and Mildred, and left them with a substantial severance that would keep them well enough for some time. Since there were only a very few business acquaintances and neighbors to say fare thee well to, it was a simple task, quickly completed.

Thus, on that glorious Wednesday morning, with a yellow sun shining brightly in the cloudless sky, a glad heart beating rhythmically within my emboldened chest, and a broad smile across my face, I left New York Harbor behind once again, this time on the good ship the NEW YORK MASTER, a very fine merchant vessel, for the port city of Papeete, Otaheite. Once there, I would make arrangements with the captain of some other vessel to deliver me to my island, to which I retained the compass directions, having obtained their reciprocals from the navigator on the ANNABELLE LEE.

During the voyage, which was planned to last some four and a half months, there was nothing for me to do, having paid in full my passage fare. I spent many hours each day writing in my journal, updating it, and with so much to write about, it demanded much of my attention throughout my journey.

Still, being a man given strongly to business endeavors, I could not resist making my talents known to the captain, a wonderful man whose name was Richard Wilson, and he was only too happy to utilize them to his advantage at each and every port we sailed into.

He was also a very appreciative and generous man, and by the time we came into the docks at Papeete, after a rather calm and uneventful journey, I held a substantial sum in my purse.

Captain Wilson and I parted as good friends, and I immediately made inquiries as to a capable captain to take me back to my island.

With gold coin aplenty jingling in my purse, it did not take me long to find such a captain. A gracious and tall man, Captain Willoughby McGuire, undertook the task to follow my navigational directions and return me to my island.

Thus, on the morning of October 21, 1835, we departed Papeete on the last leg of my journey home. The weather was fair, the winds most accommodating. I was told that we should expect to make landfall within thirty-six hours if my directions were accurate. I assured both the captain and the helmsman that they were, and I prepared myself mentally, emotionally, and spiritually to be greeted with warm and loving smiles when my foot struck upon the home sands once again.

I tried to continue my journal entries along the way, but my mind raced with visions of my triumphant return. So many and vivid were my imaginings that I found it impossible to form a sufficiently coherent thought to record. Thus, during the last few hours of the voyage, I abandoned all effort to write and chose, instead, to stand at the bow to bear witness to the first glimpse of my island arising from the undulating sea.

As is usually the case, it was a young seaman sitting atop the ship in the crow's nest who first spotted land.

I heard his call and strained my eyes to see the bit of black rising up, but I could not see it. I knew that his greater height gave him an advantage that I did not possess, but still I could not turn my eyes from such a quest even if I had wanted to.

It was several frantic minutes before I spotted the tiny speck of black. The ship bobbed about so in the swells that its moving up and down made the island difficult to see.

Since I had turned away before I could see the island disappear into the sea on my journey away, I could not know what it looked like as we approached.

I pushed my eyes to see the familiar summit of the extinct volcano, and it was with wondrous joy that I finally confirmed vision of it.

Slowly, upon our approach, it grew larger, and I began to recognize the other outlines of the island. My heart surged with excitement.

It was three hours before we finally dropped anchor and launched the small skiff. The seamen had loaded the chest containing my manuscript and my other chests, filled with several changes of clothing, several pairs of shoes, many more candles, and other things I determined I would need eventually.

I had expected my family to be waiting on the shoreline for me, having seen the approach of the ship, but not one was there. I then realized that they might be currently on the other side of the island and had not seen the ship's approach, and I grew very excited anticipating their delighted expressions when I walked up and surprised them. I could almost imagine their elation and their welcoming grins and shouts.

Before long, the skiff's bow ground to a halt into the sand. Thus, on October 22nd, my foot settled onto my shoreline for the first time in almost five years. The moment I stepped once again onto the sand, I swore I heard the joyful sigh of the island—her first son had finally returned home, where he belonged.

Chapter 17

Once ashore, the crew moved my chests to the sand well above the high-water line.

"Where are the others you mentioned, sir?" asked the young seaman.

"They're probably enjoying the day on the other side of the island and did not see us approach. Fear not, I shall fetch them later."

"Aye, sir. Do you want us to take the chest to your campsite?"

"No, good fellows. I and the others shall move them later. It was good of you to row me ashore. Please give my best to your captain. And, as arranged, I shall see you in about two months, then."

"It would seem so, sir."

"The captain has the list of supplies I'll be needing. I look forward to your meeting my family upon your return."

"As do we, sir. Good day to you, then."

"Good day, lads. Be safe upon the sea."

"Thank you, sir. Be safe and live well upon your island, Mr. Cantfield."

One seaman climbed into the launch and readied the oars as the other pushed the bow back into the water and then leapt aboard. I waved to the captain back on the ship. I saw his return wave, and then I turned inland.

So excited was I that a slow stroll up the beach turned into a dash to the trail and up to the campsite. As I suspected, the campsite showed definite signs of recent occupancy. The embers of a morning fire glowed in the usual place. There, strewn about, were wooden plates filled with fresh and partially eaten mango and papaya.

I called out but received no response. Yes. They are either on the far side of the island or at the spring falls and unable to hear my calls, I assumed.

I decided to surprise them, so I dashed first for the falls. As I drew nearer, I heard the falling water as always, but upon reaching the spring I saw no one.

Then surely they must have taken a midday stroll to the other side of the island as I first suspected, I then reasoned. I decided to surprise them there.

I ran like the wind down and up the path toward the north side, in excitement to see their surprised expressions. Along the way, I imagined Charlie's silly face squeezed into some odd expression, ready to make a joke.

It was Gretchen's face that I saw before me most, though. What would she do when she saw me sprinting toward her? Would she just stand there waiting for me to run to her and take her up in my arms? Would she run to greet me? I had no idea what to expect, and in that did I tingle full of anticipation.

I bounded down the trail at full speed and went thundering through the underbrush out onto the beach. Looking left, then right, I expected to see them. There was no one except me, and I was very confused as I retraced my steps.

Arriving back in camp, I was perplexed as to where my family could be. Then it dawned on me. They were hiding from me, watching me make a fool of myself tearing about the island like a crazed buffoon.

"The cave!" I said aloud.

I ran through the camp, through the thicket, and into the cave. I was alone, yet on the table sat a nearly used-up candle. Also upon the table sat a piece of parchment, placed as if someone had been writing on it only moments before my arrival.

How odd, I thought.

Then my heart sank into my belly as I noticed my chest, opened full, my manuscript sitting in the bottom of it as was usual when I lived on the island.

Recovering from the shock, it dawned on me that they must have gone to the beach while I was on the far side of the island and hoisted it up to the cave for me. The sneaky little devils, I thought. They were probably down there now, retrieving the other chests.

I turned and raced down the path toward the landing spot. My feet, feeling more like wings, carried me down the path with the exacting speed of a racehorse, and yet, when I reached the spot, they were not there. All my chests were absent also. The only tracks in the sand appeared to be mine alone.

I looked about me and saw the rotted wood of the signal fire, untouched by any flame but well touched by the ravages of time.

As I gazed out toward where the ship had been, I saw nothing there either. If there was a ship, surely it would still be highly visible and not yet a far way off even if it were under full sail. There was no ship, however. And, clearly, there had never been a ship.

It was then, in that very moment, that all truth spilled out before me onto the shoreline. I fell onto my behind into the sand, my legs buckling under my weight, unable to stand any longer. Tears welled up in my eyes, and my heart beat irregularly.

Glancing down, I then saw my hands, old and wrinkled, weathered from the elements as an old man's would be. I reached up and touched my face. It, too, was wrinkled and heavily weathered.

When full truth strikes you, you will find that it comes often as both a surprise and a shock, as a sharp smack across the face. Yet, when *reality* strikes, it most often sends you completely off your feet.

And here was I, an old man on his buttocks in the sand, overwhelmed completely with the realization that I had never left the island. I had grown old here and was only now coming to both the knowledge and the truth of the matter.

I arose from the sand and walked slowly up the path toward my cave.

Upon reaching my camp clearing, another shock stilled my heart for a moment. Dangling from the wooden poles were three rotted grass figures, now torn apart. One, Charlie's, even contained a bird's nest where the heart should be. I think Charlie would have thought that an uproarious sight. Still, in all, they lacked the definition of being anything humanlike, being just dried, twisted twigs and brown grass. Even the poles themselves had begun to rot and separate.

Obviously, the uneaten fruit on the wooden plates was mine. I, alone, had started the fire. The page of parchment sitting on the table in the cave had been placed there by me, most probably at a much earlier moment, although I had no idea when.

I wondered how much time had passed. The journal page on the desk had a light layer of dust covering it; obviously, it had lain untouched for a while. From the words written upon the page, it had last been touched by quill on March 30, 1879. A peek into the chest revealed several written journal pages, most of them mundane ramblings of even less important happenings. From their contents, it appeared that nothing of any great interest had occurred on the island in many, many years.

I was able to find interesting "chapters" of my life after being "rescued." And it seems that over the last year I had been consolidating them into some kind of book format.

As I read, it was now becoming further apparent to me that all semblance of sanity had left me long ago, long before the day I was "rescued," only to return to me now. I had no idea what day it was, nor what year, nor even what decade, but from the looks of the parts of my body I could see, the passing years had been many. Indeed, it seemed that several decades had passed without notice by my sane mind.

I understood, finally, that there had never been a family, no ANNABELLE LEE, no returning home, no life away from this island. In all the time that I had lived here, I had been completely alone and most surely forgotten by all of mankind.

A new thought then drifted through my mind. I turned and walked the long path down to the other side of the island. Once there, I looked for the gravesites and easily found them. The markers had been tipped over and lain untouched for what must have been years.

Perhaps the murder of those two lost souls had actually taken place, I pondered. Perhaps that event was the sole reality of any visits I'd had during my time here.

Dropping to my knees and plunging my hands into the sand a little ways, I found only a rotted and dried coconut gourd, which I assumed at the time, in my diminished mind, would have easily passed for a decapitated head. I dug a bit more in each grave and realized that the graves contained no bodies at all. It was just through a deteriorated mind that I had seen the battle and the murder of both men. In my delirium, I had prepared the graves, placing the headstones so as to accommodate a false purpose, only to knock the markers over later.

I stood up and in anger kicked at the sand. I left

the markers where they lay, seeing no reason to raise them up and give further evidence to my former insanity.

Then, to my heart's total destruction, I also realized that there had been no Gretchen either. She also was only another figment created from a saddened and lonely heart, a scantily remembered vision from days long ago that I had created in my sick brain, a cry from a desperate soul in response to a wish to not be alone in this world. My world. The world of a small and isolated island, lost somewhere amongst the waves of a great ocean.

"Dear God," I bellowed loudly, still standing before the fraudulent graves, "how did I exist this long alone and in such a diminished state?"

It seemed the first time that I had spoken His name in many, many years. But if He did exist at all, then He had proven himself to be a hateful creature, for He had allowed me to live in the depths of a lie for all these years, misplaced in my own sick and empty mind. If He had been a god of love and compassion, I would have died long ago and been spared this unholy awakening. "Damn you!" I screamed aloud. "Curse you, you wicked and foul creature, you heartless cur. Why did you let me live? Why are you so cruel? Was I so foul a soul to deserve this necessary end? I shout to you! Hear me! No crime committed deserves this fate, you accursed being!"

After a bit more cursing and shouting, I surrendered my anguish and anger to a more pensive state. What a fool I had become, shouting out to a non-existent deity, or to one who had no wish to hear me, or worse, to one who heard but cared nothing about my troubles and woes. To me, in my cursed state, it was all the same.

A few minutes later, I finally settled down, dropping back into the sand upon my rickety knees, realizing now that it had nothing to do with any god at all.

The island had called me back to clarity. Or, to be boldly honest, I had called myself back to clarity. It was within my own mind that I had suffered the losses, heard the shouts, and experienced the beckonings. But why? Why had I reached out from a diseased and fragile mind? What had been the point of doing so? I was happy there, in that land of insanity, that land of unbridled fantasy, at least for a while anyway. And now, if I was sane again, what would I do for the rest of my life—my now sane but pitifully lonely life?

For days after my appalling return, I tried to make sense of it all. Why had I chosen to return to this beleaguered and bewildering life at all? Why, when I was so blissfully unaware, did I choose this life over no life at all? A better question then rose above all the others. If indeed the island had called me back, what was her reason for doing so? What sinister secret did she have yet to reveal unto me?

I should make it clear that I harbored no ill will against my wonderful island. In fact, I still have only sweet blessings for her, for she had cared well for me all these years, always providing enough to eat and to drink, and protection enough whenever I had presumably needed it. She had taken me deep into her bosom with all compassion. She had been like a mother to me, cradling me in her gentle arms, always there when I was in need.

The sinister nature of the secret yet to be uncovered was not of the island's creation. Nay, it hailed from the darker side, the unseen thing that lurked about, seeking whom it could destroy just for the sake of destruction. The island had tried her best to protect me from such evil. And she had done so for many years, it seemed, but alas, I knew well enough that even *she* could not sustain me forever.

And it was then I felt that she was preparing to surrender me to whatever lies beyond life. She had done me very well, my gentle and loving island, and when the day comes that she finally gives me up, I am resolved to speak well of her in the great beyond to whomever will listen.

On day ten since my awakening, I began writing into my journal again, reorganizing my thoughts and tales into what you see now. I also began truly counting the days once more, from a sane perspective this time. I did so if for no other reason than perhaps a small bit of an accountant yet remained somewhere within these ancient bones even after all these years.

From my reflection in the spring water, I guessed that I was eighty years old, or very near to it. If that was so, then I had lived alone on this island for almost fifty years. In all likelihood, I had lived most of those years completely deranged, the obvious result of a painfully desperate loneliness, one which I apparently could not bear.

I can only guess that it must have been a strong, instinctive will to survive that had caused me to fill my belly and quench my thirst each and every day. And in that there existed a healthy menagerie of edible fowl, I guessed that I had eaten well over all those years.

From my surroundings it would appear that my imagination had utilized small bits of reality to create a plausible framework for my make-believe world. For the areas that lacked reality, it seemed that my mind, through my apparently adequate memories, was able to fabricate a sufficient world in which I could live in some blissful form. Thus, it seems that the incredible creative nature of the human mind was in full bloom for many years. I marvel still at the strength of the brain's creative power when such force is so desperately required.

I came to understand also why it was that I had called

myself back to reality. I needed to return so that I might prepare myself to leave this world with some measure of dignity. I felt odd within. It was like a great clock winding down while still needing to count each second, or a traveler reaching the end of some fantastic journey, yet still full of wanderlust.

As I sat at my desk on one fine day, contemplating the end of my journal and thus the end of my life as I saw it approaching, I was seized by an illuminating thought.

I don't think anyone can say when the last entry of a life can be securely recorded into his or her own journal with any degree of accuracy, for none of us, of course, know when the end moment will arrive. I think it is important, therefore, to faithfully record all of which you are able, up to the last moment that can be reasonably achieved given the limitations of a dwindling life. Knowing, then, that the moment of our end is hidden from us, we may not ever achieve the point of effectively writing the last word that will suitably define our selves or our lives.

I wonder this instead: if it could be accomplished, what would be *your* last written words in the book of your life? Think carefully on this before you answer, just as I have over these last few days.

In reaching my own conclusions regarding my life, I would hope that such words would include a grateful recognition of all the good things that have happened to me during my inestimable journey. I would also hope that I am able to describe in an effective manner the truthful illumination of my own mind and spirit, and that there be contained within the pages that is the book of my life no lies or embellishments. I would rather it be an honest assessment of what and who I was, even if it turns out to be an inglorious life.

Through the illumination of truth, I hope that I, in the end and to all who might one day read my account, find the justification for my having lived a life that was worthy of all the good fortune that befell me either by heaven or by chance.

In any event, I hope that the question of whether or not I deserved any of it, good or bad, can be finally answered with certainty, for it is doubt that I fear most. To leave this life with any doubt as to whether my contributions or accomplishments were justified would be a tragic legacy for one who had tried his best to complete this journey with some measure of both integrity and honesty.

And speaking of illumination, what a wonderful, inspiring word it is. Outwardly, to me and most likely also to the world outside, it is defined as an observable property of light, or an effect of light, but inwardly, deep within my heart, I know it to be the clarity of truth—the illumination of both my heart and my soul to all that has ever happened.

To that end, I heard it said once that "*a wise man receives in joy all that ever befalls him, for it is only unto a man alive that these things happen—the well or ill of it being relative to the experience.*"

After I had heard this said, I remembered at the time finding myself in sharp dispute with its philosophy. Reflecting upon it of late, however, I have now come to consider it to be wise counsel, for it is a person full of wisdom who is able to look upon any situation and see some good in it and, in some form, to learn from it.

As for the dead, they learn nothing.

Upon even further reflection, I have found that a lesson can be learned from any happening only if the observer is of a truthful and congenial spirit, and of a mind open to such possibility.

Is the good or bad of anything merely relative to the experience of it, as has been suggested? Perhaps. But I have come to believe that along one's journey, two real questions will necessarily arise which will demand honest answers: How is it that we determine the truthful nature of anything? And by what standard of measure do we make such determinations?

If we cut our hand on a blade, it hurts, and the blade has proven itself to be an injurious instrument. We are then confronted to decide if it is either of an evil creation or of a benevolent creation. Based on the blood and pain in our hand at the time, we might conclude it to be of an evil nature—a cursed thing.

However, later, having then a need to slice a rope binding the hands of an innocent person, we recall the blade and use it to achieve that person's freedom. Is the nature of the blade now changed to one of benevolence and, if so, is it then considered a blessing instead of a curse? To the one who was bound and is now free because of it, might it not be considered a good creation—a blessed object?

So what, then, is the blade's fixed and true nature? For that matter, does it even have a fixed and true nature, or is it a relative and evolving nature that is ever changing?

So now you can see my dilemma. Was being a castaway a good thing or an evil thing?

One could argue that it was an evil thing, for during my time away, my parents had surely succumbed to the horror and stress of my loss and had passed on without ever knowing my fate. My friends had surely forgotten about me over time and had moved on, with no more thoughts of me or my outcome.

Another could conclude, conversely, that my situation was a blessing, for I had discovered, solely in my head, of course, good friends and a beautiful wife to love and care for me, and I suffered no economic catastrophe for all these years.

So, then, what is the true nature of my circumstance?

Because I am not a man constricted by religious doctrine, and free to ride on whatever thought I may choose to think at any given time, I submit that, like the blade, each event in my life represented an opportunity. I alone, by conscious choice, accepted it for well or ill and thereby defined its nature.

I had not intended to drag you through such a dissertation, but such thoughts have occupied my mind of late. Further, I do not wish to force you to any conclusion. I wish only to present an opportunity for you to define your own true nature. I ask you only to observe what surrounds you and determine for yourself what is true and what is not true, what is good and what is not good, what is a blessing and what is not a blessing.

As for me, however, it was just a series of thoughts that shot through my mind one recent day as I lazily sat at my desk in this darkened, cool cave, considering the true nature of my limited perspective. And in this, I cannot say that I came to any glorified conclusion as to what it all means.

But if I were hard pressed to put forth my own theory as to the true meaning of all this wild thing we call life, it would be this: life is a journey that must be taken alone. Certainly, along the way, you may be accompanied by someone who might be a mate or a friend, but only so far as they wish to travel alongside you and only so long as their path remains parallel with your own. Ultimately, though, each must decide his own direction, and it is a discovery to be realized only by each of us alone.

I urge you, take from the journey together what you can. Take from your travel companion what you are able. Take from this journal what you wish, or dismiss parts of it as mindless drivel, or, still, discard it entirely as a completely unsupported fabrication without any merit at all.

In the end, however, you will be left with the task of finding the true nature of everything, for yourself, on your own. And what you allow to be manifested within your own heart as truth will determine what is the honest conclusion for yourself. I can only wish for you that your discovery comes more easily than did mine.

For the sake of argument, then, allow me to consider all that has ever befallen me as *blessings*, defined herein as occurrences being particularly endowed with exceptional good fortune, and leave it at that.

During the reconstruction and cataloguing of my life over the past several days, it has become overwhelmingly apparent to me just how many blessings befall me still. I believe that if you give the matter sufficient thought, you might find that it is the same for you as well, and yet it is amazing to me how such blessings are so easily overlooked or dismissed with callous indifference so soon after their arrival.

Perhaps, I believe, we receive so many blessings so often that they are seen as normal occurrences instead of the little miracles they actually are. Perhaps it is blessings and not curses which predominate the universe. Perhaps this is why, when we are suddenly struck by devastating occurrences in our lives, they are so traumatic and difficult for us to accept.

As I have apparently reflected over the last several years through this journal, it seems that even I have not remained immune to such capriciousness or cavalierism when it comes to my own daily expectations of blessings.

As castaways go, it seems my ordeal was not as interesting as most. There were, however, some noteworthy moments that were mildly enchanting.

It is for this reason, then, that I urge you to seize not upon the things of a dastardly nature, for they have no good measure with which to sustain you. Instead, set your hand firmly upon the things of a good and kindly disposition, for they are capable of lifting you up on high and sustaining you forever.

And when you reflect upon your deeds of the past, I urge you, call not to remembrance those things of a reprehensible character, for there is no warmth in them, nothing upon which you can rely. They are only memories likened more to dust in the air, choking you and causing you great discomfort. Expel them from your being and consider them no more.

Chapter 18

From the evidence of the journal pages, I realized that complacency had finally won out over reason. I noted that after a time, I had settled into a mode where I wrote in the journal only one chapter a year, on my birthday. I had picked that date for no other reason, apparently, than to confirm once a year that I still lived.

Once a year, thought gave way to deed. And for the last forty-nine years, I had but one event to look forward to, it seems: sitting down at my desk and scribbling another chapter on my birthday, a reprieve, if you will—a one-year extension of my life as such it was.

It was not that I lacked suitable visions and good stories throughout the year. It was that I had only so much parchment and ink, so that conservation became a necessity for me. During the year I fabricated my plots, playing them out every day until each moment, well rehearsed, was clearly set into my brain, absent any wasted words or actions. Rewriting any portion was out of the question because I simply lacked the necessary materials. Thus on each birthday, I would take the day and scribble the chapter out and then begin to invent the next.

I had nothing else to do.

Other than falling into debilitating despondency

and seeking new ways to end my miserable life, writing my annual chapter was something to occupy my mind. Having surrendered long before to the realization that I lacked the courage to take my own life, I was left with finding new ways to come to terms with my isolation. After fifty years, I had explored all possible methods. Some even multiple times. So, here I had existed for all this time, alone and empty of all hope that I would someday see my rescue ship on the horizon. My imagination, however, would take control and not allow me to descend into self-destructive behavior. It built a world for me to live in, a world that made some sense to my beleaguered mind, a world into which I could exist for a time, at least, with some measure of joy.

Now, nearly eighty years old, I feel the life within me dwindling toward its end. I have only ten pieces of parchment left and this quarter cup of ink. I am using my twenty-second quill to write these words. To my relief, I do not believe that I shall last long enough to need a new pen.

Of late, I have turned more introspective, thinking about all the things that could have been but could never be, the secret thoughts I could not tell anyone, not because of their surreptitious nature but simply because there was no one around to hear them spoken.

Having now read each page of my journal, I clearly understand the results of the ravaging disease that plagues the mind when it finds itself in the depths of despair and loneliness. I also understand to what lows a normal man sinks when he is confronted with hopelessness. Still, it seems to me that inventing grass friends in order to keep some grasp on reality is the act of one desperate to remain sane.

If this thought is so, then could it also be a shout into the universe of my desperate desire to live? I feel, at this moment, that I have just returned from my descent into the depths of insanity, climbing out of the pit, as it were.

After further consideration, I have determined that it is either that, or I am still somewhere inside myself battling for life. At this time I cannot say which it is.

While on the island, life itself, nourishing my physical body, has been neither a battle nor even a brawl. Maintaining some semblance of sanity, on the other hand, appears to have been much more of a challenge over the years—a challenge in which the outcome, I fear, is still very much in doubt.

Whether I have been sane or insane, it is clear that I have journeyed far beyond my restrictive island. Another question arises. Was it in spirit that I traveled or just in mind? That, also, I cannot at present answer with any degree of knowing, for I am not even certain that I live at all. For all I know, I died decades ago and it is only my spirit, bound to this earth for some ungodly reason, which walks the island now.

Being unsure of whether or not I have expired, I am necessarily and thoroughly confused, for I feel the sand between my toes on the beach. I feel the breath of the wind against my skin. I feel the warmth of the sun against my face. It all seems quite real to me; but in this very moment that I believe it all to be true, I find myself wondering if it is only the memory of those things that gives me such physical sensations. And what of my time off the island? Did I not feel that also? And then I am confronted by the thought that what I feel might not even be a physical sensation at all, but the mental recollection of what those feelings were once like long ago, when my physical form walked the island.

How strange it is to wonder if I am alive or dead. I think that such wondering can usually be confirmed by the actions of others. Their touch, the sound of their voices, the vision of their physical being would seem to be a most logical and ample justification that one also exists.

On this I have reconsidered the title of my book yet again. "The Wondrous Journey of a Long-Ago Man" seems more apropos at this moment, for I have indeed been on a journey. I will never be certain of the form or manner of such a journey, but it was a journey worth it all in any regard, for if I have been forced to remain here physically, my mind was allowed to travel freely, and perhaps my spirit also. That, given what it is, in the final analysis, will necessarily have to be enough.

This morning, it being the twenty-first day since my awakening, I have experienced the awful terror of loneliness set in hard upon me once more. I have tried to rationalize my circumstance, but it seems that my mind cannot handle my isolation. I understand fully now why it moved to create such a fantastical life. I only hope that I can bear up until my end, which I feel is rapidly approaching.

Waking early this morning as I did, I felt the morning sunlight warming my face as my tired eyes opened slowly. I smelled the fire and heard a scratching sound off to my right. I squinted in the bright sunlight, and there was Matthew performing his usual chore of scrubbing clean the flat rock in the middle of the fire in preparation of cracking eggs for our morning feast.

"Dear me," I said, "what a strange dream I had last night."

"Tell me of it, lad," he responded in his usual calm demeanor.

"It was so frightfully odd. I dreamed that you all were only figments of my deluded imagination."

"Again. Thomas, my boy, what is going on in that head of yours?"

I arose and walked past Matthew and sat down, placing my back against the log as usual. "I do not know. Perhaps I ate something that did not agree with me."

Matthew smiled. "We come and we go in your head, Thomas. Make up your mind, dear boy."

I laughed. "Where's Gretchen?"

"She is washing up down at the spring with the others. Perhaps you should join them. You look a mess."

I rose up and walked down the path to the spring. As I neared, I heard the familiar sounds of frivolity. The boys were even making a sport out of cleaning themselves, but they seemed well able to make sport out of most everything.

I rounded the bend in the path and there, as I suspected, was Gretchen, sitting on her favorite rock, gleefully watching the others splashing and making merriment as usual.

When she saw me approach, she smiled broadly and jumped to her feet and ran to hug me.

"Good morning, my love. Did you sleep well?"

"I had that dream again, the one in which you are all not real. Very disturbing."

"What am I going to do with you, husband? You have the oddest dreams."

Splashing off to my right caught my attention. "Look at Annabelle," I said. "I think she's getting the best of Charlie."

Annabelle laughed as she splashed Charlie directly in his face. Charlie then dove for her but missed and sank out of sight, only to arise with a great roar, frightening Annabelle, who dashed for the shore but laughed heartily as she did so.

"I never tire of their merriment," I said softly, still holding Gretchen tightly to my chest.

"I also, my dear. Are you going to clean up?"

"Apparently I need to, according to Matthew."

"He is correct," she replied with her own smile.

I released her and strode to the shore of the spring and stared down into the water. With relief, my young face stared back up at me. I dipped my hands into the water and brought a handful up to my face. "In this dream," I announced, "I was almost eighty years old."

Gretchen laughed. "With your imagination, Thomas, I have no doubt of that."

Just then my brothers all noticed me and called out their morning greetings to me. I waved back.

It was so good to be fully awake now, having put that awful dream to an end. How could I invent a make-believe family, I wondered. Whatever was going on inside my head, I resolved not to give it any more thought, if I was able.

After breakfast, Gretchen, Annabelle, and I took our normal walk along the path. I was informed that Annabelle's eighth birthday was only two days away. It was Annabelle, of course, who reminded me. She was exacting about those things.

"After our walk, my dear," said Gretchen, "I think you should spend some time updating your journal. You are falling a bit behind."

"Yes, yes, you slave driver," I joked, "I shall work on it all day if it pleases you."

"It would."

I chuckled, for of late it was Gretchen who insisted that I work on my journal, consolidating much of what I had written over time. I don't know why she was pushing so hard, but I learned that with her, there was always a good reason for it. Therefore, I yielded each time and complied without argument.

I have given much thought to the real potential that we may never be rescued. In thinking it through, I have concluded that our life here was for all good fortune, but neither having the way nor the freedom to live life any other way, it mattered not in the end. Here was I, contented and surrounded by such love and caring, the thought of being rescued seemed almost frightening to me. With such an easy and wonderful life here with my family, how could a life away from this island be any better. In fact, the horrible thought came to me that it could perhaps be so much worse if we ever were to leave.

A singular point does press me to speak out. One day, you will find our bones here somewhere on this island, for I am rudely aware that we are not immortal. But being sure that we will each expire in our own way and in our own time, it is sufficient to admit that at some time in the future, you, dear reader, will stumble upon this journal and take it up to read about our life here.

You will, no doubt, read about my desires to visit other places on this earth that I will most likely never visit. In this vein, then, I have only one request of you. I beseech you to become more than just a reader of these events. Become more than just an observer of this life.

I ask you now, dear one, to become the *writer*. Just one new chapter a year will be sufficient to keep me young and able to travel. Become the writer and take me with you that I may live just a bit longer. I do not wish for my story to end here in this manner—forgotten and alone on this island, never to see the wondrous sights yet to be seen through your eyes.

I want to travel. I want to travel the world with you and to greet all the glorious and inglorious people that you have yet to meet. I want to stand by your side and stare at the world's great works of art. I want to read over your shoulder the greatest books in all of literature. I want to stand with you when you visit the grand and artful buildings of the greatest architects. And yes, I even want to travel to the stars with you, if that is ever possible. And beyond, if you are willing to make it so. Together, with your kind indulgence, we could go onward to other amazing adventures that even my mind cannot yet comprehend or conceive.

Take me with you, therefore, this long-ago man, for your sake. Take me with you so that *you* should never feel alone or forgotten. I encourage you to do this, dear friend, with all my heart, my soul, and my good intent. Take me with you as you leave this island that I could not leave. Take me with you from this pitiful speck of rock which has held both my soul and my body in kindness, yet without mercy, these long years, to somewhere far beyond these wretched shores, for I, dear soul, in now such a sorry state yet still full of wanderlust, am no longer able to do it alone.

"Lay your pen down, my love," said Gretchen. "Lay your head down upon the table and close your eyes to sleep."

"But why, my dear? Should I not retire to my bed to sleep?"

"Here, Thomas. Rest your head here. When you open your eyes next, it will be a glorious new day."

"Father," said Annabelle, "Mother is right. Rest your head here on the table. Mother and I shall remain here with you until you open your eyes next. We will not leave your side, and we will be here also when you awaken. You are not alone, Father. We are here with you."

"It gives me great comfort to hear you say that, child, but I'm perplexed as to why I should remain here."

"It is the way necessary, Father. Rest here."

I being the obedient sort, having never disagreed with either my wife or my daughter, will, of course, in this also comply.

I shall soon stop writing. I shall lay my head

down onto my arms and close my eyes as instructed. I shall feel Gretchen's hand on the back of my head, stroking my neck softly.

Abigail has graced us with her presence once again with the flutter of wings and a rush of air past me. Her heavy body makes quite a thud on my desk. She is a very lovely bird. Looking up from my parchment page, I am most delighted to see her once again, her dark mysterious eyes blinking at me as usual.

I, of course, reach out my hand and stroke her long, slim neck. "I'm very happy to see you again, my friend."

Of course, I get the look as her response.

"I'm afraid I cannot engage you in a conversation at the moment, for I'm feeling a bit worn. But after I have rested, we shall converse. Until then, my friend, fare thee well."

Once more, the look.

As I record this, a new consideration has settled gently down upon me, and as Gretchen continues stroking my neck, I feel compelled to add two more sentences before a deep slumber overtakes me.

For every story ever told finally comes the end, and so it is also for every life ever lived. Even so, very soon I feel, for this long-ago man.

Epilogue

The DESTINY's bow struck firmly against the sandy shoreline, bringing the new yacht to an abrupt stop. Moments later, Loretta Callison leaped down, her young bare feet sinking into the soft, dry sand with a small explosion.

"It's simply beautiful, darling," she sang back to her new husband. "This just *has* to be the most wonderful honeymoon anyone has ever been on."

"There certainly *is* a magical feel to it, dear," responded Henry Callison, still standing on the bow of the yacht.

"Darling, would you please get the picnic basket? It's on the table in the galley."

"Of course." Henry spun about on his heels and walked across the deck, stepped down onto the main deck, and then cheerfully floated down the steps into the galley. He quickly found the wicker basket on the table and scooped it up, but before turning to go, he noticed the calendar hanging on the wall.

Setting down the basket, he picked up a grease pencil and bent over the calendar, which read March 1900. All the dates but three were carefully crossed out with a single diagonal line beginning in the upper left corner of each date box and ending precisely in the lower right corner. Henry drew a diagonal through the date of the 29th.

With a short nod of his head, he smiled, picked up the basket, and trotted back up the gangway stairs.

He leapt down off the bow into the sand and immediately noticed the large spire of rotted wood. He walked straight to it and placed his hand upon one of the logs.

"Loretta, dear, do you see this?"

"Yes. What is it?"

"If I'm not mistaken, it looks like a signal fire stack."

"Really? How odd."

"It's pretty rotten. It must have been built years ago."

"Are you saying that someone was marooned here?"

"So it would seem, but they obviously never used it. It's been here a long time, though."

"Fascinating! This is so exciting. Let's explore. Maybe there's some buried treasure around here."

"I doubt it. According to the brochure, it's never been inhabited. It doesn't even have a name."

Loretta then discovered the well-beaten path. "Henry?" she called out. "There's a path."

"Are you serious?"

"Yes. Come here."

Henry trotted over to his young wife and immediately confirmed the existence of the worn path. "Interesting. Let's follow it."

The two followed the path toward the island's interior until Loretta gasped at the site of the camp.

"Look, Henry. A complete campsite. The brochure was obviously wrong. Someone *has* lived here."

"A long time ago, too, from the looks of it."

"Hello," she shouted out. There was no response. "Hello. Anyone here?" she shouted again. Still no response.

"Look at that," announced Henry, spotting the broken and rotting bird cage, then the three wooden poles with the torn and tossed grass figures, and the remnants of the now tattered tent. Around the dead campfire laid dried and cracked wooden bowls, and a rusty knife, its tip still buried in the top of a stump.

"Dear Lord," Loretta gasped. "There *was* someone marooned here."

"Sure was. I wonder who it was," said Henry. "It looks like they just picked up and left."

It was Loretta who first spotted the path through the thicket and followed it, disappearing behind it as Henry continued on into what was left of the tent.

A few moments later, he heard Loretta's frightened scream and rushed through the thicket and spotted Loretta on her knees in a shocked state, in the sand near the cave entrance.

"What is it?"

She did not answer but pointed toward the cave. Henry walked directly into the cave and saw what had caused her fright.

Sprawled across the desk lay Thomas

Cantfield's skeleton, his skull resting on his left arm, his bony fingers still clutching the cracked quill pen, the bottle of long-since-dried ink sitting just off to the side from his skeletal hand.

"My God!"

Loretta then returned, having recovered from her initial shock. "The poor man."

"Indeed, my darling. It looks as if he's been here for ages."

"He died all alone, Henry. I can't even imagine what it must have been like for him."

Henry noticed the faded writing on the parchment and then the chest. He bent and opened the lid of the chest and discovered Thomas's written account. "Dear me. Look at this."

Loretta moved over and looked into the chest. "He recorded his life here?"

"It certainly looks like it." Henry carefully picked up a fragile sheet of parchment, now dried and brittle, and read the first page. He then read several more pages, skipping down to the last pages, including the faded page upon the desk, under Thomas's hand.

"1830. That's when he arrived here. On his thirtieth birthday, March 30, 1830."

"Today is the 29th."

"I know. Seventy years ago tomorrow, this fine man was marooned here after a hurricane and he lived here completely alone. How sad. How dreadfully sad."

That evening after an accelerated dinner, having hauled the chest back to their yacht, both Henry and Loretta began reading Thomas's journal.

They didn't sleep that night, and the next morning found them standing in front of the two false graves on the far side of the island. Henry replanted the markers at the head of the graves.

"Dear," said Loretta, "there are no bodies there. They aren't real graves."

"I know that, but I think Thomas would want them reset anyway."

"I'm sorry, dear. You're right, of course."

Upon returning to the cave, they were both shocked to see a large albatross squatted on the table, its head resting on Thomas's hand.

"My God! It's Abigail," Loretta yelped excitedly.

"Her descendants, darling."

"I know that, but how does it know to do that?"

"They must have been taught by their mothers over the years to do this."

The albatross then stood up and flew away, winging its way just over their heads.

"There is one more thing that we need to do," declared Henry.

Henry pounded in the grave marker with a large basalt stone. Giving it one more good strike, he then tossed the stone to the ground off to the side and stood up, staring at all three grave markers.

"That should do it. Rest well, Thomas Bartholomew Cantfield. Right here next to your brothers, rest well, my good man."

As they turned away, hand in hand, they both heard the flapping of wings. As they turned back toward the grave, the albatross landed and waddled over to the grave. It crawled up onto the mounded sand, squatted down, and remained still.

It was late in the afternoon when Loretta walked out onto the deck and sat down next to Henry. He was lost in a deep contemplative thought. She wasn't sure if she should interrupt him, but she instinctively laid her left hand upon his right shoulder. He stirred.

"Yes, my love," he said softly, his own left hand rising up to her hand.

"What are you thinking about?"

"I'm going to do what he asked."

"What is that?"

"He condensed his journal down to a book containing eighty-five chapters. I'm going to begin tonight with chapter eighty-six and write a new chapter each year on this date. Today is the thirtieth. It's his birthday. I'm going to write one chapter each year to keep him alive, just as he asked. He's going to travel with us. I shall show Thomas every sight that I can. And I shall teach our children to do the same, and then our grandchildren."

"That would be a wonderful tribute to the man, darling. I think Thomas would have liked that very much."

"I *know* he would have. Happy Birthday, Thomas."

He thought a moment more before speaking.

"Without question, my dear, he truly lived a wondrous life."

The cursor on the computer's holoscreen blinked as a man sat down at the table. He was a gentle-looking older man, with graying temples and kindly eyes. He glanced at the digital calendar on the wall. It read March 30, 2146.

He then leaned back in his chair and thought deeply for several moments. When he returned his attention to the computer's holokeyboard, he began typing the words:

"Chapter 331."

He stopped and turned his head to stare out the starboard port window of the spacecraft at the beckoning stars. He finally nodded and began typing once again, the words forming on the screen:

My very good friend Thomas Bartholomew Cantfield and I had never before visited the Martian Colonies, so on one fine day we decided to go.

The End?

ABOUT THE AUTHOR

Val Edward Simone was born in Seattle, Washington, and has been writing since 1980.

Val has published adult-themed action/adventure novels; historical fiction; western novels; short stories; a collection of thoughts, musings, and observations; a collection of children's short stories; and several children's picture books. He continues to work on many other novels, short stories and screenplays.

He is also a strong advocate of early childhood development through the arts, and continues to support all efforts toward helping children discover their own creativity through reading, writing, and drawing.

Val currently lives and writes in Arizona.

His websites:
EkidslandPublishing.com
MorningsidePublishing.com
Ekidsland.com (For kids only)

Connect with Val
and Other Books

Connect with Val Online:
Twitter: @valsimone
Instagram: @valedwardsimone

Other Books by Val Edward Simone
Novels/Novellas
Blood Trackers: One Crazy Love Story
Blood Trackers 2: Revenge of an Angel
About Things I Lost Long Ago…scribblings from a foolish heart
The Wondrous Life of a Long-Ago Man
Comes the Devil to Crooked Creek
Captain Delightable's Magical Tales of a Minchon Warrior
A Minute of Forever
Into the Light Boldly…an odyssey of self-discovery
The Firestone…Is Mankind Ready?
The Story
Adventures at Dead River
The Art of Living Between Hell and Breakfast
5th Avenue Whore

Short Stories
Manifest Destiny
The Secret Life of Goner Andling
Love Bytes
Dragons Within
The Problem with Dragons
The Unfortunate Dragon
The Fairy Collection
Through the Waterfall
Fairy Forgotten
Emily's Wish
Kaylee's Secret
The Wizard of Sebastianville

Children's Picture Books
Felix
The Gingerbread Pony
The Littlest Bell
Mean Muley McGrudge
Otto and Kevin
Proton Gator
Sammy Sparrow Spy

Children's Coloring Book
Proton Gator & Friends Coloring Book